THINGS
I SHOULD
HAVE
KNOWN

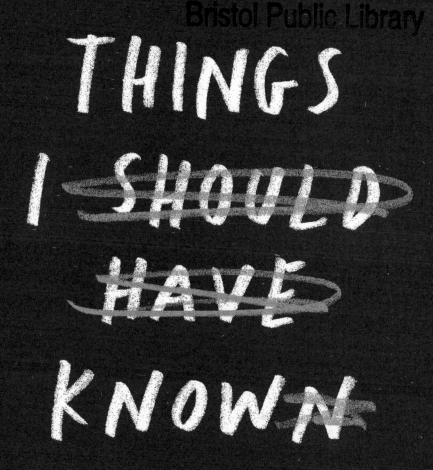

THINGS
I ~~SHOULD~~
~~HAVE~~
KNOWN

A NOVEL

CLAIRE LAZEBNIK

HOUGHTON MIFFLIN HARCOURT
BOSTON   NEW YORK

Copyright © 2017 by Claire LaZebnik

All rights reserved. For information about permission to
reproduce selections from this book, write to Permissions,
Houghton Mifflin Harcourt Publishing Company,
3 Park Avenue, New York, New York 10016.

www.hmhco.com

The text was set in Adobe Garamond Pro.
Title hand-lettering by Lee Crutchley
Book design by Sharismar Rodriguez

Library of Congress Cataloging-in-Publication Data
Names: LaZebnik, Claire Scovell, author.
Title: Things I should have known / Claire LaZebnik.
Description: Boston ; NewYork : Houghton Mifflin Harcourt, [2017]
Summary: "A popular Los Angeles teen tries to find love
for her older, autistic sister"— Provided by publisher.
Identifiers: LCCN 2016010017 | ISBN 9780544829695 (hardback)
Subjects: | CYAC: Sisters—Fiction. | Autism—Fiction.
Dating (Social customs)—Fiction.
Classification: LCC PZ7.L4496 Th 2017 | DDC [Fic]—dc23
LC record available at https://lccn.loc.gov/2016010017

Manufactured in the United States of America
DOC 10 9 8 7 6 5 4 3 2 1
4500643001

I've mentioned my husband, Rob,
in several previous dedications,
but he's never had one all to himself.
And he deserves one all to himself.
He also deserves a wife who's as patient,
capable, and kind as he is,
but since that's not going to happen . . .
this book is dedicated to him.

ONE

THERE'S A SWEET burnt-jelly smell in the air. When I enter the kitchen, Ivy's standing by the toaster.

"Hey, Ives. Making a snack?" I stick a mug of water in the microwave and get a tea bag out of the cabinet.

"Yeah." In her pajamas, with her round face, big eyes, and blondish ponytail, she looks like an oversize five-year-old. She doesn't say anything else. Ivy's not a big conversationalist.

The toaster clicks, and by the time my tea is ready, Ivy is installed at the table, a Pop-Tart on a plate, a glass of cold milk at its side. She's got her iPad in front of her, and she's doing something on it—probably playing a game. I open my laptop to work on an English paper, and the two of us fall into companionable silence.

There are footsteps in the hallway and then Ron's in the doorway, filling it up with his broad shoulders. He's wearing his after-work uniform: sweatpants and a T-shirt with sleeves short enough to show his bulging biceps.

Ron's beefy without being cut. His face is heavy, especially down at the jaw and chin, but he wears his light brown hair on the longer side in front, so he can thrust the mass of it back with his fingers—it's a ridiculously youthful gesture for someone edging toward sixty, and I'm convinced he practices it in front of the mirror.

My mother married him over a year ago. He still feels like an intruder in our house. I don't think he'll ever not feel like one.

"Hey, there!" he says with unconvincing geniality. "Look at you two girls, working away! I'm going to assume you're doing homework and not messaging boys." He crosses to the refrigerator. "Your mom's thirsty, and as usual, I'm waiting on her hand and foot." He snaps his enormous hand like he's got a whip in it. "Coosh-oo! She orders, and I obey."

Neither of us responds. He grabs a half-empty bottle of wine from the fridge and two glasses from the cabinet. He's heading back out when he notices the plate in front of Ivy.

"What's that you've got there?"

"Pop-Tart."

He sighs. "Oh, Ivy," he says in the overly gentle tone he always uses with her. "We've talked about this, haven't we? About making better choices? About eating to fuel our bodies and not just because we're bored?" Ron's always trying to micromanage Ivy's diet. He acts like it's all about her health, but I eat just as much junk as she does and he never says anything to *me* about it, because I'm thinner than she is. Not that Ivy's fat, exactly, just kind of solid. She'll never be a supermodel, but that's not exactly her destiny anyway, so who cares?

Other than Ron, I mean.

"I was hungry," she says.

"Were you?" Ron says. "Were you *really* hungry? Because

you ate quite a bit at dinner tonight. Quite a bit." He leans against the side of the doorway, wineglass stems threaded through the fingers of one hand, bottle in the other. There's a scar on the side of that hand — he claims he cut it as a teenager working in a lab one summer, but I bet it was from a broken beer bottle. He acts all cultured now, but I'm convinced he was a total bro back in the day. Probably beat up all the nerdy kids and high-fived his friends afterward. "A lot of what you ate was carbohydrates — potatoes and bread. You didn't touch your salad."

"It had peppers in it." She appeals to me. "I don't like peppers, right, Chloe?"

"No one does."

"Chloe," Ron says. "Don't." His voice tightens when he talks to me, but I prefer that to the patronizing tone he uses with my sister. Which he now slips back into. "You don't have to finish that, Ivy. We can wrap it up, and you can have the rest for breakfast tomorrow. Or we can just throw it out — processed food like this belongs in the trash anyway, as far as I'm concerned."

"But I'm hungry."

"No, you're not."

"Don't tell her whether or not she's hungry," I say. "It's her body."

"Can you just stop?" he snaps at me. "I'm trying to help her out here." He flashes a strained smile in her direction. "I want to keep our sweet Ivy healthy."

"Her health is fine," I say, because it is — Ivy never gets

3

sick. "You're the one with high cholesterol. Worry about yourself. You really need that wine? Lot of calories in wine, you know." I deliberately eye his waist—he's always complaining to my mom that no matter how many sit-ups he does, he can't get back to a size twenty-eight, so I know he's self-conscious about it.

Ron stands up straighter, sucking in his stomach—it's the kind of thing people do when you stare at their love handles. "When I want your advice, Chloe, I'll ask for it. But don't hold your breath." He turns back to Ivy. "You could be so pretty," he says. "I mean, you *are* so pretty. You don't want to go and mess that up by eating so much junk food you get fat and pimply, do you? Don't you want a boyfriend one day? And a husband? My mother got married when she was younger than you! Doesn't that blow your mind?"

"I know," Ivy says. "She was nineteen when she got married, and your father was twenty-three. You were born two years later in 1961. Mom was born in 1972. She's eleven years younger than you."

For a moment he blinks at her, overwhelmed by the sheer volume of accurate information she's just thrown at him. Then he recovers. "Yeah, well . . . good. It's good you remember. My point is you're old enough to be thinking about boys and to care about how you look. Like Chloe." He jerks his chin at me. "She always looks nice. I'll give her that."

I stifle a sarcastic retort—I don't want to prolong this.

"Chloe's really pretty," Ivy says.

"So are you," says Ron. "But you won't be if you keep eating junk."

She considers that, and while she considers it, she absently picks up the Pop-Tart and takes another bite of it.

"Stop eating that!" he says. "You're not listening to me."

"I *am* listening."

It would be funny if I thought Ivy was deliberately provoking him. But Ivy doesn't do stuff like that. All she wants is to eat her stupid Pop-Tart in peace.

"What's going on in here?" It's Mom, coming up behind Ron. Her hair is styled and she's wearing makeup — she's Ron's receptionist, and he likes her to look "put together" for the office — but she changed when she got home and the T-shirt and sweats make her mascaraed eyes and curls look ridiculous. I don't like when she wears that much makeup, anyway — it settles into every crease and makes her face look older than it is. Without it, she's pretty, with big, wistful blue eyes and a small nose and mouth. She and Ivy look a lot alike.

Mom says, "What's a girl got to do to get a glass of wine around here?"

"I was on my way." Ron holds up the bottle and glasses. "But the girls and I started talking."

Her eyes flicker from face to face, gauging the moods of everyone in the room. She says, a little too brightly, "I sound like the worst kind of mother, don't I? *Stop talking to my kids and bring me my wine!*" She forces a girly laugh, then gives me a vaguely pleading look. I glance away and notice that Ivy has taken advantage of the distraction to quickly cram the rest of the Pop-Tart into her mouth. *You go, Ivy.*

"It's okay," Ron says to Mom. "I've exhausted my parenting skills for the evening anyway. These girls of yours . . ." He leaves it at that and steers her back into the hallway, where she tosses out another giggle-laugh.

She never used to laugh like that. She used to have this rare deep chuckle that often ended in a sigh. Nothing girlish about it at all. But a lot's changed since she met Ron and even more since the day she told us she was going to marry him, "because you girls need a father."

I said, "No, we don't, and even to say that is an insult to lesbian parents everywhere," which at least got her to stop saying it, but did nothing to prevent her from going ahead and marrying Ron, a guy she had met through some online dating site and whose profile she had first clicked on because a) she thought he was handsome (meh) and b) he said he didn't have kids of his own and regretted it. (He'd been married once and divorced.)

Mom came back from their first date dazed and ecstatic. Things moved quickly after that. I think Ron must have liked how pliable she was, how willing to follow his lead when it came to exercise and diet—and raising kids, even though he had no experience in that last area. And Mom definitely liked having someone around to direct her. She's never liked to be in charge of anything.

The thing about Mom is that she's the kind of needy that makes people want to do stuff for her, not the kind that repels them. Ron was basically her white knight, charging in to fix her life for her. But I'm not so crazy about being a part of her life that he thinks needs fixing. And I'm even less crazy about watching him pick apart Ivy, who doesn't have any anger or malice in her and so can't defend herself against his attacks.

I'm her younger sister, but I can't remember a time when I didn't feel like I needed to protect and take care of her.

TWO

Ms. CAMPANELLI TAKES her job very seriously. "I mean, fine," Sarah said to me at the beginning of the school year. "You like books? You like talking about them? Go ahead and become an English teacher. That's great. But don't expect everyone else to get as excited as *you* about Shakespeare or whatever. Have some perspective. People have lives."

"*She* doesn't," I said. "I'm assuming. Given the way she dresses."

But even though I make fun of her, I kind of love Ms. Campanelli and the way every class she teaches veers off into whatever tangent interests us the most. We'll start off recapping the last few chapters of *Wuthering Heights,* and then a kid will say he thought the whole book was totally incestuous, and the next thing you know, we'll be deep into a discussion about whether it's okay to think your cousin is hot, and how the ancient rulers all married their own sisters, and stuff like that.

During these discussions, Ms. Campanelli (we call her "Camp" when she can't hear us) gets more and more excited, running her hands through her wildly wavy hair until it stands out like a mane around her head, tugging at her long boho skirt until it's so twisted that the side pocket is over her crotch, pleading with us to raise our hands and not just shout out. But you can tell she doesn't really mind—she's just happy we're all into the conversation, and the truth is that most of the time she's shouting over everyone else just as much as the rest of us. In any other classroom, we'd all be secretly checking our texts under our desks, but we pay attention in English.

Anyway, today it's all about *Romeo and Juliet.* The usual complaints are made—Shakespeare's boring; he uses way too much imagery; the story's over the top; half the words are made up, etc., etc.—and Ms. Campanelli duly notes them and moves on. She asks us to describe Romeo in our own words. "What if he were a student at this school? What group would he be in? Who would he date?"

Sarah raises her hand, and Camp calls on her. "Everyone would want to date him," she says. "He's, like, perfect boyfriend material—"

"Oh, please," David Fields snorts. "He's an idiot."

Figures. David only talks in class to attack what someone else has said. Otherwise, he ignores the discussion and spends the class surfing the web on his computer. People say that he gets such good grades that all the teachers let him do whatever he wants.

David has one of those bland faces that would get him off for murder because not a single eyewitness would be able to describe him. They'd all be saying stuff like, "Oh, you know . . . hair that's kind of brown . . . not that straight, but not curly either . . . His nose? Just kind of normal, I guess . . .

Dark eyes, probably brown . . . Average size . . ." Meanwhile he'd be off killing a bunch more innocents. And they'd come interview everyone at our school, and we'd all be, like, "Yeah, I'm not surprised. Guy was *weird*."

"Has anyone here actually *read* the play?" he says. "The guy's a flake, falling in and out of love with any girl who crosses his path. If he and Juliet hadn't died, he'd have moved on to someone else the second the excitement was gone. Only a moron would find that romantic."

"Hey, watch it," James growls—defending Sarah because she's my best friend and he's a good guy. James is tall and broad-shouldered and dark-haired and blue-eyed—he basically looks like Clark Kent when he takes off his glasses just before he turns into Superman. Everyone at school is either in awe of him or in love with him, but he's *my* boyfriend.

David ignores the growl. "Shakespeare's making fun of lame teenagers who convince themselves that lust is love." He deliberately glances at me and James and then raises a hand to his lips with comically exaggerated embarrassment. "Oh, dear . . . I hope I didn't offend anyone in this room."

"We should give David a break," I say, addressing Ms. Camp, but making sure everyone can hear me. "It's not his fault he doesn't get it. I mean, he doesn't get *It*. Ever." Lots of laughter at that—the crowd's on my side.

"Oh, gee," David retorts. "I've missed out on all the delights of a public high school relationship. What *will* I have to cringe about in my old age?"

"I'm sure you'll find something."

"I think," Ms. Camp says with an edge of desperation, "that we've lost track of our discussion."

"No, it's good," I say. "It's like Shakespeare's come alive for us."

"Really?" she says hopefully.

"Definitely," I assure her with my sweetest smile.

James drives me home from school like he always does if he has time. Otherwise, I have to take the bus or walk—it's about a mile, which isn't too bad unless you have a heavy backpack and it's, like, eighty-five degrees out . . . which is most of the time in LA.

I invite him to come in, but he says he has to go to soccer practice. I pout and tell him he's no fun.

"You're a bad influence," he says. "I'm late every time I drop you off, and Coach is threatening to bench me for the next game if I'm late again."

"Oh, please. You're his best player—he's never going to make you sit out."

"Yeah," James says with the slow twitchy grin that was the first thing I noticed about him and which still sends a thrill through my body. "I know. Give me a goodbye kiss?" He holds out his arms, and I wriggle out of my seat belt and across the gearshift into his lap, where I do some more wriggling and try to change his mind about coming upstairs with me.

I know I've succeeded when his breath turns ragged and uneven.

"All right, fine," he says with an exaggerated sigh. "I'll go in with you. But I can't stay longer than five minutes, Chloe. I mean it."

"A lot can happen in five minutes," I say as we tumble out of the car. I break free and sprint toward the front steps. He catches me at the door as I'm unlocking it. We move inside together, and he pins me against the wall. He's got his tongue in my mouth, and I'm moving my hips against his . . . and then my phone buzzes. I duck away to check it and curse.

"What's wrong?" he asks.

"I have to get Ivy. Mom said things got busy at work and she can't leave." I look at my watch. "Crap. It's almost four, and I have to pick up the car. I'm going to be so late."

"You need me to do anything?"

"Yeah—can you drop me off at Ron's office? It's on Wilshire. Not too far."

"Okay, but we'd better leave now." He casts a last wistful glance at the sofa.

"Sorry," I say. "I'll make it up to you."

"You'd better."

THREE

My friend Sarah has this theory about life, which is that no one has it all, even though it looks like some people do. The kids who have a happy home life don't have a lot of friends; the popular, athletic kids have mean parents; and the rich kids are stupid and get bad grades. "*You* have a great boyfriend and you do well at school and everyone likes you," she said to me when she was explaining her theory. "You're even *blond*. So of course your family situation is a little, you know . . . challenging. That's life keeping things in balance."

"What about you?" I said. "What's not good about your life?"

"I do really badly at school," she said, which is ridiculous — she gets decent grades in mostly honors classes.

"No, you don't. Anyway," I said before she could start arguing with me about how stupid she was, "I'm not a true blonde. I highlight it, you know."

"You're blond enough."

"I'll trade hair with you any day."

Sarah has these amazing black curls. Her mother's Latina and has black hair, and her father's Jewish and has curly hair (well, *had*—he's lost most of it now), and somehow she got the best of both. Her skin is this great light olive color that turns to burnished copper in the summer. She complains a lot about her nose (too crooked) and her eyebrows (too intense) and her thighs (not as thin as she'd like them to be), but I love the way she looks.

Anyway, she *does* have a point about my sucky home life.

Ivy was diagnosed with autism when she was seven. For a long time after that, that was all Mom and Dad could talk about—what to do for her and whether they were doing enough. (The answer was always no.)

Then Dad started having trouble swallowing.

Esophageal cancer moves fast: our lives stopped being about Ivy's diagnosis and started being about all the medical stuff.

Then, after a couple of years of that—about five years ago—Dad died and Mom lost it. She plunged into this depression where she just didn't want to get up in the morning, and Ivy and I had to learn to get ourselves out the door in the morning without her help.

Even when the worst was over, we never knew if Mom would be okay or not. Some days she was totally present and wanted to do everything right, but other days the smallest thing would unsettle her—a leaky faucet, an old photo, Ivy freaking out about something—and she'd slide back. I learned to be relieved on the good days and to just deal on the bad ones. She was always worried about money, too—Dad had had some life insurance, but not a ton, and the work Mom got as a medical transcriptionist allowed her to be home all the time but didn't bring in a lot of income.

And then Ron came along and Mom felt saved.

Me, not so much.

Maybe Sarah's theory is right that everything evens out. School's kind of easy for me—not just academically, but socially too. The thing is, I have a dead father, a needy mother, and a sister who struggles to communicate, so getting into a clique or wearing the right clothes doesn't even come close to making it onto the list of things I worry about. And when you don't worry about that stuff, you seem cool without trying. Instant social success.

But I'm not sure that makes my life even with other people's. Deep down, I still feel like I've been cheated out of something.

James drops me off in the parking lot of the mini-mall where Ron's chiropractor practice is, and I run inside.

"I'm so sorry, Chloe," Mom says, rising from behind the reception desk. "I wouldn't have taken my car to work if I'd known I couldn't pick up Ivy."

"I thought Wednesday was your short day."

"It is. But Ron—" She glances at a couple of patients who are sitting on chairs within hearing distance and lowers her voice. "He's trying not to turn away any appointments, and we got a few last-minute requests." She retrieves her purse from under the desk and digs out her keys. "Tell Ivy I'm sorry about the mix-up." She drops them in my hand.

"She hates when she's picked up late."

"I know, but what could I do?" She shrugs, helpless as always.

The drive is stressful. I don't mind picking up Ivy—I'm used to it—but I usually leave much earlier when I do. I'm already late, and there's a lot of traffic. When I finally pull through the school gate onto the circular driveway where cars are normally stacked up at pickup time, it's empty.

Ivy's standing in front of the main entrance with a young female aide, who waves me toward them with obvious relief. Ivy's hammering her fists against her hips, which means she's upset.

"You see?" the aide is saying as she opens the car door. "I told you she'd be here any second." She bends down and sticks her head in. "You're the sister, right?"

"Yeah, I'm Chloe. Hi."

"Pickup's at four, you know."

It was already past four thirty. I flashed my biggest, brightest *Love Me!* smile, the one with lots of teeth, a scrunchy nose, and wide bright eyes. "I'm so sorry!"

She relents. "That's okay. I'm just glad I was able to stay late today."

I thank her, she steps back, Ivy gets in the car, and I drive away.

"Where's Mom?" Ivy asks. "She's supposed to pick me up at four on Wednesdays."

"She didn't text you?"

"No."

Argh. I had assumed Mom had taken care of that. She knows as well as I do that Ivy hates it when plans are changed without warning. "She had to stay at work and then I had to go get the car, and that's why I'm late. But I'm here now, right?"

She doesn't respond out loud, but I can hear her whispering to herself, something she does when she's unhappy. I can't actually make out the words, but the slight hissing sound gets on my nerves, and I have to bite my tongue not to snap at her to stop — when I do, she always looks stricken and embarrassed.

The last person in the world I want to hurt is Ivy. But sometimes I do anyway.

"I'm hungry," she says.

I glance over. Her curly fair hair is pulled back in its usual ponytail, so I can see her profile clearly: she's sucking on her lower lip, and her slightly overgrown eyebrows are drawn together in concern.

Anxiety is Ivy's constant companion — she's always afraid that there's something she's supposed to be doing and isn't, some magic word or action that everyone else has figured out that she hasn't, some catastrophe that's waiting for a break in her routine to come crashing down on her.

But she won't — or can't — put these feelings into words.

"You want to stop at Starbucks?" I ask. "Get a muffin?"

"Yes, please." Ivy is often oddly polite, mostly because she learned to talk by memorizing phrases and sentences and when to use them.

While we're waiting in line at Starbucks, a barista turns on a blender. Ivy puts her hands over her ears and moans. Loud sounds cause her almost physical pain.

I see a couple of other customers stare at her.

I move closer to my sister and square my shoulders.

FOUR

WHEN MOM AND RON come home later that evening, Ivy and I are sitting at the kitchen table together—I'm on my laptop, and she's using her iPad. Mom greets us in that overly energetic and cheerful way she does when we're all in one room together, like if she's just bright and sunny enough, we'll be a *real* family.

Ivy looks up. "You didn't come today. I was waiting and waiting."

"I am so sorry, baby." Mom never calls *me* baby, only Ivy, even though I'm three years younger. "We got so busy at the office—"

"Chloe came, but she was late."

"Not exactly my fault," I say. "I didn't know I was picking you up until it was already too late."

"You girls have to learn to be more flexible," Ron says, putting a bag of groceries on the counter. "Learn to roll with the punches a little. Life isn't always predictable."

"So true," Mom says. "I hope everyone's hungry! We picked up some salmon and asparagus. I can have it ready in half an hour."

"I'm going out for frozen yogurt with Sarah," I say.

"Have you eaten anything healthy yet today?"

"Yeah, I'm good."

"She had a muffin at Starbucks," Ivy says helpfully.

Mom frowns. "You need to eat a real dinner, Chloe. You can't live on muffins and frozen yogurt."

"What are you talking about? Yogurt's, like, the healthiest thing in the world."

"Can't you meet Sarah after dinner?"

"I already told her I could go at seven. It's not my fault you guys came home late."

Ron turns around, fists firmly planted on his love handles. "Don't argue with your mother. She told you she wants you home for dinner. End of discussion."

"You're not part of this."

"Maybe you can just postpone with Sarah for half an hour?" Mom says, darting anxious looks back and forth between me and Ron. "I'll just feel better if you have a few bites of salmon first, Chloe."

"Fine," I say, because I can hear the plea in her voice, and I don't want *her* to feel bad—Ron's the one who makes me crazy. I text Sarah with the new plan.

Ron goes to the refrigerator and takes out the half-empty wine bottle from the night before. He pours them both a glass of wine, and Mom stops what she's doing to take a long, grateful sip from hers. Ron picks up his and leaves the kitchen, saying he's going to change.

"Muffins and frozen yogurt," Mom sings out as she puts her glass down and starts sprinkling a piece of fish with salt and pepper. "I will say I'm jealous of how you can eat whatever you want and stay thin, Chloe. I never had your metabolism. Or maybe it's just that I'm so much shorter that I end up wearing everything I eat."

"Yeah, I'm glad I got Dad's tall genes."

"Dad was six feet and two inches tall," Ivy says with sudden interest, looking up from her game. "I'm five feet and ten inches tall, and Chloe is five feet and seven inches tall, and Mom is five feet and three inches tall. Mom is the shortest."

"Rub it in, why don't you?" Mom says cheerfully.

"Was that a bad thing to say?" Ivy asks anxiously. "I wasn't being mean, was I? I was just saying how tall we all are."

"Mom's just teasing you," I say.

"How about my metabolism?" Ivy asks. "Is it like Chloe's?"

"No one's is like Chloe's," Mom says. "She's unnatural."

"Is mine bad?"

"Metabolisms aren't good or bad," Mom says.

"But you made it sound like Chloe's is better than yours."

My phone buzzes, and Mom quickly jumps on the chance to change the subject. "Who's texting you?"

I check. "Sarah—she's fine going later."

"Can I go too?" Ivy asks.

"You want me to bring back some fro-yo for you?"

"It will melt. I'd rather go with you."

"Sorry, but Sarah and I have stuff to talk about."

"That's okay. I'll let you talk."

Argh. Sarah and I do a lot of gossiping and giggling about the people in our class, and I know from past experience that if

Ivy comes, she'll ask awkward questions and we'll start to feel self-conscious and a little guilty . . . and all the fun will go out of our conversation.

"I'm sorry," I say again. "I really need to see Sarah alone this time. But I'll bring you back whatever you want."

"You always get to go out and have fun." She slumps in her seat and morosely swipes her finger across the iPad. "I never do."

"We'll have fun tonight," Mom says as she empties a bag of prewashed lettuce into a bowl. "We can watch TV together!"

Ivy may be autistic, but she's not an idiot—you can't fool her into thinking that an evening on the sofa with Mom and Ron is a good time. She says, "Please, Chloe?"

I feel bad, but I still shake my head. "Another time. I promise."

I do bring her back a cup of frozen yogurt. She's already in her pajamas and in bed, and she points out that it's mostly melted. "It's like eating a puddle."

She manages to scarf it down, though.

FIVE

I HAVE A PROBLEM," I tell James on Friday as I walk him over to practice.

"What's that?"

I nuzzle into his neck, kitten-like. "I don't know what to wear on our date tonight."

"That is a problem," he agrees. "If it helps, I like tight jeans. Or that tight little black skirt you wear sometimes. Actually, anything tight works for me."

"Oh, I can choose an *outfit*," I say airily. "It's what I should wear underneath that's the issue."

That wins me a growl and a grab.

We duck behind a tree and give each other a decent preview of the pleasures waiting for us later that evening.

"Stupid practice," he mutters eventually and tugs me back out into the courtyard with a sigh.

I pout. "You need to get your priorities straight."

"They *are* straight," he insists. "You, then soccer, then . . . nothing, because nothing else matters. What are *your* priorities?"

"You. And then you. Followed by you." We kiss. Deeply. Lots of tongue.

He moans and pulls away. "Now I'll have to limp to practice."

"Poor baby," I say without a trace of sympathy. He makes his way—not limping at all, more like swaggering—toward the locker rooms over by the field. I check the time on my phone and realize I'll have to run to make the bus, so I turn, and that's when I see David Fields sprawled out on a nearby rock with a book in his hand, watching me.

"What are you looking at?" I snap, embarrassed and irritated by my own embarrassment.

"You," he says. "But only because you want me to. I mean, the only reason anyone would get as physical in a public place as you two just did is because they get off on being watched."

"Don't be disgusting."

"Me? I'm sitting here peacefully reading while you and your boyfriend grind against each other in a public place—and *I'm* the one who's disgusting?" He shakes his head. "Trust me, I would have enjoyed the last five minutes a lot more without having to see or hear any of *that*."

"So sorry," I say. "I forget how upsetting other people's pleasure is to those who have none." I'm trying to make it sound like we're just joking around, but inside I'm seething, and there's nothing good-natured about *his* tone.

He says, "You know, studies show that couples who have a lot of public displays of affection are insecure and unstable."

"You just keep quoting your little statistics, and maybe someday a girl might be willing to overlook your personality long enough to actually let you hold her hand."

"I just hope she won't be a conceited, self-centered blonde," he says. "I find those unpleasant."

"She won't be blond. She probably won't even be *breathing* if she's willing to stay in a room with you." I turn on my heel and walk away before he can see that I'm not just pretending to be annoyed.

Mom comes into the room Ivy and I share to ask us what kind of pizza we want—it's Friday night and she's tired, so we're ordering in.

"None for me," I say over my shoulder before going back to flicking through the dresses in my closet. "I'm going out for dinner with James and his parents. Which I told you."

"Oh, right," Mom says. "I forgot. I should really have their whole family over for dinner sometime—they're always hosting you."

"Yeah, we'll take a turn soon," I say with absolutely no sincerity whatsoever. Introducing James's classy parents to my dysfunctional family could only ever take place over my rotting corpse.

Ivy looks up from the screen. "James is your boyfriend. Before you went out with him, you went out with Juan. And before Juan, you went out with Brian. You also went on dates with Nick, Loren, and Braden, but you said you weren't actually 'going out' with them."

"Wow," I say, both amused and uncomfortable. Some things you want to forget—like Brian and Loren, for example. I'm glad I never told Ivy about the other half dozen or so guys I've hooked up with at parties. "I can't believe you remember all that." I turn back to my closet—well, technically, Ivy and I share it, but it's almost entirely my clothes in there. Ivy only likes to wear pants and tops, which she keeps in drawers.

"You've had a lot of boyfriends," Ivy says. "So did you, Mom. You went out with Rick, Bill, Jim, and the guy whose parents owned a seafood restaurant."

"Bobby," Mom says, a little wistfully. "His name was Bobby."

"You got married when you were twenty-four and then again when you were forty-six. Dad would have been forty-six in August if he hadn't died. You were married for sixteen years when he died, and if he hadn't died, you two would be celebrating your twenty-third anniversary in November."

"Yes," Mom says, "but I started counting anniversaries again from the beginning when I married Ron."

"The twenty-fifth anniversary is called the silver anniversary," Ivy says. "And you're supposed to give people gifts made out of silver. In two years, you and Dad would have celebrated your silver anniversary, but you probably won't now because Dad died."

"But I *will* celebrate my third anniversary with Ron that year," Mom says with a forced smile. Her fingers are twining around each other, like she's trying to braid them together. She doesn't have any huge problem talking about the fact that Dad died, but it's probably hard for her when Ivy casually tosses it out the way she does. Or maybe I just think it's hard for her because it's hard for *me*.

It kills me to think about Dad. Sometimes when I see Ron strutting around the house, filling up rooms with his bulky chest and kissing Mom like he has a right to, I want to scream at him that she's not his, that she'll never be his, that she belongs to someone else.

I miss my dad, even though we never really talked that much. He wasn't the "sit down and tell me what's going on in your life" kind of father. He worked long hours, and when he was home, he was usually on his computer. His eyes could slide right past you without seeing you — just like Ivy's. You had to *work* to get him to pay attention to you, but if you made enough noise or tugged at him hard enough, he'd suddenly blink and look at you like he'd just returned from a long trip and was glad to see you again.

I can't remember a single mean thing he ever said or did to any of us. He still drove Mom crazy, though — he was always forgetting to do stuff she asked him to and she'd yell at him and he'd apologize. And then forget to do what she asked again.

He was tall and slender, with dirty blond hair like mine and Ivy's, except his was thinning on top. He walked oddly, up on his toes, the rest of him tilting forward, so his head and shoulders arrived at a destination before his legs did.

He ate so slowly that the rest of us always finished before he did, and Mom would eventually say, "Oh, for God's sake,

Chris. It'll be breakfast before you finish dinner." He'd push his plate away then and say he was done, even if he wasn't. I don't think food mattered much to him.

But maybe I'm confusing the way he was at the end — when he couldn't eat at all — with the way he was before. It's so hard to keep it all separate. I try to picture him before he got sick, but it all blurs.

He was so tired during those last few months, and so were we — tired of the *idea* of cancer, of its presence in our house. I wanted it to just go away.

And then it did, but it took him with it, which wasn't what I'd meant at all.

Anyway, since the skeletal, defeated, exhausted guy he was for the last few months of his life keeps blotting out the happier, younger version of him in my mind, it hurts to think about Dad.

But I can't get mad at Ivy for bringing him up a lot. She's just figuring stuff out, the way she likes to, adding up bits of information to see where they lead. She wants to find patterns, to be able to predict things and find some sense in the chaos, but what sense can you find in a father who died too young and a mother who remarried too quickly?

"I'm going to be twenty-one in June," Ivy says. At least she's off the topic of wedding anniversaries. "And that's why I can't go to school anymore after this year. I'll have to get a job. And I'll live in my own apartment and pay for it myself."

"Let's take things one step at a time," Mom says.

"When I turn twenty-one, I'll be able to order alcohol at restaurants and bars," Ivy says. "And also buy it at stores."

"Oh, God," Mom says.

"One step at a time," I remind her.

SIX

A LITTLE BEFORE SEVEN, James texts me to say he's waiting out front.

I call out a goodbye to everyone in the kitchen, but before I make it through the front door, Ron appears in the hallway. He expands his chest and sets his feet far apart—he's like a peacock, trying to impress and intimidate by spreading out. "Hold on there, Chloe—are you getting picked up?"

"Yeah. James is waiting." My hand is twitching on the knob.

"Not cool," Ron says, shaking his head. "He should come in and get you."

"He would, but we're running late."

Ivy's face appears behind Ron's shoulder. "Are you leaving, Chloe?"

"Yeah."

"Can I go too?"

"Sorry. James's parents are taking us out."

"Because you're his girlfriend?"

Ron puts his arm around her waist. "Let Ms. Chloe go out to her fancy dinner," he says jovially. "You and your mother and I will have fun here. Maybe we'll play a board game."

"I don't want to play a board game." She pulls away from him. "I want to go out too."

"I can ask your mother if she'd be up for a movie—"

"Not with you guys. With Chloe."

"Not tonight," I say, and quickly slip out the door.

In James's car, I lean over for a quick kiss and then he steps on the gas and his BMW roars off. His parents bought the car for him for his seventeenth birthday. It's used but in perfect condition, and if I weren't his girlfriend, I could easily hate him for all the stuff he has and the life he leads.

He totally blows apart Sarah's theory that no one's life is perfect, because his *is.*

He glances over at me. "You're quiet. I'm not complaining or anything—actually it's kind of a relief—"

"You are so going to pay for that."

He flashes a wicked grin. "But just to cover my ass, is everything okay?"

"Yeah, fine." I smooth my parent-friendly demure skirt over my thighs and wonder if I should tell him how guilty I feel going out and having fun when Ivy's stuck at home with Ron and Mom.

I turn my head and study him for a moment. He's wearing a collared shirt under a blue crewneck sweater. His short, dark, wavy hair is still damp from the shower, and his sleeves are rolled up just enough to show his strong forearms. He looks sexy and handsome and carefree.

And I think, *Don't be the girl who can't have fun, who drags everything down, who can't ever leave her sister behind.*

"Stop staring at me," James says. "I'm not just a pretty face, you know. I have a brain." Mock sigh. "But you never seem to notice that part of me."

"I promise to only pay attention to your brain tonight. I'm going to ignore your body completely."

"Yeah, I'm not sure that's going to work for me either."

"Your choice," I say. "I can love you for your mind or for your body. I can't do both."

He reaches over and finds my hand, which he puts on his leg. He presses it hard against his thigh. "If have to choose . . . I'd say that brains are overrated."

"Mmmm," I agree. "So after we have dinner with your parents, any chance of finding somewhere quiet and alone to be?"

"Not at my house." James has a younger brother and sister, and his mother likes to send them in with messages for us when we're alone in a room, to make sure we're not having sex.

"We'll figure something out," I say.

We eat dinner at a fancy Italian restaurant where the appetizers cost ten dollars and the entrees thirty — Ron would have a heart attack if our family ever tried to eat there. He's either very cheap or just kind of poor, but I'm not sure which, since he and Mom are both secretive about finances.

After dinner, James and I hang out at his house for a while and then he takes me home and comes inside with me. It's dark and quiet downstairs, which means everyone else has gone to bed.

We don't turn on any lights, just creep quietly into the family room, where we feel our way to the sofa, kick off our shoes, and fall onto the cushions together.

"See?" James whispers in my ear. "All I am to you is a body you can use."

"Do you have a problem with that?"

The noise he lets out in response suggests that he doesn't.

And then we're blinded by a sudden and brutal flood of light.

I fling myself off of James so fast I fall on the floor. I scramble upright, tugging my clothes into place, while James does the same with his as he swings into a sitting position on the sofa.

"Ivy!" I say, because she's standing by the light switch. "What the hell?"

"I'm sorry." She switches the light off.

"Oh, for God's sake," I snap. "Just leave it on."

She flicks it back on. "I'm sorry," she says again. "I heard some noises and didn't know what you were doing. I'm sorry. I'm sorry."

"It's okay," James says. "Don't worry about it." He glances at me ruefully. "I'm sure my heart will start beating again any minute now." He reaches down for his shoes. "I need to get home anyway."

I walk him to the door, where we kiss each other goodbye, but we're both too aware of Ivy watching us from the other side of the room to do more than just touch lips, and then he leaves.

I turn around. Ivy's standing there in her pajamas—old-fashioned ones, in matching red and gold stripes, because Mom buys her clothing and that's the kind of thing moms buy.

"Are you mad at me?" she asks, her hands cycling anxiously through the air. "I probably shouldn't have turned on the light."

"It's fine." I'm annoyed, but if Ivy thinks you're angry at her, she gets more and more anxious and starts hitting herself —it's not worth it. And she didn't do anything wrong. She just has this talent for being in the wrong place at the wrong time.

"What were you doing with the lights off?" she asks.

"Come on, Ives," I say. "You know what we were doing." She's twenty years old, and Mom bought picture books when we were little that explained all about changing bodies and sexual attraction. And Ivy watches tons of TV. There's no way she doesn't know what goes on between a guy and a girl in the dark.

"Were you having sex?"

"Jesus!"

"What?"

"You don't just ask stuff like that."

"I'm sorry." She clutches the collar of her pajama top and tugs down hard like it's choking her. "I didn't know."

"It's okay. Just don't ask stuff like that in front of other people, okay? And we were making out, that's all."

"That's different from sex, right?"

I feel a surge of anger—not at her, just at a world where I

have to explain what making out is to my older sister. "Yeah. You don't go as far."

"Far? What do you mean?"

"It doesn't matter. I'm too tired to talk now, Ives. I want to go to bed."

"How do you know what to do?" she asks, raising her head to stare briefly at me before sliding her eyes away again. "When you're with James?"

"I don't know. It's not something you think about. You just kind of know."

"What if you don't?"

"You just *do*." I walk past her into the hallway and up the stairs.

But, then, in the bathroom, as I'm brushing my teeth, I freeze suddenly, struck by a whole new thought. What if Ivy isn't asking questions just because she's curious about my life?

What if it's not all about *me?*

When I come back into the bedroom, Ivy's curled up with her iPad, and I can hear dialogue coming from the tablet.

"What are you watching?" I ask.

"*Ten Things I Hate about You.*"

"That's the one with the two sisters and Heath Ledger?"

"Yeah."

"You don't usually watch movies." Ivy's more of a TV show fan. Especially police procedurals — she eats that stuff up.

"I like this one," she says. "I've seen it before."

Interesting. She's not only watching this movie; she's *re*watching it. "That's the one with the father who won't let the younger daughter date until the older one has a boyfriend, right?"

"Yeah. If Mom made that rule, you couldn't go out with James because I don't have a boyfriend."

I don't know how to respond to that.

"It's a good thing Mom didn't make that rule," she says. "I probably won't ever have a boyfriend."

"Sure you will."

"I don't think so. Chloe?"

"What?"

"I want to watch my movie." She leans over the screen again so her face is partially veiled by her hair. She's absorbed by what she's watching. Curious—the way she was curious about me and James.

I lie awake for a long time, thinking about Ivy and her curiosity and how sad she sounded when she said she might never have a boyfriend of her own.

SEVEN

THE NEXT MORNING, Mom says she needs to do a supermarket run. Ron's at the gym and Ivy hates food shopping, so I offer to keep Mom company—it'll give me a chance to talk to her alone. We grab some canvas grocery bags and head to the car.

I launch into the subject as soon as we're on our way. "Hey, Mom? Do you ever worry that Ivy seems a little lonely?"

"Are you kidding? I worry about that every single day."

"It just feels like there's nothing in her life except going to school and playing on her iPad and watching TV."

"I know. I wish I could change that, but I've got a lot going on these days and just don't have the time or energy to figure out a solution."

She's never had the time or energy to solve problems—just throws up her hands and waits for someone else to deal with them.

And I'm the only other person who really cares about Ivy.

"I think Ivy wants a boyfriend."

"What?" Mom brakes too hard at a red light and turns to stare at me, horrified. "Why would you say that? She's never said anything like that to me."

"Last night she saw me and James . . . you know . . . kissing and stuff."

"And stuff?" she repeats.

"She wouldn't stop asking me questions about what we were doing." The light changes, and we move again. "And then she was watching this romantic movie and started talking about how she doesn't have a boyfriend and probably never will. She sounded really sad about it."

"Oh, poor baby. I honestly never thought she cared about any of that."

"She's *twenty*, Mom. Most twenty-year-olds in this country have already had sex. She's totally an adult—her boobs are bigger than mine. I bet she's way more interested in guys than we realize."

"She never talks about boys in her class. I mean, she *talks* about them . . . names go by . . . but no one name more than any other. Oh, wait!" Mom raises a finger off the steering wheel. "Now that I'm thinking about it, she *has* mentioned an Ethan a few times. A lot of it is complaining—she thought he had taken her pencil a couple of days ago—but she's definitely noticed him."

"Getting annoyed at him could totally mean she likes him. Back in seventh grade, I thought I hated Brian Kessler. I used to come home and complain about what a jerk he was. And he was the first boy I ever went out with."

"He was one of your boyfriends? I don't even remember the name."

"The relationship never got past the texting stage—but

that was considered going out in seventh grade. Anyway, I'll ask Ivy about Ethan. She needs to start getting out of the house without me before I go to college. Otherwise—" I stop before I say what I'm thinking, which is that it would kill me to leave knowing that Ivy has no escape from Ron and Mom. I switch to, "A boyfriend would be amazing for her. She'd have someone to do things with and to talk to and to help her grow up a little. Plus she probably has all these physical feelings—I mean, I *know* she does since she was asking me all those questions."

Mom groans. "That's what I'm terrified of—Ivy and some boy exploring each other's bodies, trying to figure it all out, letting nature take over. She could easily wind up pregnant, Chloe."

"If we tell her exactly how people get pregnant and how to avoid it, I bet she'll be careful. She sets the alarm clock every night and brushes her teeth for exactly three minutes—she's a total rule follower. If you explain about condoms, she'll use them—and also probably lecture to death any guy who tries to get away without one."

Mom's laugh ends in a sigh. "I'm sorry, Chloe, but even if I can get over my own fears, I honestly don't see this ever happening. It's just so hard for her to be social in *any* way, and then adding in romance . . ."

Shocker: Mom's giving up before even trying. Which just makes me more determined. "I'll figure something out. I'm going to make this my mission—to get Ivy a boyfriend before I leave for college. You didn't hear how sad she sounded last night. She's so lonely. I'm going to make this happen for her, even if I have to help her along every step of the way."

"*Every* step of the way?"

"Okay, not every step of the way," I concede. "Some things they'll have to figure out for themselves."

"That's what terrifies me."

"Get over it," I say.

Ivy's hungry when we get home, so Mom makes her a grilled cheese sandwich with the American cheese and sliced white bread we just picked up at the market. Ivy likes her food bland and colorless.

I pull up a chair to sit opposite from her as she's eating. Mom lurks nearby, listening but letting me do the talking.

I keep it casual. "Hey, Ives? I was just thinking . . . Are there any boys you like to hang with at school?"

"I don't know." She examines the edges of a grilled cheese half and then bites into it. She chews and swallows. There are traces of gluey orange cheese at the corners of her mouth as she says, "They don't talk that much to me."

Yeah, well, that's probably true: the class is specifically for kids on the autism spectrum. There's probably not a lot of conversation for conversation's sake.

Then she says, "Ethan likes to talk. Usually about movies. He's obsessed with movies."

"Ethan, huh?" I say with a meaningful glance in Mom's direction.

"But he's really annoying sometimes. He talks about movies even if no one cares. Diana always says to him, 'Stop talking so much, no one cares,' but he still talks about them. Diana says he's boring." She pronounces Diana the Spanish way, *Dee-ah-na*.

"Do *you* think he's boring?"

"Sometimes." She puts down the sandwich and reaches for her glass of milk. "If I've seen the movie, it's okay."

"Maybe you should ask Ethan if he wants to go see a movie sometime."

"He sees movies all the time."

"I meant with you."

"With me?" She puts her glass down without drinking from it. "That would be weird."

"Why? James and I go to movies together all the time."

"That's because he's your boyfriend."

"He wasn't always. Things have to start somehow."

"Things?"

"You know . . . Stuff between a girl and a guy."

"Oh." She thinks for a moment. "Did you and James see a movie before he was your boyfriend?"

"Yeah," I say, even though it's not entirely true. We hooked up at a party last spring and then hooked up again at another party and then we hung out together at each other's houses a couple of times and then we just slipped into being boyfriend and girlfriend. Somewhere in there we probably saw a movie or two, but never just as friends.

"Huh," Ivy says. "Ethan really likes movies. He'd probably like it if I invited him to one."

"So do you want to?"

"I don't know. I need to think about it." She crams the rest of the sandwich into her mouth and excuses herself from the table.

"She's so hard to read," Mom says, coming forward after Ivy's left the room.

"Not for me," I say. "She's interested. A little nervous, but interested. I'll keep trying."

"I have such mixed feelings about her growing up. You too. I'd like to keep my little girls little for as long as possible."

I don't say anything. It's been a long time since I felt like a little girl.

EIGHT

In Ms. Campanelli's class on Tuesday, we're discussing tragic and comedic endings, and Jana Rodriguez brings up *Jane Eyre,* which we read back in September. "I know it's supposed to count as a happy ending," she says, pulling her thick ponytail over her shoulder, "but it doesn't *feel* happy to me. Rochester's such a mess by that point — blind and missing a hand and scarred and everything —"

"Not in the movie," Carolyn Horinberg says. "Michael Fassbender was a little blind, but otherwise he was perfect."

"He's too beautiful to ruin," Sarah says.

"Ew," Jana says, and the girls in the class start arguing about whether he's cute or not.

"Hold on!" Camp says. "Jana made a really good point, and I want to talk about it. Why couldn't Jane just come back and find Rochester strong and virile but now free to marry her? Why does he have to be a wreck?"

"He had to be punished," I say.

"For what?" Jana asks, turning in her seat to look at me.

"Um, for trying to commit bigamy?"

"Oh, who cares?" she says with a shrug. "His wife was cray.

And he took care of her and even tried to save her life, which was more than anyone else would have done."

"Trying to marry someone when you already have a wife is pretty bad."

"Sucks to suck," Lambert Vini says helpfully.

Jana says, "But it's so not fair that Jane gets punished too — instead of getting the handsome, strong Rochester she fell in love with, she gets stuck with lame, blind Rochester. He's not nearly as sexy."

"Except when he's Michael Fassbender," Sarah says.

Jana ignores that. "Why should Jane have to lose out? She should get to end up with someone hot."

"But that's part of the point, right, Camp?" I'm so eager to appeal to the teacher that I accidentally call her by the nickname we usually only use behind her back. "That Jane gets to be the strong one now? Like the way she tells him another guy wants to marry her, just to torture him. He was kind of mean to Jane before, and now she's kind of mean to him."

Jana says, "I still say she'd rather have him the way he was before. Sexy and strong."

"Like Michael Fassbender," Sarah says.

"Maybe she likes him better this way," David Fields says. He's sitting over by the wall and, as usual, has been staring at his laptop, but apparently he's deigned to eavesdrop on the class discussion, because he looks up now. "Some girls prefer their men thoroughly emasculated. Right, Chloe?" He jerks his chin meaningfully in James's direction.

Someone makes a low *ooooh* noise. James glares at David

and opens his mouth, but I get my response in first: "If that were true, David, you'd probably get a date once in a while."

That gets a pretty big laugh.

Ms. Campanelli says, "Guys, guys, please don't get personal in classroom discussions. I expect better from you, Chloe."

"Sorry," I say. "He started it."

David puts an offended hand to his chest. "*I* was just discussing *Jane Eyre.*"

"Let's get back to Shakespeare," Ms. Camp says wearily.

At lunch, Sarah and I talk about what happened in English.

"James looked like he was ready to kill David," Sarah says. "Do you think he'd ever actually do anything to him?"

"Nah." I tear a chunk off my bagel. I have to bring my lunches from home — Ron says school lunches are a waste of money — but I'm too tired in the morning to make anything other than bagels with cream cheese or peanut butter and jelly sandwiches, both of which I'm royally sick of. "James isn't the violent type."

"Lucky for David. James could crush him with a single blow. He's, like, twice his size."

"David's such a jerk. I don't know what his problem is."

"He's *so* arrogant." She pulls a half-chewed cherry tomato out of her mouth, examines it, makes a face, and drops it on her tray. "He thinks he's smarter than everyone else because he gets As really easily."

"I will vomit if you do that with another tomato."

"It's not my fault — it was slimy." She pushes the salad

away and reaches for a brownie. "Hey, want to do something after school today? I can drive."

"I can't. I told my mom I'd pick Ivy up from her school —I'm heading out right after bio."

"It's so annoying that she has to go to a different school that's farther away. Why don't they just let her go here?"

"No class for her here. Can I have a bite of your brownie?" I don't feel like launching into the story of Ivy's educational choices.

Ivy actually went to a regular public elementary school, but by fourth grade, the other girls had figured out that she was gullible and played some pretty dirty tricks on her, like locking her in a closet and stealing her stuff. Mom pulled Ivy out as soon as she realized what was going on and has kept her in special needs classes ever since. They may not be all that great academically, but at least no one's mean to Ivy and she feels safe there.

She's been in the same class at Vicente High for a couple of years now. There aren't that many options for special needs kids who are already over eighteen, so we're actually lucky it isn't even farther away—for LA, half an hour's a reasonable commute. The school district is theoretically responsible for transportation, but Ivy hated riding the bus with all the other special needs kids. A lot of them had serious behavior problems, and by the time she got home every day, she was a wreck from spending over an hour in a confined space with kids who were bucking wildly in their seats and banging their heads and shouting at the aides who rode the buses with them, so Mom resigned herself to dropping her off and picking her up. It wasn't a problem until Mom got married and Ron realized he could save money by replacing his paid receptionist with his free wife. Which leaves me picking up Ivy a lot.

That's the complete story, but my friendship with Sarah is built on laughing and teasing and gossiping and both sincere and insincere flattery. No reason to inject too much of my family life into it. It would just drag us both down.

I get to Ivy's school about half an hour before classes end so I can go in and scope out the boys in her class—I'm especially interested in seeing Ethan. Since it isn't pickup time yet, the gate's closed, and I have to park on the street and walk in. A security guard buzzes me through the door and escorts me to the main office, where they check my ID and give me a stick-on name tag. Los Angeles public schools have gotten pretty intense about security in the last few years, and this one's in kind of a dicey neighborhood, so they're extra careful.

I've only ever picked Ivy up outside, in my car, so it takes me a while to find the right room number. In the hallway, some guy yells at me to get to class, but I point to my badge and he backs off.

It's total chaos in Ivy's classroom, and I sneak in without anyone noticing. The teacher and a couple of aides are at the front of the room, sitting behind tables covered with small treats (plates of M&M's, pyramids of Hershey's Kisses, bowls of pretzels) with prices written on big pieces of paper near them (*5 cents, 30 cents, 10 cents*). The students are carrying around fistfuls of plastic coins, and after I watch for a minute or two, I realize they're buying snacks with their play money.

Not everyone's into it. About a third of the kids in the room are sitting at tables, rocking or shaking their heads or staring into space, their stash of coins ignored on the table in front of them. An aide is circling around, trying to coax them to get up and join the fun.

I'm glad Ivy's up at the front, picking out red M&M's (the only color she likes), carefully counting each one as she adds it to the small pile in front of her. A thin, pale girl with bad skin and French-braided dirty blond hair is standing next to her. She's wearing overalls. Her lips are moving, but I can't tell if she's talking to Ivy or just to the air.

The aide who's walking around spots me. "Hi," she says, coming over. "You've *got* to be Ivy's sister." She's a short, pretty woman with light brown skin and cropped hair, probably not that much older than Ivy in years, but totally an adult in a way that I can't imagine my sister ever being.

"How'd you know?"

"You look a lot alike—those beautiful blue eyes and all."

"Aw, thanks. I'm Chloe."

"Kimberly."

"Hey," I say. "Maybe you can help me. We're trying to get Ivy to be more social? We were thinking of inviting a friend from school to do something with her, but we weren't sure who we should ask."

"That's a great idea." She surveys the room. "Let me think about who she usually hangs out with . . ."

"Who's the girl standing next to her?"

"That's Diana." She pronounces it the way Ivy did: *Dee-ah-na*. "Ivy definitely likes her—when they need to buddy up, it's always those two. She'd be a good choice for a get-together —if you can work out the logistics. Unfortunately she lives pretty far away, in, like, Alhambra or something. Poor thing is on the bus for hours every day."

That's a problem. I want someone who Ivy can see easily. Plus she seemed into the boyfriend idea, so . . . forget Diana. "How about Ethan? She talks a lot about him."

"I'm not surprised. He's a real cutie." Kimberly nods toward a slim boy who's leaning against a wall near the tables, soberly chewing on a pretzel, a bunch more cupped in his half-open upturned hand. He has light brown wavy hair and a slightly pixie-ish face that looks vaguely familiar—I've probably seen him at pickup. "All the girls in the class seem to have a special place in their hearts for Ethan. And he lives on the west side. You do too, right?"

"Yeah."

"Well, there you go. Give him a try. You can get his number out of the class directory." She glances at her watch. "Oops, time to clean up." She claps her hands and makes an announcement to the room and then there's a lot of movement as the teachers shout commands and the students rush around to obey them. Well, some of them do, anyway.

Ivy obediently sorts her coins out on the front table

according to the teacher's instructions and then grabs Diana's arm and tugs her back toward a table. They pass Ethan, and his eyes follow Ivy.

I don't know much about autism, but I know a lot about high school guys, and it looks to me like he's interested in her. And why wouldn't he be? She's pretty cute, and totally sweet.

"Chloe?" She's turned around and is staring at me. "Why are you here?"

"I was early for pickup and figured I'd come in and see what your class is like. Did you—"

"Shhh," she says. "The teacher's talking."

I nod sheepishly and fade back until class is officially dismissed.

NINE

In the car, I say cautiously, "That kid Ethan seems nice."

"Did you talk to him?"

"No."

"Then why do you think he's nice?"

"He just seemed nice, that's all."

"He doesn't do anything wrong."

"What do you mean?"

"The other boys drive everyone crazy. Like, Roger hits himself in the head, and sometimes the teachers have to take Ajay out of the room because he won't listen."

"Who do you like the best?" I ask. "Of those three? Ethan, Roger, or Ajay?"

"Ethan."

Just what I was hoping she'd say. "Cool! I think you should text him and see if he wants to do something this weekend."

"Do something?" she repeats. "Like what?"

"You guys could go to a movie or out for ice cream or to a bookstore . . . Whatever sounds like fun to you."

"Could we get frozen yogurt?"

"Sure."

"But you have to drive me," she says. "Not Mom. He'll think I'm a baby if she drives me."

"No problem. So we'll text him when we get home?"

"I guess, but it will be weird."

"What will?"

"Going for frozen yogurt with him. We're not really friends."

"That's how you become friends with someone. Doing stuff like that."

"You and Sarah were already friends when you started going out for frozen yogurt."

"But doing stuff like that made us better friends. You and Ethan are already friends too, right?"

"No, we're not. That's why it's weird."

"You're in class together, and you like to talk to each other. That's what being friends is."

"I don't think so. And we almost never talk to each other at school."

"Well, you will when you go out for frozen yogurt."

She doesn't say anything to that, or at least nothing out loud. She turns her head away, but I can hear soft hissing as she whispers to herself.

Back home, we look up Ethan's number on the online school directory and write a text together (actually, I write it, but I make her hit Send).

This is Ivy from school. Would you like to get some frozen yogurt with me this weekend?

Ethan's answer comes back quickly: Yes, please

The *please* kills me. It's so sweet.

"Ask him if Saturday afternoon works," I say. "At, like, three or four?"

Ivy composes another text, her tongue caught between her teeth as she concentrates on punching out each word. She shows it to me for my approval before sending it.

We're at the kitchen table, doing our homework. Mom and Ron are staying late at the office, which means it's nice and peaceful right now.

Ethan texts back that three is fine and asks where they should meet.

"There's a place at Bundy and Santa Monica that I like," I say.

"What's it called?"

"I can't remember. Just tell him the intersection. He'll find it."

"No, no." She jumps up out of her chair and starts pacing around the table, pounding at her hips with her fists. "What if there's another frozen yogurt place near there?"

"I'm pretty sure there isn't." But she's getting more agitated, bouncing her hands harder and faster against the sides of her thighs. So I say, "Fine. Let's just go to Yogurt Palace on Montana." It's more expensive and smaller, but at least I remember the name.

"Okay." She stops hitting herself, but her hands stay rigid in the air near her waist. "You sure that's the right name?"

"Positive."

She still does a Google search to double-check it before sending the text.

There's a photo of me and Ivy stuck with a magnet on the refrigerator in our kitchen. I'm a toddler, and Ivy's five or six. We're holding hands tightly. I'm looking right at whoever is taking the photo, but my sister is looking past the photographer, her gaze elusive.

It's been up there as long as I can remember, along with a bunch of other family photos, a torn-out gazpacho recipe from a magazine, a partial alphabet of letter magnets, and a drawing I did in second grade of my family, my mother looming larger than my father, and Ivy and me together to the side, drawn with identical long hair and eyelashes.

Nothing on there ever changes, so I'd stopped even seeing any of it, but then one day a few years ago, I suddenly stared at the photo of me and Ivy. For the first time, it seemed weird to me — why were we holding hands? We'd never held hands that I remembered. Ivy has never liked being touched.

Mom was at the table doing some work, so I looked over my shoulder and said, "When was this photo of me and Ivy taken?"

She raised her head and squinted at it. "That one? I think we were at one of those indoor park things, with the slides and balls and stuff. They had an area that was for kids only. So we said you two could explore it, but only if Ivy held your hand and watched out for you. You were only three."

"But she hates holding hands."

"She knew she was responsible for you and wanted to be a good big sister. She guided you in and out very carefully and was so worried you might get hurt that she marched you quickly through and right back to us."

"Huh," I said. "I have no memory of this."

Most of the time, when I'm opening the refrigerator, the photo is just part of the background—I don't even notice it. But every once in a while, I stop to look at the two little blond girls, holding hands, a tiny team facing the world together.

TEN

On Saturday afternoon, I'm curled up on my bed binge-watching a nineties TV show when Ivy comes into our room and says, "We should go."

I check the time. "It's too early. It only takes ten or fifteen minutes to get there."

"There could be traffic."

"On a Saturday? Unlikely. Is that what you're planning to wear?"

"Yeah." She's got on her usual: stretch pants (black today) and a short, worn cotton tee (yellow today). She looks not un-bee-like.

Ivy doesn't like clothes that are tight or uncomfortable or have a lot of buttons, hooks, or zippers. She also hates shirt tags and long sleeves and necklaces, watches, and rings. That leaves her with a pretty limited wardrobe.

"Maybe change first?" I say. "You have a gray skirt, right? You could wear it with that blue top I gave you for your birthday. That would look really nice."

Her hands start vibrating at her sides. "I don't like wearing skirts. I can feel my legs too much."

"Okay. Then how about you keep the pants but change your top?" The one I gave her is longer and looser, and will cover up the lumpy elastic waistline of those pants.

"Why do you want me to look nice?"

"It's just nice to look nice when you're meeting a friend." Okay, I sound like an idiot. I don't know what else to say, though. I don't want to make her more nervous . . . but I want her to look decent. For her sake.

"Okay," she says, but you can tell she's not happy about it, and once she's put the top on, she keeps plucking nervously at the gauzy fabric.

She starts pacing around our bedroom. "We should go," she says. "Why aren't you ready?"

I tell her again that it's too early, but after about twenty minutes of enduring the exact same exchange every thirty seconds, I give up. "Fine, let's go. We'll be early, though."

Joke's on me—a lane of Sunset is blocked by a moving truck, and traffic's backed up, and once we get past that and down to Montana, I can't find parking close to the yogurt place.

"It's three-oh-four," Ivy says when we finally get out of the car and start walking. "We're late. It's bad to be late."

"It's okay. You're allowed an extra five minutes to show up somewhere before you're considered late."

"Five minutes late is late."

We reach the shop. I open the door and follow her inside. "I bet he's not even here yet."

"Yes, he is." She points across the shop, halting so abruptly that I bump into her.

"Don't *stop*," I say, and give her an impatient little shove toward Ethan, who's slouching by the frozen yogurt machines, his hands stuck deep into his pockets. There's a guy next to him whose back is toward us; he's reading the yogurt information above the machines. "Come on," I say, because Ivy is hesitating again. Her hands are snaking at her sides, and any second she's going to start slapping at her hips. I grab her by the wrist and tug her over to Ethan, who regards us gravely.

"Hi, Ivy," he says.

Ivy looks down at the floor and mutters a barely audible "hi," and I try to make up for her apparent lack of enthusiasm by practically shouting, "Hey, Ethan!" The guy next to Ethan turns around, a polite smile on his face, which fades the second he gets a look at me.

It's David Fields.

"Chloe?" he says. "What are you doing here?" He looks back and forth from me to Ivy. "Oh, my God. Is she your sister?"

"Just for my whole life." Now I know why Ethan looked so familiar: he's a thinner, more-hunched-into-himself, and less-savage version of David. "Ethan's your brother?"

"Just for my whole life."

"Huh." I don't know what else to say. If he were a friend, it would be a cool coincidence. But if he were a friend, we'd probably have figured out a long time ago that we both had siblings in the same special needs class.

"We need to get frozen yogurt," Ivy says, shifting nervously.

"Right," I say. "But isn't it funny that I know Ethan's brother? He goes to my school. Ivy, this is David. David, Ivy."

"Nice to meet you," David says, and shakes her hand. He then introduces his brother to me, even though I said hi to him already, and *we* shake hands.

It's strange how much the two of them look alike and also don't look alike. Ethan is thinner and more slope-shouldered, and his light brown hair is longer and bushier than David's, which is pretty short. But there are subtle differences too—there's all this awareness and calculation and judgment in David's brownish/grayish eyes, and Ethan's just look innocent and uncertain.

I separate a couple of paper bowls from a stack and hand them to Ivy and Ethan, who wander down the row of yogurt machines, checking out the different flavors, not consulting or even acknowledging each other, but sort of together anyway.

"Are you staying?" David asks me.

"Yeah—Ivy wants me to. How about you?"

"I have to."

"Why?"

He just shrugs. "You and your sister look a lot alike."

"I was going to say the same thing about you and your brother. He looked familiar when I saw him before, but I didn't know why."

"It's such a weird coincidence."

"So weird."

There's an awkward pause. Then we both start to speak at the same time and stop.

"Sorry, what?" he says.

"I was just going to ask if you were going to get some yogurt. What were you going to say?"

"Just that I almost didn't recognize you without James at your side. I thought you two were permanently attached at the hip."

Ugh. His brother may be my great hope for Ivy, but David's still a jerk. I don't even bother to respond—what do you say to something like that, anyway?—just grab a bowl and stalk away to the other end of the row of machines, where I splurt some chocolate yogurt into it.

Ivy's moved on to the toppings bar and is ladling a ton of colorful sprinkles onto her yogurt. Ethan's waiting for her to finish—apparently he likes his yogurt plain.

"I'm going to pay for yours," he tells her when she's done. She looks at me uncertainly. I nod, and she lets him take her bowl and put it on the scale next to his.

The cashier is a smiley young Asian American woman. She's keeping up a stream of patter, either oblivious to the fact that Ivy and Ethan aren't really responding or savvy enough to sense that they need some help making conversation. She counts out Ethan's change and then Ethan picks up both yogurt cups and says to Ivy, "Come with me," and leads the way to a table. She looks back at me, but I gesture to her to follow him, and she does.

"Excellent," David says. He's come up next to me. "We talked about how this would go, and he remembered everything I told him to do."

"You guys close?"

"I mean, yeah." He puts his cup on the scale.

"Are you together?" the bubbly cashier asks.

David and I say no at the same time. She tells him the price, and he pays before heading over to an empty table.

While the cashier is weighing my cup, I say, "Hey, any chance you're hiring?" Seems like a decent place to work — *she* certainly seems to be enjoying herself.

"I think we're set right now," she says, "but you can fill out an application, and we'll keep it on file in case something opens up. I'll bring one over to you. Three forty-seven, please."

I pay, then turn and hesitate, wondering whether I should sit with David or not. I don't really want to have to make conversation with him, but sitting a few feet away and ignoring each other for the next half-hour or so seems even more awkward.

I decide to let him decide. "You want company?" I ask, approaching his table.

"Up to you." He already has his phone out and is flicking at it with one hand while he shoves spoonfuls of yogurt into his mouth with the other.

I sit. He just keeps looking at his phone, so I pull out mine.

I text Sarah about the situation and get back a Holy crap, David Fields???????

David and I both look up from our phones at the same time, so I nod toward the other table, figuring I might as well be friendly—it might make things more comfortable for *me,* even if he doesn't care. "How long do you think they'll last?"

"As a couple?"

"No, I mean right now. I'm guessing not more than half an hour. Ivy's never been much of a sit-and-chat kind of girl."

"Ethan can sit and chat all day long. It's *listening* that's hard for him."

"How long has he been in that class at Vicente?"

"This is his second year."

"It's Ivy's third—and last. She turns twenty-one this summer. No more school after that."

"Just the big bad world."

"I wish she could stay in high school forever."

"Yeah, I know. It's safe for them there." He shifts in his seat. "How about you? What's in the future? College, I assume?"

"Definitely. You?"

"I don't know." He swipes at his mouth with the back of his hand, which he then wipes on his jeans. "I don't want to leave Ethan all alone."

"All alone? What about your parents?"

"Divorced. Dad lost the custody battle, so we live with him."

"You mean he won it."

"Do I?"

I don't know what to say to that.

"Anyway, Mom moved to another state and sends us

postcards of some lake at sunset. And Dad's all about the new wife. She just had a baby, so . . ." He trails off, then shrugs. "Whatever. I'll make sure Ethan's okay. You going to take AP English next year?"

It takes me a second to catch up with the change in subject. "Uh . . . yeah. Planning to. You?"

"I'm taking as many APs as I can."

"But why, if you're—"

He cuts me off, his finger raised. "Shhh—listen."

Ethan is talking more loudly than he needs to in such a small space. "I like the X-Men movies but not *Wolverine Origins* or *X-Men: The Last Stand.* Those are the worst ones. A lot of people think the best one is *X-Men: First Class,* but I think *X-Men: Days of Future Past* is better. What's your favorite?"

Ivy's voice is quieter; I have to strain to hear her response. "I've only seen the first one. It was on TV. I watched it with Chloe and my mother and my stepfather."

"The first one's pretty good," Ethan says.

"It was okay."

"Wolverine is the best character. He's played by Hugh Jackman, who's originally from Australia. He was also in the movie that was called *Australia,* but it's not very good. A lot more people saw him in *Les Misérables.* Some people really liked that movie, but a lot of people didn't. I didn't. Did you see it?"

"No."

"She doesn't go to a lot of movies," I whisper to David.

"Too bad," he whispers back. "Ethan lives and breathes movies. I told him he could talk about them if he didn't know what else to say."

"You should have told him to talk about TV shows. Ivy's strong on those."

"I'll remember that for next time."

"Do you think they're having fun?"

"Ethan looks pretty happy right now. What about her?"

I study my sister, who's gazing down at the table, her hands twitching by her sides. She doesn't exactly look ecstatic, but she might just be nervous. "I don't know. I hope so. I really want this to go well. She needs friends."

"Ethan has friends—or says he does—but they're all online. He's probably being catfished by half of them." David fidgets in his seat. He's devoured his frozen yogurt, and seems restless without it. He picks up his phone and flips it in his palm.

"We don't have to talk," I say. "You can use your phone."

His neck kind of retracts at that—hard to tell if it's relief or annoyance. "Yeah, okay," he says. He slouches in his seat and stares at his phone screen as his thumbs skim over the keypad. I curl up in my chair with my own phone.

A minute later, the cashier comes over with the promised job application, which she hands to me. "Drop it off whenever you want," she says with a friendly smile. "No rush." She goes back to the counter.

"What's that?" David asks.

"Job application." I put it in my purse to fill out at home

—I don't have my social security number with me, and she said there was no rush.

"You looking for work?"

"No, I just have a job application collection. Don't you?"

He doesn't respond, just studies me uncertainly, like something doesn't make sense to him.

ELEVEN

Ivy CALLS AN END to the date about five minutes later. She gets up abruptly—Ethan's in midsentence, still talking about the X-Men franchise—walks over to our table, and says, "I'm done."

"You sure you don't want to hang out a little longer?" I ask.

"No, I'm done."

"Okay, then . . ." I stand up. "It's been real," I tell David flatly.

"Yeah," he says. "Later."

Ethan has leapt to his feet and joined us. "I'll walk you guys to your car," he says.

"That's really nice, but you don't have to," I say. "We're parked a couple of blocks away."

"My brother said I should."

"Yes, I did." David gets up, jamming his phone in his pocket. "Come on. Let's accompany these two lovely ladies to their car."

I catch a whiff of sarcasm, but the other two are oblivious to it. Ethan resumes his X-Men discourse, but the rest of us are silent, and the walk feels endless. We come to a halt at our Subaru hatchback.

"This is yours?" David says, like he's surprised.

"My mom's."

"Where's *your* car?"

"Nonexistent?"

"Seriously? I pictured you always cruising around in some hot girl car like a Porsche or something."

"A 'hot girl car'? What does that even mean? That the girl is hot or the car is?"

He flushes. "I don't know why I used that word. I never do."

"Hot or girl?" I ask sweetly.

"Come on," he says to Ethan. "We have to get home."

"Wait." Ethan turns to Ivy and holds out his hand. "I've had a very nice time," he says politely.

Ivy stares at his hand.

"Shake it!" I hiss.

"I know!" she says, annoyed, and puts her hand in his.

He bends forward and kisses her quickly and lightly on the cheek, then rocks back on his heels, glancing over at his brother.

David nods his approval. "Well done. You ready to go?"

"First you have to say goodbye to Ivy's sister."

"Right." David holds his hand out. "Goodbye, Chloe."

I pump his hand, as aware of our audience as he is. "Goodbye, David. It was nice to see you."

"Let's do this again sometime," he says gravely.

"Yes, let's."

We release each other's hands and step back. Ethan studies

us for a moment, his grayish eyes flickering back and forth quickly between our two faces.

If I had to make a guess, I'd say he's waiting for David to kiss me on the cheek.

That's not going to happen.

"Well?" I ask Ivy once we're safely in the car.

"What?"

"Did you have fun?"

"It was okay."

"Ethan seems really nice."

"I guess."

"It's funny that I know his brother from school."

"Are you guys friends?"

"Not really." The goal is to get Ivy to like Ethan, so that's all I say. "But we do have a class together."

"That's like me and Ethan—we're in the same class, but we're not friends."

"Even after today? You don't think you're friends now?"

"Maybe. We went out for frozen yogurt, and that's what you and Sarah do, and she's your best friend."

"Yeah." I dart a sideways glance at her as I brake for a light. "It's also what James and I do, and he's my boyfriend."

She doesn't respond to that, just slumps in her seat and chews her lip for a while.

Back home, I shower and get dressed to go out.

"What do you think?" I ask Ivy, twirling around for her

in our bedroom to show off my circle skirt and short, tight sweater. "Will James like this?"

"You look great." She always says I look great—I accidentally trained her to give meaningless compliments. A few years ago, Mom put on a dress for a friend's fiftieth birthday party, and Ivy said, "You look like you're pregnant, but you're not pregnant, right?" Mom tore the dress off and said she was just going to stay home. I lectured Ivy for a while about how it's important to make people feel good about themselves, and now when Mom and I get dressed up, she always says we look great.

I'm able to slip out of the house without running into Ron. I don't want to go through the whole "James needs to come inside" thing with him again.

In the car, I tell James about how Ethan turned out to be David's brother.

"Well, that sucks," James says. His car purrs under his skillful handling. I like watching his hand work the shift—it's kind of sexy, but I'm not going to overthink the metaphor. "Guess you'll have to keep looking."

"Nah. Ethan's totally sweet."

"How is that possible if he's that douchebag's brother?"

"Siblings can be really different. Look at me and Ivy."

"Yeah, but you guys are different because she's messed up."

My face feels suddenly hot. "She's not messed up."

"Sorry." He takes his hand off the stick shift so he can pat my leg briefly. "You know what I mean."

For a moment, I think about being sullen and saying that

no, I don't know what he means, that calling my sister "messed up" is really lousy.

But I don't want to be *that* girl, the one who takes everything too seriously and has weird reactions to things. I've never wanted to be that girl. I want to be the cool, fun—and, yes, *hot* girl—who doesn't think too deeply about anything at all, at least not when she's with her adorable boyfriend.

So I just change the subject, ask him to tell me about the game he played that morning, and when he says, "We won!" I tell him he's awesome and that I wish I'd been there to cheer him on.

The movie we want to see is sold out, so James buys us tickets to our second choice, which turns out to be about as good as you'd expect a second choice movie to be.

We split up to use the bathroom before heading out into the mall to grab some dinner. I check my texts while I'm waiting for an empty stall and see one from a number I don't recognize.

Ethan wants another date with your sister. He's texting her but wanted me to text you too

I'm almost at the front of the line, so I quickly write back I'll check with Ivy when I get home and leave it at that. I'm glad Ethan's eager to see Ivy again. I just hope she's as enthusiastic about seeing him.

"Again?" she says when I bring it up the next morning. "We just had frozen yogurt."

"I know. He must have had a lot of fun. We're probably talking next weekend anyway—so it's not *right* away."

"You have to drive me and stay again. I don't want to go alone."

I'm just glad she wants to go at all, so I promise to chauffeur and hover over her as she and Ethan text back and forth for a while. I check her texts before she sends them to make sure she doesn't say something super rude or awkward.

I'm very happy, he writes, when they finally settle on going bowling that Saturday.

"He's so sweet," I say.

"Is James sweet?"

"Totally."

"Is that why you like him?"

"That and his enormous biceps."

Her brow furrows. "His arm muscles?"

"Yeah. I like the way they look. And feel."

"I don't want to touch Ethan's biceps," she says, her eyes flickering about the room in sudden panic.

"Don't worry about it. You're not up to the biceps-touching part of the relationship yet. And by the time you are, you may be more into the idea."

She just shakes her head.

Well, Mom definitely doesn't need to be worried about Ivy's rushing into having casual sex. Right now that seems about as likely as her landing the starring role in Channing Tatum's next romantic comedy.

I wish I could ask David if Ethan's equally nervous

about the physical stuff, but I don't feel comfortable doing that.

Why couldn't Ethan's brother be someone I could talk to? I feel so alone in this.

In Camp's class on Monday, David briefly looks up from his laptop as I walk past him, and we nod at each other. Even that tiny acknowledgment of each other's existence feels weird.

Camp assigns a paper for Friday, and at lunch we all complain that it's way too much work.

"Maybe Camp's really evil," Sarah says. "Maybe this whole *I love teaching kids* is a cover for her sadism."

"She probably has a dungeon in her house," Jacob Gordon says. "With all sorts of sick tortures and handcuffs and shit."

"Yeah, and that's why she wears skirts with those big pockets," Sarah says with a giggle. "She keeps cattle prods and Tasers in there."

"I bet she has leather versions of those skirts for when she's working in the dungeon," he says.

"Yeah, that's sexy," James says. "Big shapeless skirts made out of leather."

"Look who's getting turned on thinking about the Campster," Jacob says.

"Right," James says. "That lady is *hot*."

"Get in line," Jacob says. "Those saggy boobs are all mine."

They laugh, but I don't. They're being too mean. Camp's

a good teacher, and she's always nice to us. And there's something innocent and vulnerable about her that makes me want to protect her. Something almost Ivy-like.

I don't say anything, though. Just eat my lunch and wait for them to talk about something else.

TWELVE

THE DAY BEFORE Ethan and Ivy's date, I get nervous about the fact it's at a bowling alley— Ivy doesn't do well with loud noises.

"Have you ever been to one before?" I ask.

She shakes her head. "I don't think so."

I've been a bunch of times, but it was always for other kids' birthday parties. Ivy doesn't go to a lot of parties. Or any, really. I explain how noisy they can get with all the crashing pins and all. "You going to be okay with that?" I ask her.

"I don't know," she says. "Should I tell Ethan I don't want to go?"

"Wait—I have an idea." I find some videos online of people bowling, and I play them for her, increasing the volume with each one until it's as loud as I can make it. It's still not as loud as the real thing, but at least it gives her a sense of the kind of noise she'll be dealing with.

She doesn't mind watching the videos and, in fact, looks for more on her own and plays them at top volume in our room until Ron yells from the master bedroom that he can't hear himself think.

Then she puts on her headphones and listens to them some more.

The desensitization actually works. As soon as we walk inside the bowling alley, the noise is pretty intense. Ivy winces and her hands float up toward her ears, but then they pause and drop down at her sides again.

"Bowling alleys are always noisy," she informs me. "But it's okay. It's just the ball hitting the pins."

"Yeah," I say. "I don't like the noise, but I can live with it."

"Me too," she says.

The guys are waiting for us at the front desk. Ethan comes forward eagerly and reaches toward Ivy. I'm not sure what he's going for—hug? Handshake? Kiss? It doesn't matter: Ivy ducks away, and his hand lands on her arm, which he pats awkwardly.

"Hi," he says.

"Hi," she says. "I don't know how to do bowling."

I should have told her before that you don't "do" bowling. I just assumed she knew.

"That's okay," Ethan says. "I can teach you. I'm good at it."

David says, "We already got a lane. You guys just need to get your shoes."

"Are we bowling too?" I ask him.

"Might as well. We're stuck here, right? Or are you leaving?"

"No, don't!" Ivy clutches at my arm.

"Guess I'm staying." I knew as soon as I saw David there that Ivy wouldn't let me leave.

"Here's where you get the shoes," Ethan says, and leads Ivy away.

David says in a low voice, "If we play against them, they can be on a team together instead of bowling against each other. It's probably better that way — Ethan can get competitive."

I nod. Not a bad idea.

After Ivy and I give our sizes to the overweight, balding guy behind the counter, he slaps a couple of pairs of bowling shoes down in front of us. I notice a sign on the wall saying they're hiring and ask him what the job is.

"You really interested?" He gives me an up and down sort of look.

"Sure."

"It's an old sign, but you never know — people come and go a lot. Something might open up. I'll get you an application." He goes into the back room.

"You don't want to work here," David says.

The guy comes back with the application before I can respond, so I wait until we've moved over to the nearby bench to put on our shoes to ask him why not.

"Well, first of all there's the noise," he says.

"It's probably better in the back office."

"Maybe. But did you see the way that guy looked at you when he handed you the application? This place would be a daily creepfest for a girl who looks like you."

"A girl who looks like me? What does that mean?"

"You know," he says irritably.

"Do I?"

He turns away and asks Ivy how the bowling shoes feel.

"Weird," she says.

Ethan says, "Are they too small? The first pair I tried on was too small, but the second pair felt okay. I'm usually a ten, but here I'm a ten and a half. Do you want me to get you a bigger size?"

"I don't know. They just feel weird." Ivy's worn the same brand of sneakers for the last five years and hates wearing any other shoes. It's always an issue when we need her to get dressed up.

"Mine feel weird too," I say. "But we're not wearing them for long—let's not worry about it."

"Come pick out your balls," David says, and leads us to the racks.

I reach for a pretty blue and white one. "Perfect! It matches my shirt."

"You have to check the weight and finger holes."

"No! I want this one." I hug it defiantly against my chest. He rolls his eyes.

Ethan says to Ivy, "I could pick one out for you if you want."

"Okay."

"I use a pretty big one, but I think you should have one that's not as heavy."

"Girls can be strong too, you know," I say to Ethan.

"I know!" he says, raising his voice. "I know girls can be strong!"

"Relax," David says. "Chloe was just joking. Help Ivy with her ball."

"Okay." Ethan shoots an annoyed look at me before turning back to the balls. He selects a dark blue glittery one and says to Ivy, "See if this fits."

She touches the ball uncertainly, sliding her palm over the finger holes. "What do you mean?"

Ethan shows her how to put her fingers in the holes and then loftily declares that the ball is too big for her. He picks out another one that he says will be better. He drops it into Ivy's arms, and the weight makes her sag forward.

"Too heavy?" he asks.

"Maybe. I don't know."

"It's the lightest one they have."

"Then it's fine," I say impatiently. The ball selection already feels like it's taken forever. I don't want to spend my entire Saturday in a dark noisy place that smells like sweat and fried food. "Just take it, Ivy. And stand up straight. It's not *that* heavy. What's our lane number?"

"Eleven," Ethan says. "Between ten and twelve." He leads us over there. "We need to make teams."

David jumps in. "Chloe and me against you and Ivy."

Ethan looks delighted, but Ivy says, "Can't I be with Chloe?"

"No," I say. I'm worried she'll hurt Ethan's feelings. "It's more even this way — they're both better than us."

She looks like she might cry, and I want to shake her. Why can't she be nicer to Ethan? She's not stupid—she knows that this is sort of a date and that he's happy to be on a team with her. It's embarrassing that she's acting like this, especially with David there watching and understanding far more than his brother.

"Let's just try it this way," I say. It's always best to keep things moving forward with Ivy. Too much time to think, and she finds reasons to feel anxious. "You guys can go first. Who wants to keep score? I don't remember how to."

"I'll do it," David says. He drops into the chair behind the table, and I nab the only other chair, next to him, leaving the bench for the other two. "Ethan, you're up."

"Ivy can go first," Ethan says gallantly.

"I don't know how to," she says.

"I'll help." He guides her fingers into the holes before leading her to the bowling line. "Hold it in both hands and then one hand and then roll it," he says.

She lowers the ball to the floor, pulls her fingers out of the holes, and pushes at it. It rolls slowly into the gutter.

"What we have here," David whispers to me, "is a failure to communicate."

Ivy's next attempt doesn't go any better than her first one; she doesn't manage to knock down a single pin with that ball either.

"That's okay," Ethan says, patting her shoulder as they watch her ball slowly—slooooowwwllyyy—roll along the gutter and eventually vanish into the back.

Ivy chews at her lip. "I'm bad at this. I didn't get any points."

"I was bad my first time," he says.

"When was that?"

"I was really little."

"Do you want another turn?" David asks her. "It's fine with us."

She shakes her head vehemently. "No! That would be cheating!" She and Ethan come back to the table. Her face is bright red, and she's thumping her hands against her thighs.

"It's fine, Ivy," I say. "We're all bad at this."

"I'm not bad at it," Ethan says. "I'm quite good."

It's funny how sometimes you can tell that someone's autistic from a short sentence that's not even technically *wrong* in any way.

I get up. "My turn."

They sit down while I cradle my ball and survey the lane. Then I send both my balls wobbling into the gutter. I don't knock down a single pin.

I turn around with an indifferent shrug and a cheerful "oh, well!"

Ivy's mouth is wide open. "Chloe! You're so bad at this! I thought you knew how to do it."

"I thought so too. Guess I forgot how hard it is."

"It's okay," Ethan says. "Don't worry about it, Chloe. You're still tied with us."

"Yeah." Ivy sits up, her face brightening. "We're tied."

I slip back into the chair next to David.

"Bad luck," he says gravely.

"The worst," I agree.

Ethan's up next. He really is a decent bowler—better than me, anyway, even when I'm *not* deliberately aiming for the gutter. He just misses the spare and has to settle for eight pins down.

Then it's David's turn. He easily knocks down seven pins with his first ball but sends his second sailing into the empty space between the remaining pins.

When he returns to his chair, I whisper, "Takes a lot of skill to knock down exactly the number of pins you want to."

"Yeah," he whispers back. "Would have been easier to get a spare." He records his score.

Ethan gets up when Ivy does and watches from a foot away as she bowls.

Her first ball is a flop, and you can tell she's bummed, but her second one creaks slowly down the alley and actually manages to nip off two pins before disappearing. She gasps, and Ethan pats her shoulder, saying, "That's so good!"

I hit four pins with my first ball and aim for the gutter with my second.

And so it goes.

David and I work hard to stay within a point or two of our siblings' scores, which turns out to be just as challenging as trying to get a strike every time—and maybe more fun? The team scores stay close, and Ivy loses her worried look. She even starts to jump up eagerly when it's her turn.

Ethan cheers for her every time, raising his arms and

pumping his fists into the air when she knocks down a pin. She happily high-fives him after each of their turns.

David and I don't bother with the high-fives, but we do shoot amused glances at each other following the success or failure of our attempts to keep the score as even as possible. At one point, he gets a strike, and the others congratulate him, but he whispers to me when he sits down that he's pissed at his bad aim: he was trying to knock down nine pins, not ten.

"I suck," he says with disgust. "No control."

Because of that strike, he and I end up winning, but only by a couple of points, and Ethan and Ivy take it well.

"We'll beat them next time," Ethan says to her.

"We might not," she says.

THIRTEEN

IT'S ACTUALLY GOOD we won," David says to me a couple of minutes later. He and I are making a pilgrimage to the vending machines at the far end of the bowling alley to score some sodas and snacks before the next game. "Don't want them to think we're not trying."

"It's sort of like we invented a whole new game," I say. "Trying to get just the right number of points without getting too many."

"We're like Harold Swerg."

"Who?"

"You don't know Harold Swerg?"

"Is he in our grade?"

He laughs. I've never seen David Fields laugh before. Amazingly, the earth doesn't stop turning.

"Not a kid," he says. "A character in a Jules Feiffer cartoon. You know Feiffer's stuff?"

"I think so?"

"He did the illustrations for *The Phantom Tollbooth*. You ever read that?"

"Oh, right! Okay, I know exactly who he is."

We reach the vending machines and stand side by side,

studying the choices, while he explains. "So he made this car-toon about a guy named Harold Swerg, who's, like, the greatest athlete in the world at every single sport. And he gets sent to the Olympics, and the Americans are really excited because he's going to win for them. Only he doesn't win. He ties at everything—even the long jump. Everyone's mad at him for not winning, but he says he wasn't trying to win, that he was trying to tie, and that tying is much harder than winning."

"I like that."

"Yeah, you should see it with the drawings. They're pretty great. I read it in this collection in my grandmother's house. When she moved to a nursing home, I asked my dad if I could have it, but he said he was hiring someone to box and sell all her books and it was too big a pain to start picking stuff out."

"Doesn't seem *that* hard to grab one book."

"I know. I could just buy my own copy, but it pisses me off that I have to."

"Do you have any other grandparents?"

"Well, I *had* the usual four, but my father's father is dead, and his mother doesn't recognize anyone anymore—Alzheimer's."

"What about your mother's?"

"They're alive. They send us birthday cards and stuff and see us once in a while, but it's weird. My mother has this whole other family now, and I think they feel much closer to those kids."

"Why did your mother leave? Do you mind my asking?"

"It's fine," he says as he pulls out his wallet. "After Ethan was diagnosed, she said she'd always thought there was something wrong with my father, and now she knew why, and that since my dad was the reason their kids weren't normal, he should have to deal with us, not her." He starts to feed a dollar bill into the slot. The machine rejects it, and he says irritably, "These stupid things never work."

I get the sense he's done with the topic, and I don't want to push — it's got to be painful even if he acts like it isn't. As weak as my mother is, I can't imagine her abandoning us. I leave him to his struggles with the soda machine and move over to the snacks, where I buy some peanut butter crackers. Once David finally manages to coax a couple of Cokes out of his machine, we change places, and he gets chips while I get drinks.

Booty cradled against our chests, we make our way back toward our lane. Four middle-aged women have been bowling in the alley next to ours for the last half-hour. I sort of registered that they were there and constantly talking to one another, but otherwise was too focused on our game to pay them much attention. Now, as we walk behind their bench, one of them says to another, "I'm surprised they left those two alone." She nods in the direction of Ethan and Ivy. Her back is to us. "Clearly there's something wrong with them," she says. "I think the other two must be the caregivers — they look normal. Why they think it's okay to leave them alone like that is beyond me. It doesn't feel safe."

"I know," her friend says. She tucks a strand of her chin-length hair—bright red except for a thick gray stripe lining her part—behind her ear. "I'm worried that they'll damage the floor—the girl is throwing the ball all over the place. She doesn't have any control at all."

"And the way the boy talks . . . He's so loud. It's disturbing."

David suddenly pulls his arm back and hurls a bag of chips into the air, way up high in an arc that lands it on the floor right in front of the two women. They gasp in unison and turn to see where it came from.

One's face is rounder, and her salt-and-pepper hair is brutally short, and the other has that badly dyed hair and a longer face . . . but their expressions are identical: confused and uncomfortable.

"Have some chips," David says, his voice calmly hostile.

There's a pause while the two women glance at each other nervously, and then the red-and-gray-haired woman leans forward, picks up the bag, and tosses it back.

"No, thank you," she says as David catches it neatly in his free hand.

"I insist," David says, and whips it back at them. It can't possibly hurt anyone—I mean, it's a *bag of chips*—but the gesture is violent, and they both cower away from the Lay's with little noises of distress. He adds politely, "It's the least we can do when we've added so much stress to your morning."

The contrast between his pleasant words and angry action

seems to render the women speechless. They clutch each other's arms, leaving the chips untouched on the floor, while I hastily tug David toward our alley. I don't want them to get so freaked out they call the manager. Or the police.

"Sometimes I fucking hate people," he mutters as I drag him the few steps over to our lane.

"I know what you mean."

"No, you don't." He shakes off my hand.

One good thing about Ivy and Ethan: neither of them seems to notice David's change in mood.

We play another game, sisters against brothers this time. Other than encouraging and reassuring Ivy, I don't say much, and neither does David or Ivy.

Ethan on the other hand . . . He talks and talks, mostly about TV shows. Apparently he's been binge-watching a bunch since Ivy told him last weekend that she likes TV more than movies. He's studied the Wikipedia and IMDB pages for every one of the shows and proceeds to tell us pretty much everything he's learned from them, at an impressive volume. Our friends at lane number ten keep glancing over at him, then exchanging raised-eyebrow looks with each other.

Makes me furious. What's their problem? Were they expecting a quiet morning at the *bowling alley?*

And then Ivy, who's getting tired—you can tell from the sag in her shoulders—nothing wears her out so much as being social—aims a ball so carelessly that it pops in and out of the gutter and onto the next lane.

The women whisper to each other, and then the red-and-gray-haired one calls from a safe distance, "You really should be using bumpers, you know."

"We're almost done," I say, responding because she's looking right at me and only me—not at David (who probably scares her) and not at the other two (because they also probably scare her, just in a different way). "Sorry about that."

She moves closer to the bench that divides their lane from ours and beckons to me. I'm curious enough to get up and go over. She leans forward and lowers her voice. "I just think you should make it easier for them, cut down on the frustration. It might be . . . you know . . . safer."

"We're doing fine," I say stiffly. "Thanks for the suggestion."

Ethan has overheard. He edges toward us. "I don't need bumpers! They're for little kids. I got a one-sixty in the last game, and I could get a one-seventy in this one if I bowl only strikes from now on." His voice, as always, is a little too loud.

"Oh, okay," the woman says, with a big fake smile. She takes a step back. "That's fine. I just wanted you to know it's an option." She flees back to her friends, who are huddling on the other side of their lane, as far from us as possible. Staring. Staring.

"Let's just go now," Ivy says, her face stricken. "I don't want to bowl anymore."

"We're not done," Ethan tells her. He doesn't seem bothered by the woman the way Ivy does. But then, she was the one who just flung a ball into the other lane and she knows it.

"It doesn't matter," David says, standing up. "We don't have to finish."

"You guys were destroying us anyway," I add. "You definitely get the win."

"That's cheating." Ethan grabs his bowling ball out of the ball return and hugs it tightly like someone's going to try to take it away from him. "I don't want to cheat."

"It's not cheating," David says. "Everyone's good with it."

"Yes, it is!" Ethan shouts. "You can't stop in the middle of a game! We have to finish! We have to!" He's getting louder and more frantic, and everyone in the bowling alley is staring at him.

"Crap," David whispers to me. "What do we do?"

I glance over at Ivy, who's watching Ethan, her eyes big, her lower lip caught under her top teeth. She's uncomfortable, but less upset than *he* is, at least for the moment.

"Let's finish the game," I say.

"But I want to leave," Ivy says.

"We'll play fast."

"But—"

"We'll be done soon. I promise. Please, Ivy."

She reluctantly sits back down.

Ethan slowly and carefully bowls his turn, while Ivy rocks unhappily on the bench, her hands fluttering softly through the air. Then David and I speed through our turns, grabbing and pitching the balls as soon as they emerge from the ball return. When I tell Ivy it's her turn, she clutches the edge of the bench seat with both hands and shakes her head, casting shamed glances over at the lady in the next lane who said we should get bumpers.

"Want me to take your turn?" I ask her.

Ethan says, "That's not fair, she—"

But his brother cuts him off. "It's fine," he says. "Chloe can bowl for Ivy." So I do. Neither Ethan nor Ivy is very happy at this point, so it's all about keeping things moving and getting us out of there.

The game ends—the guys win, of course—and we return our balls and grab our street shoes from their cubbies. I'm fascinated to see that Ethan ties his sneakers by making two rabbit ears and knotting them (instead of looping one lace around the other) because Ivy does the exact same thing.

I want to point it out to David, but he's scowling down at his own shoes and tying them with such sharp, savage motions that I decide it's not worth it.

"That was fun!" Ethan says when we're in the parking lot.

"So much fun," I say with way more enthusiasm than I'm feeling.

Ivy's silent.

"Can we do something again soon?" Ethan asks her.

"Okay," she says. "Just not bowling. I don't like bowling."

"It's because you're not very good at it." Ethan pats her shoulder consolingly.

I almost laugh out loud, but another glance at David's closed and angry face kills my amusement.

Ivy and I get into the car.

"You okay?" I ask once we're settled.

"I don't like bowling. I'm bad at it."

"You did great. Seriously. For a first time—"

"My ball went onto the other people's floor."

"No one cared."

"That woman did. She said I needed bumpers, and Ethan said those are for kids."

"It's not a big deal, Ives."

"I don't want to go bowling again." She leans forward in her seat and turns up the radio volume. "Can we listen to 102.7?"

"Since when do you listen to 102.7?"

"Diana says they play the best music." She switches stations and sits back.

I wish I could talk to her about David, about how angry he is at the world, and about how sometimes he seems to think I'm on his side and sometimes he seems to think I'm not, but dissecting other people's emotions isn't exactly her strong suit.

"What are we going to do tonight?" she asks.

"I don't know what you're doing, but James's parents have tickets to a play and they invited me to go with them."

"I never go out at night," she says wistfully. "Only during the day."

"Would you want to go out with Ethan some night?"

"Yeah, okay."

Progress! "Text him. Invite him to go to a movie next weekend. He likes movies."

"And you'll go with us?"

"I'll drive you. But maybe I don't need to stay for the whole thing."

She doesn't respond, just gets that worried look on her face before turning her head toward the window and whispering quietly to herself.

FOURTEEN

"How ARE THE LOVEBIRDS doing?" James asks when he picks me up that night. We're driving downtown by ourselves, since there isn't room in his parents' car for their whole family plus me. And it's kind of a relief—as nice as they all are to me, it's a lot of work to be all adorable and cheerful and bright and *perfect,* the way I feel like I have to be to make them think I'm good enough for the son and brother they all dote on.

"Ivy and Ethan? I wouldn't call them lovebirds, but I think they both had fun today."

"What's the long-term goal with them, anyway?" James asks. "I mean, do people like them get married? Do they have kids?"

"People like them?"

"You know what I mean."

"Do I?"

There's a pause and then he says, "Why do you get so weird when we talk about your sister?"

"I don't."

"It's fine. I totally get it, and I'm not mad or anything. But you should just know that I always feel like I have to be extra careful what I say about her, or you'll get mad at me."

"When have I ever gotten mad at you?"

"You know what I mean. Not like *mad* mad. Just quiet mad, like you're annoyed but don't want to show it."

"I don't feel that way," I say, and, to prove it, I lean toward him and kiss his cheek, my chest straining against the tightening seat belt. "Sorry."

"No need to apologize. Just cut me a little slack now and then."

"I will. I mean, I *do*. I mean, I don't *need* to because you don't do anything wrong. I'm sorry if I seem weird sometimes —I'll try not to be."

And for the rest of the evening, I'm as not-weird as a girl can be. I'm so normal I'm practically invisible.

On Sunday, Sarah invites me to come over and do homework at her house. I find Mom in the kitchen with Ron and ask if I can borrow her car.

She's nodding and reaching for her purse to get her car keys, when Ron raises his hand in a *halt* gesture. "Hold on, there. We were hoping we could all do something together this afternoon. Your mother was interested in a family hike."

"I have a ton of homework," I say. "And I already made plans with Sarah."

"If I had a dollar for every time you say both of those things to get out of being with your family . . ." Ron shakes his head.

"Then what?"

"Excuse me?"

"If you had a dollar for every time I say those things, then what? What would happen?"

"I'd be rich," he says irritably. "And I don't love your tone."

I appeal to my mother. "What's wrong with my tone?"

"I don't think you mean to, but sometimes you can sound a little . . ." She gropes. "Challenging."

"Fine. I'll try to be less 'challenging.' May I please have the car keys?"

She looks at Ron. He thrusts his fingers through his hair, tosses his head, and says, "It's your call, Jeannie, of course. I thought you wanted to go hiking with the girls, but if you don't care—"

"It's okay," she says, and gets her keys out of her purse and hands them to me.

"Thanks," I say. "Text me if you need the car back at some point. Oh, and just so you know, Ivy hates hiking."

"She can use the exercise," Ron says.

"Tell her that. I'm sure that will *completely* change her mind about it."

"Hear that?" he says to my mother. "That's exactly the tone I'm talking about."

"It may be too warm to hike anyway," Mom says. "We can do something else."

"Whatever you want," he says, but I can still feel the heat of his angry gaze as I leave the kitchen, and I'm glad I'm escaping for the day. And sorry for Ivy that she's not.

• • •

Sarah's mother greets me at their front door and says, "I made cupcakes!" She sounds like a little kid who's proud of herself.

I love Sarah's mother. She totally homey and maternal, with her cheerful, round face, graying hair, and comfortably sturdy body, and she's an amazing cook—but she also co-runs a travel blog that's won all these awards and lets her score a ton of free trips for her family.

"Holy crap," I say when Sarah and I are alone in their family room with an entire plate of her mother's chocolate-frosted peanut butter cupcakes. "Your mom sets the bar high. You know what the last thing *my* mother baked was?"

"What?"

"A cake for my fourth birthday. And it was from a mix."

We curl up on the sofa with cupcakes, tonguing the frosting and moaning with practically orgasmic delight.

Sarah loses interest in hers once the frosting's gone. She drops the sticky remains right on the coffee table—she's an only child and gets away with making a mess everywhere—then licks her fingers clean. "Hey, didn't you have another thing with David and his brother yesterday? How'd that go?"

"It was weird." I finish my cupcake and drop the paper liner on top of hers. "For a lot of reasons. But mostly because of David. He's different away from school."

"I hope he's nicer."

"I wouldn't go that far. I mean, he's, like, a decent brother to Ethan, but he's still pretty brutal to other people."

"So how is he different?"

"I don't know. More tortured, maybe? Less sure of himself?"

"Interesting." She hugs her knees to her chest and rests her chin on them. She's wearing a tank top and our school sweatpants, rolled down at the waist and up at the ankles, and has her thick curly hair piled in a topknot. It's a totally sporty look, which is funny, because she's the least athletic person I've ever met, won't even go for a walk if she can avoid it. "So he's not a smug asshole *all* of the time?"

"Not really. He seems a little sad, actually. He's got a rough home life. His mother left — I mean, like, *totally* left, started a different family — and his father remarried."

"Ugh," she says. "Don't make me start feeling sorry for him. Even if his life sucks, he's still a jerk, and you shouldn't have to spend time with him. Couldn't you find someone else for Ivy to date?"

"It's not that easy."

"Well, can't your mother drive her to the dates?"

"Ivy wants *me* to."

"So?"

I raise my eyebrows. "You are such an only child."

"Are you calling me spoiled?"

"Not spoiled . . . You just don't know what it's like to have a sibling who needs your help."

"We used to have a dog," she says, and at first I think she's making a joke but then I realize she's serious.

FIFTEEN

I WALK JAMES to his practice on Monday afternoon and then head back to my locker, where someone calls my name. I look up. It's David. I can't tell if he was waiting for me or just happened to spot me.

"Hey," I say. "What's up?"

"Hold on a sec." He pulls out his phone and sends a text. It doesn't take long, but still . . . it's pretty rude, given the fact *he* flagged me down. "Sorry." He pockets his phone. "I wanted to ask you about this weekend."

"Wait," I say, because now *I've* gotten a text and I figure I might as well be as rude as he was about it.

I look at my phone and laugh out loud—the text is from him.

More used to texting you than talking to you

I text back. yeah me too. should we keep going like this?

Nah

We look up at the same time. He says, "Ivy invited Ethan to go to a movie next weekend."

"I know."

"He's really excited about it. He's watched a ton of trailers. You should have heard him trying to decide which movie Ivy would like best . . ." He shakes his head. "Actually, it's probably good you didn't hear him. It was kind of endless. And loud."

"Our bowling friends wouldn't have approved."

"They don't approve of Ethan's existence," he says bitterly. "Assholes."

"So . . . maybe it was a mistake to invite them to go to the movie with us?"

He flashes a brief reluctant smile. Which feels like a minor victory.

"Anyway," he says, "does Ivy want you to stay this time?"

"I'm hoping not. At some point she's got to start having her own social life."

"Right," he says. "And leave you free to enjoy yours."

"I don't mind coming along."

"Even if you have to hang out with the most hated member of your class?"

"Don't flatter yourself," I say. "No one cares enough about you to hate you."

Another begrudging smile. "Listen to you," he says, almost admiringly. "And you're supposed to be so nice."

"I *am* nice. You bring out the worst in people."

"Maybe I just free people up to say what they really want. Don't you get tired of being so . . . you know . . . sweet and pretty all the time?"

"Aw." I bat my eyelashes. "He thinks I'm pretty."

"That wasn't my point."

"So you *don't* think I'm pretty?"

I'm trying to torture him a little, but he just shrugs. "I couldn't possibly think you're as attractive as *you* think you are."

"It is a high bar," I agree cheerfully. "So what were you planning to do about the movie?"

"I'm not sure. It's kind of a tricky situation with Ethan." He sticks his hands in his pockets. "When things are going fine, he's great. But when he gets upset . . ."

"Yeah, I know. Ivy's the same way."

"But does she run? Ethan's a runner."

"As in track and field?"

"As in running away. If he gets overwhelmed, he just . . . takes off. Used to happen all the time when he was little. He'd slip out a door when no one was looking, and we'd have to hunt him down. A couple of times, we couldn't find him and had to call the police. At first, it was mostly from school, but after my mother left and my dad got remarried, he started to run away from home too. Freaked out our stepmother so much, she started talking about how maybe he needed to be put somewhere 'safe.'"

"Meaning what?"

"Some kind of special needs institution, I guess."

"Oh, God. That's horrible."

"I know. I've warned him he has to stop with the running away, but it's not like he's thinking rationally when he does it. Or thinking at all, really. He did it once last year, but I found him so quickly they never even knew about it."

"What upset him?"

He sighs. "So . . . the fourth Bourne movie was on TV
—the one that Matt Damon wasn't in . . ."

"And?"

"And he was upset they'd used a different actor. He liked
the first three a lot." He glances at me sideways. "It's okay to
laugh. I think it's funny too."

"It's kind of sweet . . . Shows he's loyal. How'd you find
him?"

"He went to the little supermarket on Montana Avenue.
It was hot out, and he was thirsty and wanted something
to drink. They know us there and could tell something was
wrong, so they used his phone to track me down."

"But he likes going out with Ivy. He wouldn't run away on
a date, would he?"

"Probably not." He takes his hands out of his pockets and
stands up straight. "But he's really invested in things going
well—you saw him with the bowling, how upset he got when
we wanted to end early. He wants everything to go exactly the
right way, and if something went wrong . . ."

"Got it." Another thought occurs to me. "What about
when he's at school? He must get upset there now and then."

"Yeah, but you can't get on or off that campus without
going through security."

"Oh, good point."

"And when he's not in school, I'm pretty much with him."

No wonder David has no social life. He can't really go to
parties and stuff dragging an autistic brother with him. Well,
he *could*—and people would probably be nice about it—but

someone as proud as he is probably wouldn't want to have to ask if it's all right or risk having people feel sorry for him. It also explains why he doesn't play any sports or do any extracurriculars.

"You're a good brother," I say.

"I make up for that by being a horrible human being in every other way."

I laugh.

"Feel free to argue the point," he says. "Anyway, this Ivy thing . . ."

"Yeah?" I adjust my backpack on my shoulder and glance at my watch. The bus leaves in two minutes. I'm going to have to make a run for it soon. "What about it?"

"It could be amazing for him. And for me. If they really like each other and she becomes someone he can trust . . ." He stops, then says, "I mean, I don't want to put too much pressure on the whole thing . . ."

"No, it's okay—I feel the same way. There's freedom for both of us if this thing works out."

"Exactly. Anyway, I just wanted you to know that I'm going to hang out at the movie on Saturday, and I wouldn't mind some company."

"All right. I'll see whether or not Ivy wants me there." I nod toward the front of the school. "I'm going to try to make the bus."

"Good luck," he says, and is gone before I can say goodbye, like he needs to be the one who walks away, not the one who gets walked away from.

· · ·

The bus is already pulling away from the curb. I run toward it, shouting, and either the driver doesn't see me or she's kind of a jerk, because she doesn't stop.

My backpack's super heavy and the sun is hot, so I decide to just stay at school, do my homework in the library, and hope James will be in the mood to give me a lift after practice. If not, I can take the late bus.

He responds to my texts on his way into the shower to say that he can drop me off but can't stay at my house—he has two tests tomorrow, and he needs to study.

"I can't help feeling that you only love me for my car," he says when we meet up in the parking lot after he's clean and ready to go.

"Not true!" I say. "I also love you for your big house and the nice meals you buy me."

"Want to guess what I love *you* for?"

"My rapier wit?"

"Definitely not that," he says, and I stick my tongue out at him. "Right," he says, and leans over and catches my tongue between his lips.

I'm so glad I have a boyfriend who's fun and happy and good-natured and successful. The way James floats through the world—that's how life should be. Easy. Painless. When I'm with him, it feels like maybe that could be my life too.

SIXTEEN

It's Friday night, and I'm studying my sister's face from across the kitchen table.

I feel like I haven't really looked at her in years. I think of her as being blond, but her hair has darkened over time and always hangs, lank and limp, in that eternal unflattering ponytail. Her face is so pale that you can see thin blue veins under her eyes. She almost never goes outside, hates the sun, hates exertion.

"Why are you staring at me?" she asks, looking up from her iPad. "Are you mad?"

"Why would I be mad at you?"

"I don't know," she says seriously. "Sometimes people just *are*."

It breaks my heart how confused she can be about what people are thinking and how anxious that makes her. I shake my head. "I was just thinking we should have a girls' beauty night — paint our nails, highlight our hair, that kind of thing. What do you think?"

"No, thank you."

"Come on! Don't you want to know what you'd look like with lighter hair?"

"You mean like Diana's hair?"

"Sure. Or like mine. It just takes a few minutes. I'll do all the work, and if you don't like it, you don't ever have to do it again."

"Okay," she says, and stands up. "Let's do it."

"Hold on—I have to run to the drugstore and buy the stuff first."

She instantly plops back down on the chair. "Can you get some potato chips?"

"Absolutely," I say. "Junk food is a necessary part of a girls' beauty night."

I have to ask Mom for the car keys again. I wish I had my own car. I really have to get a job. If I start working now and work all through the summer and save every dime, maybe I'll be able to afford my own (old, used, beat-up, semidisgusting wreck of a) car by next fall.

That's a lot of *if*s and *maybe*s. And until then, I'm stuck asking for Mom's keys.

Mom and Ron are sitting close together on the family room sofa, drinking martinis and watching some reality show. We ate dinner earlier—cheese pizza Mom had picked up on her way home from Ivy's school and reheated unevenly so the edges were burned and the cheese was cold. She may be the worst cook ever—I mean, who ruins *pizza?*

Ron's slung his thick leg over her knees. It's made his sweatpants ride up at the ankle, and I can see his brown leg hair. Ugh. Nauseating.

I say, "Can I borrow the car? I need to make a drugstore run."

Ron looks up. "I could use a few things myself."

"Text me a list."

"You know what?" He lifts his leg off of Mom's lap and climbs to his feet. "I'll just go with you."

Crap. Crap crap crap crap crap. "I don't mind getting your stuff," I say. "Really. It's no problem."

"It'll give us a chance to talk."

There's no getting out of this.

He insists on driving, which freaks me out since his breath smells like alcohol. But he drives steadily enough.

A few minutes in, he clears his throat. "You're quiet this evening, Chloe."

"Long week."

"Two words! I got two words out of her! Victory is mine!" He pumps his fist in the air, taking his eyes off the road long enough to admire his own biceps muscle. "Just teasing. So what made this week particularly long? Seemed like the usual Monday through Friday kind of thing to me."

Bleah. Apparently we have to have a *conversation.*

"Oh, you know," I say. "Junior year and all." *Please let that be enough.*

It's not. "I'll bet," he says. "Lots of pressure about college, right?"

I make a noncommittal sound.

"I will say I'm always impressed by your grades. You're lucky you're naturally smart. School was tough for me."

"Yeah?" I stare out my window so I don't have to look at the dyed wings of brown hair flying back from his widening temples.

"Today they'd diagnose me with a learning disorder, and I'd get help," he says. "But back then they just said you were stupid if you couldn't learn to read."

"Sounds rough."

"I survived. I'm a survivor, Chloe."

Oh, great. Now the Destiny's Child song is earworming in my head.

"I want you and Ivy to be survivors too. That's why I push you both the way I do. For your sake. Your mom doesn't like to make demands on you—she loves you too much—so it's up to me to teach you the value of hard work and discipline and self-control."

"Mom and Dad taught us plenty," I say tightly.

"Of course they did! You've had great parents. The best. But I like to think that I bring something new to the table."

I don't say anything, and his words linger, wither, then die in the silence.

Ivy has replaced Ron at Mom's side on the sofa. I drop bags of chips and M&M's on the coffee table in front of them and hold up the highlighting kits I bought.

"Get ready for beauty, Ives! We are going to look so gorgeous that every guy will fall in love with us and every girl will hate our guts."

"Why will they hate us?" Ivy asks, snatching up and ripping open the bag of chips.

Ron says from behind me, "Go easy on the junk food, Ivy."

"Okay." She crunches a chip in her mouth. "Why do girls hate girls who are beautiful?"

"They don't." Mom shoots me an exasperated look. "I don't know why Chloe said that. It's a sexist stereotype that women will fight each other for male attention, but women can and should support one another."

"Will other girls like me less if I use this?" Ivy asks, pointing at the highlighting kit.

"Of course not," I say. "All it does is make your hair lighter. Come on. Let's go do it in the bathroom."

She hesitates for a moment, then slowly follows me upstairs, clutching the chips bag to her chest the whole way.

In the bathroom, I try to brush out her hair, but there are a ton of tangles, and the brush keeps getting stuck.

"Ow!" she says, and pushes my hand away. "I changed my mind! I don't want to do this."

"I'm almost done. Do you *ever* brush your hair?"

"Yes, every day!"

She must just smooth the brush over the top before dragging it into a ponytail. There's no way she's really getting out the snarls on a daily basis. The mats feel like they've been months in the making.

I try again.

"Chloe, stop!" She clutches at her head.

"Just relax." I try to ignore all her moans and complaints, but I'm sweating and tense by the time I can actually get a brush clear through it.

I mix up the highlighting solution and start painting it on strands of her hair and tucking them into little tin foil packets. It would be fun if Ivy were into it, but she's tense as she watches in the mirror, her face creased with anxiety, her lower lip tucked under her upper teeth. She keeps reaching up to touch her head.

"It's itchy!" she says. "And it smells bad, and it hurts."

"No, it doesn't."

"How would *you* know?"

"I highlight my hair all the time. And it doesn't hurt at all."

"Well, it hurts *me.*"

"Whatever. I'm almost done anyway." I speed-paint a few more strands, just to keep the sides even, and then tell her to let it sit while I do my own color.

It takes me two seconds to brush out my own hair: it's layered, unlike Ivy's, which Mom simply hacks a few inches off of every once in a while. I can't afford an expensive haircutter, so I go to one of the cheap chains and micromanage the whole thing, telling the cutter exactly how I want every strand cut. I've been highlighting it since eighth grade — first just putting lemon on it and sitting in the sun and eventually upping my game to use the at-home kits.

A while later, after I've rinsed and combed us both out, we stand in front of the mirror side by side.

"It doesn't look that different," Ivy says, suspiciously eyeing her own reflection.

"That's because it's still wet. It'll lighten as it dries. Can I cut your hair just a little bit? To give it a better shape?"

She backs away. "It will hurt even more."

"Haircuts don't hurt."

"If you pull, they do."

"I won't pull. Come on. You need a new look. Enough with the ponytails."

"I like ponytails."

"Wouldn't you like to be able to wear it down too? And have it look nice?"

"I feel like—" She stops, her hand flailing around. Sometimes the words don't come easily for her.

"Like what?"

"Like you don't like what I am."

"That's ridiculous." I turn so I can look at the real her, not just the reflection. "This isn't about changing you, Ives. I just thought you'd have fun experimenting with being a little glamorous. That's all, I swear."

She thinks for a moment, her eyes cast down, searching out and consulting an invisible advisor on the floor. She looks up again. "Okay. You can cut my hair."

"You sure? I don't have to."

"It's okay." She pats me on the shoulder. "I know you want to."

"Thanks," I say. "I kind of really do."

• • •

"Holy cow," Mom says, coming into our room later to check out the results. (That's how my mother curses—she grew up in the Midwest.) "Your hair is lighter than ever, Chloe. You're heading into platinum territory."

"I like it," I say defensively, but she's already turned her attention to Ivy.

"Oh, baby! Your hair looks beautiful! Is it shorter too?"

"I let Chloe cut it."

"I'm glad you did." Mom studies us. "You guys almost look like twins now."

"I don't think I look like Chloe," Ivy says. "She's thinner, and her hair is whiter than mine."

"Whiter?" I repeat. Maybe I *did* go too heavy on the bleach.

"Well, I see it, even if you girls don't," Mom says with a shrug.

Ivy's been sitting cross-legged on her bed, but now she slides to her feet and crosses the room to examine herself in the closet mirror. "I think I look more like Diana than like Chloe."

"Like who?" Mom says.

"Diana. From my class. I look like her now."

"No, you don't," I say.

Ivy crosses her arms over her chest. "You don't know her that well. I do."

"I've seen her, and her nose is completely different from yours. And her eyes are a different color, right? Plus your face is rounder, and—"

"No, no!" Ivy shouts, putting her hands over her ears like she doesn't want to hear any more.

"Stop it, Chloe," Mom says. "You're upsetting her."

"Because she's *wrong*," Ivy says.

"Fine." I throw up my hands. "It doesn't matter. I don't care, except . . . *truth*."

Ron appears in the doorway. "What's going on here?"

"The girls were having the silliest argument," Mom says, suddenly all cheerful about it. "Not even worth discussing."

He slings his arm over her shoulders and surveys us with phony paternal pride. "Your daughters may be noisy, but they sure are pretty! Some male hearts are going to be broken this week."

"They do look beautiful, don't they?" Mom says.

"They come by it honestly." He plants a revolting kiss on her lips.

Ivy says, "Can you please get out of our room?"

I doubt she was commenting on the kiss—she probably just wants to go to bed—but I've never loved her more.

SEVENTEEN

I DON'T GET IT," David says.

It's Saturday, and we're sitting in the back of the movie theater waiting for the trailers to start. Ethan and Ivy are two rows ahead of us. He wanted to sit far away from us. She wanted to sit right next to me. This was the compromise.

"What don't you get?" I ask, tilting the popcorn bag toward David so he can help himself. We got one for us to share and one for them to share. Ethan paid for theirs, and I paid for ours.

"You and Ivy both did something to your hair, right? It looks different."

"We just highlighted it a little bit."

David wipes his fingers on a napkin. "Why?"

"Why not? It's fun to change things up."

"And it has nothing to do with the general belief that blondes are more attractive than brunettes?"

"I don't care what other people think. I just do it for fun."

"Okay, putting aside that that's just a lie, what about Ivy?"

"It wasn't a lie!"

"You care about what other people think. Everyone does. Why did Ivy do it? Was it her idea?"

"Stuff like that doesn't occur to her."

"Right," David says, digging into the bag. "So it was *your* idea."

"What's wrong with that?"

He tosses popcorn into his mouth. "Hey, if you want to impose your own advertising-driven ideas about beauty on your sister, that's your right."

"Thank you. Your permission means the world to me. And I think she looks pretty cute."

"Your sister always looks cute. She didn't need blonder hair for that." His tone changes as he lowers his voice. "Ethan has a major crush on her, you know. He talks about her all the time. I hope she feels the same way."

It's confusing—one second he's caustically berating me for being superficial, and the next he's soberly confiding in me.

"Do you think she likes him?" he asks.

"She was definitely excited about going to a movie tonight. But I can't tell whether it's because she likes *him* or just the idea of going out."

He takes a drag on his soda straw before saying, "It must be rough for her to have a sister like you."

"What does that mean?"

"You know."

"No, I don't."

He flaps his hand impatiently. "You have crazy good social skills—the whole world wants to hang out with you. It wouldn't be easy to be your sibling even if she weren't on the spectrum. But she is. So it's worse than not easy. It's got to be painful."

"Yeah, well, it's probably rough on Ethan being your brother."

"I'm not nearly as social as you."

"Oh, I know," I say airily. "I just meant because you can be such an enormous pain in the ass."

He looks at me, a little stunned, I think, and I brace myself for his return volley. I figure he'll shoot to kill. But he surprises me. "Yeah, you're right," he says. "And the sad thing is, as big a jerk as I am, I'm Ethan's *best* relative."

"I was just joking!" I'd been pleased by my insult but then he had to go and be nice about it and ruin my fun.

"No, you weren't. And that's fine. I know I can be a—"

The lights dim, and he stops before he can tell me what he can be. I have some guesses though.

We meet up with the other two in the lobby after the movie.

"What'd you think?" I ask.

Ethan says, "It was really good!" just as Ivy says, "I didn't like it."

"Why didn't you like it?" he asks her, a little anxiously.

"It was stupid." She moves away from him, closer to me.

"No, it wasn't," Ethan says, appealing to David, who says diplomatically, "It was a little stupid, but I liked it anyway."

Ivy and I go to the bathroom together and join the long line of women who drank too much soda during the movie.

I glance at her. Her lips are moving, and I can tell she's whispering to herself, even though I can't hear her with the hand dryers blasting away. "Everything okay?" I ask.

"I don't know."

"Something happen?"

"Ethan put his hand on me."

My voice gets tight. "What do you mean, 'on you'? What part of you?"

She gestures with her right hand at her left shoulder. "Here."

"Oh, that's okay. He was just trying to put his arm around you. As long as he wasn't trying to cop a feel . . ."

"What's that?"

"You know . . . like, trying to grab your boob."

The middle-aged woman in front of me turns around at that. I gaze at her blandly, and she quickly swivels back.

"That would be bad?" Ivy says. "If he tried to do that?"

"Only if you don't want him to. It's fine if you want him to."

The woman ahead twists again, pretending to look past us —but she's clearly spying on us.

"He didn't do that," Ivy says. "I wouldn't have liked it if he had, but he didn't."

"But he did try to put his arm over your shoulder?"

"Yeah. I pushed it away."

"Why?"

"I don't know." She sounds confused and maybe even a

little upset, but I can't tell whether it's because of what happened or because I'm trying to get her to tell me how she *feels* about what happened.

"The first time a guy tries to put his arm around you is always strange," I say.

The woman ahead of us goes into a stall with one last curious backwards glance.

"Do you like it when James puts his arm around you?" Ivy asks.

"Of course. You know that."

"Did you like it the first time?"

"I think I made the first move, actually. You should probably ask James how *he* felt about it."

"That would be weird." She hesitates. "I don't want to be alone with Ethan again tonight."

"Okay. We'll all get something to eat together and then we'll go home."

She nods and then a stall frees up, and I push her toward it.

As soon as we rejoin the boys in the lobby, Ethan says to Ivy, "It's okay if you didn't like the movie. You don't have to like it because I did."

"Yeah, I didn't."

"That's okay."

"We had a little talk about tolerating other people's opinions," David says to me as we walk ahead, leaving the other two to follow together.

"I figured. We had a talk too."

"What about?"

I move closer and lower my voice. "That it's okay for a guy to put his arm around you at a movie, but not for him to cop a feel."

"Wait—" He grabs my arm. "Did he—?"

I shake my head. "Just a nice friendly shoulder squeeze."

He releases me. "Oh, good. I mean, unless she's told you she wants him to make a move—"

"Definitely not. She's not ready yet. Do you think he is?"

He snorts. "He's a *guy*."

"Does he talk to you about it?"

"Not really. But I've seen his Google history. He looks up a lot of stuff."

"You mean like porn?"

"He mostly just Googles body parts—the fun ones. But he must stumble on porn now and then. I mean, it's the Internet —you can't *not* end up looking at porn."

"Ivy is definitely not looking at porn."

"Well, she's a girl."

"That's sexist. Girls can like porn too."

"Yeah?" he says with interest. "Do you?"

I laugh. "Actually, no. I think it's gross."

"Have you ever heard a girl say she liked it?"

"No, but I don't go around asking people."

"Well," he says, "from my sample size of one, I'm going to say my theory that girls don't like porn is confirmed."

At the food court, Ivy and the guys get meals at Panda Express, but I don't feel like Chinese food, so I wander around, considering my choices, before settling on a tuna roll and a Diet Coke from the Japanese place.

It takes me a minute to find the others, who are no longer at Panda, but once I turn a corner, I spot their table instantly —they're hard to miss, mostly because Ethan is standing up and shouting and flailing his arms.

"It hurts!" he's shouting. "It hurts!" He sticks his tongue out and rubs at it with first one hand and then the other—he looks like he's slapping at his own mouth.

David grabs at his hands. "Hey, hey, hey. Don't do that. Eat some rice—that'll help."

"Why did they give that to me?" Ethan cries. "It hurts!"

"They're just for flavor—you're not supposed to eat them."

"Why do they put them in there, then?" He wrenches his hands out of his brother's grasp and swipes at his mouth again.

David sees me standing there. "Chili pepper," he says wearily.

"Oh." Now I understand. "He's right about eating rice," I tell Ethan. "It stops the burning."

"The rice is hot too!"

"It's a different kind of hot. Blow on it first, and it will help, I promise."

Ivy's sitting at the table, watching Ethan with impassive curiosity as she steadily chews and swallows her own food. There are bits of rice on her shirt and in her hair, which I got her to wear brushed and down tonight, instead of in a pony-tail, and there's also some kind of brownish sauce on her chin and at the corners of her mouth.

Ethan wails some more. An elderly couple is walking by, and the man maneuvers around his wife so he can put himself between her and our group.

He's being *gallant*.

It hurts, especially because he's probably just some sweet old guy who loves his wife and wants to protect her from bad things.

But Ivy and Ethan aren't bad things.

David pushes Ethan into a chair and stands over him. "Seriously, dude, eat some rice." He plunges a fork into the mound on Ethan's plate.

Ethan glares at him but opens his mouth, and David shoves the rice in. Ethan chews and swallows. "It still hurts."

"You shouldn't have eaten the chili pepper," Ivy says. "Everyone knows they're hot."

"I didn't mean to!" Ethan roars at her, spraying chewed-up rice across the table. "It got in my mouth on accident!"

"Chilis can be sneaky," I say.

"Tricky little beasts," David agrees. "You can't trust a chili."

"Bell peppers, though—they're trustworthy."

"The really evil ones are those little shishito bastards," David says. "Some of them are hot, and some aren't. You can't tell until you bite into one. How is that fair?"

"It's not," I say. "It's not fair at all."

"And don't get me started on pepperoncini. I mean, first of all that *name . . .*"

"My tongue is better now," Ethan says. "Because of the rice." He takes the fork from David and starts rapidly shoveling more rice into his mouth. "I'm not going to eat any more orange chicken," he says through the mess in his mouth. "Just the rice. There's no chili pepper in rice."

"Good idea," David says, and we sit down to our food.

I'm drizzling a packet of soy sauce over my sushi when I hear someone say, "Hey!" and look up as Jana Rodriguez descends on us. "What are you guys doing here?"

"We just saw a movie," I say.

Her eyes flick eagerly back and forth between me and David. "You two?"

"All of us," I say quickly. "My sister and David's brother are friends."

"Yes, don't mistake *their* friendship for ours," David says jovially.

Jana turns to Ivy. "So you're Chloe's sister? Oh, my God, you totally look like her! I can't believe I've never met you! I'm Jana."

"Hi," Ivy says. Her eyes slide away from Jana's friendly gaze. I notice there's now also a smear of sauce on her forehead. How did that even get there?

"And you're David's brother?" Jana says to Ethan, who's still hunched over his plate, forking rice into his mouth like his life depends on it. "What's he like at home? Does he say really smart, scary things there too?"

Ethan says, "I don't know," through a mouthful of rice.

Jana stares at him for a moment then abruptly turns to me. "It's so weird bumping into you, Chloe—I was *just* thinking about you on the way here, about how I needed to ask you for notes from Monday's history class. And here you are!"

"Don't say it's an amazing coincidence," David says. "Just don't."

"What's wrong with saying that? It is! I mean, what are the odds?"

"On any given day, you probably think of dozens of different people at various times. But the only time anyone ever *remembers* thinking about someone is when they run into that person. It's not coincidence—it's selective memory."

"Whatever," she says, rolling her eyes. "You do you, David."

"I always do," he says calmly.

"I'll send you my notes when I get home," I tell her.

"Thanks." There's an awkward pause. She glances sideways at Ivy and Ethan. Neither of them looks at her. They both just keep eating. "I'd better go meet my friends," she says. "It was cool running into you guys—even if it wasn't a *coincidence.*"

"It wasn't," says David.

We're all quiet for a moment after she leaves, and then David says, "Smart and scary? *That's* my reputation?"

"Yeah," I say. "Except for the smart part."

"Shut up," he says, and if it had been anyone else in the world, I would have sworn he said it affectionately.

On our way out, we pass the old couple sitting at a table. They watch us furtively as we pass, and the old man protectively hitches his chair a little closer to his wife.

EIGHTEEN

"WHY IS EVERYONE so judgmental?" I ask David a little while later. We're walking through the mall on our way back to our cars. Ethan and Ivy are lagging behind us—she's slow, and he stays close by her side. "I mean, the second Ivy or Ethan does something the slightest bit not normal, people act like they're going to start serial killing everyone in sight. Where's the compassion?"

"Okay," David says. "I've thought about this a lot, actually. Want to hear my theory?"

"I do."

"You know what the uncanny valley is?"

"It sounds familiar, but no, not really."

"It's a nerd term. You know how computer animation is getting really good? Like they can do individual strands of hair and fur and stuff like that? So there's just this one problem with it: if the animation's *too* good, it starts to freak people out. Which is why most animated characters still have eyes that are too big and floaty hair and stuff like that—the goal isn't to make the most realistic animation you can, but the most *appealing*."

"Why is it called the uncanny valley?"

"Because if you graph their reactions, people like more and more realistic animation up to this one point and when you reach that point"—he makes a dipping motion with his right hand—"they suddenly find it creepy. It's usually something about the eyes—the eyes always look just a little bit dead when everything else looks totally real."

"Got it," I say. "So why are we talking about this?"

"It's just something I've thought about." He lowers his voice a little more as we turn a corner. "You know, if we were pushing our siblings in wheelchairs, people would be nice to them and to us. They'd be like, *Oh, the poor disabled people and their wonderful siblings! Let's hold doors for them!* But Ivy and Ethan . . . they basically look like everyone else, with just these tiny differences in how they behave and move. And that bugs people. They don't know what to do with that. It's like people have a place in their brain for normal, and they have a place in their brain for something obviously wrong, but they can't deal with something just a little bit different. And that makes them uncomfortable. And when people are uncomfortable, they act like jerks."

I'm silent for a moment.

"What do you think of my theory?" he asks.

"I think you're probably right. But it makes me sad. How do we get people to stop being like that?"

He shakes his head. "You're talking about basic xenophobia. We're hardwired to stay with our tribes."

"My father would have liked you."

He blinks. "Um . . . okay?"

"Sorry. That was a weird thing to blurt out. But he always liked to think about stuff like that — why we do what we do, what the root biology of our behaviors probably was . . . that kind of thing."

"Cool." A pause. "I'm sorry about him. I mean . . . you know."

"Yeah, it sucks that he died." We walk for a moment in silence and then I say, "Can I tell you something I've never told anyone else?" I'm sort of embarrassed by the question as soon as I ask it — it sounds more meaningful than it is. I've never told anyone else because my mother would freak, and no one else would care. But David will get it, I think.

"Sure."

"I think he was autistic."

"Really?"

"He wasn't like Ivy or anything — I mean, he was totally out in the world and really good at what he did and, like, this amazing scholar and researcher . . . but he was sort of hard to talk to. Mom always called him an absentminded professor type, and maybe that's all it was, but I can remember all these times when I'd talk to him about, like, kids at school being mean or something, and he never seemed to *get* it. And he dressed terribly and hated social events . . ." I trail off. "I don't know. Maybe I'm overthinking it."

"It makes sense genetically that one of your parents would be on the spectrum."

"He was a good dad, either way. I felt safe around him."

"I'm sorry you lost that." He stops, and for a second I think it's because he wants to say something more about that, but instead he says, "Our car's down this one," and points to an escalator.

"Ours is on the other side. We'd better go down that way, or I'll never find it."

Before we separate, Ethan grabs Ivy's hand, squeezes it, and manages to land a kiss on her cheek. Given all the sauce she splashed on herself this evening, it probably tasted nice and salty.

David and I just say a brief good night to each other, but he texts me later that evening.

I had a thought

??

Next E/I date at one of our houses?

You think?

Maybe less stress?

Maybe

Ok, a different KIND of stress

Right. Worth a try I guess

Ron and Mom usually run errands on Sunday afternoon, so we make a date to meet then at our house.

I wonder if David will feel like he needs to stay. He could probably just drop Ethan off, but it's also okay with me if he wants to come in and hang. I don't hate him anymore.

I'm not sure *what* I think about David these days.

I tell Ivy the plan.

"Okay," she says. "What will we do?"

"I don't know . . . Have a snack, watch TV, listen to music? Whatever you want."

"Could Diana come too?"

"Your friend from school? I don't know. Ethan might not want to have to share you."

She gives me one of her classic Ivy looks: a combination of confusion and annoyance. "That's a weird thing to say. I'm not food."

"I just meant he might want all of your attention."

"Diana's his friend too."

She's clearly not getting it. I wonder if I should try to make her at least a *little* aware of what Ethan might be feeling for her at this point. And a little more aware of what she might be feeling for him — what I *hope* she's feeling for him.

Maybe not being able to describe or put a name to your feelings makes them less accessible to you. Mom once said that they had to explain to Ivy when she was little what hunger was — she would just cry from the feeling of emptiness in her stomach instead of asking for food. Maybe romantic attraction is like that for Ivy — something she *feels* but can't yet name or even connect to its cause.

But can someone tell you you're in love? Or do you just have to know it at a gut level? And if you can't identify it, does it even really exist?

At lunch on Tuesday, Sarah asks me what's going on with "the Ivy fix-up thing," and James says, "Yeah, what?"

So I tell them that Ethan's coming over on Sunday to hang out with her.

Sarah says, "Oh, my God, that's the cutest thing ever. Can I drop by? I want to see them together. Do they hold hands? That would just kill me."

"Is he coming too?" James jerks his chin toward David, who's sitting alone at a table in the corner, staring at his open laptop as he shoves a bouquet of french fries in his mouth.

"No idea."

"Let's crash the date," Sarah says to James.

"I'm so there."

"Guys . . ." I say.

"We're just joking," Sarah says. She leans over and stage-whispers to James, "We're not joking."

Jana comes over and drops a full tray on the table. "I am exhausted," she announces before sitting and launching into a description of her day, which apparently involved a Spanish presentation, a biology test, and something else that she resented (I'd stopped listening by this point).

A little while later, when people are talking about other stuff, she turns to me and says, "That was cool meeting your sister. You never talk about her."

"Yeah, I do," I say uncomfortably. "It just doesn't come up that often."

"She seems really sweet." She's fishing. She wants to know more.

"She is," I say. "She's also autistic."

"I thought it was something like that!" she crows.

I feel a brief flash of something that's almost hatred for Jana, but I just take a sip of my water and will it away. She doesn't mean to be hurtful, any more than Ivy means to whisper incessantly to herself.

People can have nothing but good intentions and still sometimes make you want to kill them.

NINETEEN

THERE'S A MOVIE on the TV and chips in a bowl on the table, but Ethan won't eat them because Mom buys the kind sprinkled with flax seeds and Ethan does not appreciate finding seeds on his tortilla chips, as I discovered a few minutes earlier. It wasn't a chili-pepper-level crisis, but he was pretty upset. I found some plain rice crackers in the pantry, and he was willing to eat those, so peace has returned to our family room.

Ivy and Ethan are sitting next to each other on the sofa. I steered them there. I'm perched on one sofa arm and David's in the armchair on the other side of them. I'm bored. I don't like the movie—some mediocre thriller Ethan wanted Ivy to see—but I've been forbidden to talk during it: Ethan and Ivy both shushed me when I asked David a question about our English homework.

David catches me yawning and gestures toward the doorway. I nod. We both get to our feet.

As I cross in front of them, Ivy says, "Where are you going?"

"We're just getting something to drink."

"Come back," she says.

. . .

"Do you think she'll ever be willing to be alone with him?" David asks me once we're in the kitchen.

"Yeah," I say. Then: "I don't know. Maybe not . . . Why wouldn't she? But she can be so weird about it. But eventually she has to get comfortable, right?"

"Maybe think about it for a while and get back to me?"

"Sorry. Clearly I have no idea. Can I get you something to drink?"

"Sure. You have Coke?"

"Sorry. It's considered unhealthy around these parts. I have a stepfather who's very concerned about everything he puts into his body . . . except when it comes to alcohol, which he seems just fine with."

"So my only choice is alcohol? A little early for me, but if it's what the natives do . . ."

"Yeah, no. But you can have water. Or juice. Or milk. Or one of these." I open the fridge and take out a can of the weird health food carbonated zero-calorie juice things that Mom and Ron buy. I toss it to David. He catches it and sits at the table.

"Blackberry and sage?" he reads off the label. "And here I was hoping for watercress and guano." He pulls the tab and peers dubiously down into the opening before sniffing it. "Ugh." He takes a sip. "Yep. Just as disgusting as I expected." He gulps some more.

"Why are you drinking it if you don't like it?"

"I'm thirsty." He puts it down and leans back in the chair.

"I'm glad we're staying in today. It's definitely less stressful than being out in the world with them."

"Yes, because people suck."

"They do."

I'm wearing my hair clipped up in a knot on top of my head. I unclip it now and shake it free. For no good reason.

"You have nice hair," David says.

I shrug, pleased by the compliment but also a little surprised by it. "You said I was ridiculous for highlighting it."

"You are. But it's still nice hair. With or without highlights."

"Thank you."

A slightly awkward silence follows.

His fault for complimenting me.

It's gotten kind of dark in the kitchen. I should turn on a light. But I don't move. I just sit there, playing with my hair, darting glances at David Fields, who, in one of life's weirder twists, is right now sitting alone with me in my kitchen.

He says abruptly, "Oh, so Ethan told my dad that he has a girlfriend."

"What did your father say?"

He makes his voice gruff and dismissive. "'You'd better get a job, then — if she's anything like the women I've known, she'll spend all your money and expect you to thank her for the privilege.'"

"Nice misogyny."

"Well, to be fair to him, it's not so much that he's sexist as it is that he hates everyone. Also? He's sexist."

I laugh.

But he's not smiling. "Meanwhile Ethan's standing there, waiting for my father to see how exciting this is for him, how proud he is to be able to say he has a girlfriend—but Dad just says that one unpleasant thing and walks away." His fingers trace the writing on the can in front of him. Then he shifts and glances up. "You have to wait a long time if you want to hear my father say something nice. Like, forever."

"I'm sorry. Ethan deserves to be appreciated. He's so sweet."

"I've never seen him do or say a mean thing. I mean, I've seen him be anxious and loud and demanding and annoying . . . but not mean. Never mean."

"Ivy's the same way. She doesn't want to hurt anyone."

"And yet they're supposed to act more like us. That's what we keep telling them."

"Because it's dangerous to be too nice. Selfish people get ahead."

He raises his eyebrows. "Pretty dark thing for Chloe Mitchell to say."

"It's true."

"So why aren't you selfish?"

"Who says I'm not?"

"You told me your college plans depend on Ivy. Not a lot of kids our age worry about their siblings."

I shrug. "Most people aren't in my situation. You're the only other person I know like me."

"Yeah, I'm basically the male version of you." He cocks his

head at me. "And a look of horror crosses her face. Don't worry, Mitchell. I was joking."

"I didn't look horrified," I protest.

"You were terrified at the thought," he says. "Admit it."

"It was a look of *intrigue*—I was intrigued by the possibility."

"In a horrified sort of way."

"Maybe," I say, and we grin at each other and then the door from the kitchen to the garage bursts open, and Mom and Ron and James and Sarah all come flooding into the room, and we stare at them open-mouthed, and they stare at us open-mouthed, and then Sarah bursts out laughing.

"You should see your expression!" she says, coming toward us, curly hair bobbing on her shoulders. "You look like you're about to faint."

"They were parking out front just as we were pulling into the garage," Mom says. "What's this about Ivy having a date here? You didn't say anything to me about that."

"Sounds like someone didn't want the parents around," Ron says, setting a bag on the counter.

I glare at Sarah, who's clearly been shooting off her mouth. Next to her, James is watching David with narrowed eyes.

I turn back to Mom. "I just didn't want to make a big deal out of it, for Ivy's sake."

"Mm-hmmm," Ron says, like he doesn't believe me.

"Where are they?" Mom asks.

"In the family room. Watching TV."

Ron says to Mom, "We should probably check on them. Not sure how long they should be left alone. For a lot of reasons."

"I *would* like to meet Ethan," she says. She holds her hand out to David. "You must be his brother."

"Yeah." Still sitting, he shakes her hand. James would have jumped to his feet the second Mom walked in the room. It's the polite thing to do, and it bugs me that David doesn't do it. Not because I think that kind of thing matters, but because other people *do,* and now that we're spending a lot of time together, it would be helpful if he would stop alienating everyone he meets.

Mom doesn't seem to mind, though. She smiles warmly and says, "Nice to meet you."

"I'm going to the family room," Ron says, and heads off. Mom excuses herself and follows.

"So," James says. "What's up, guys?"

"Not much. We're just hanging out while Ivy and Ethan do their thing." I go over and stand next to him. I feel wary, like he might be angry, but he doesn't *look* angry. And that makes me wonder why I'm worried he might be. He knows what the story is with me and David, why we've ended up spending so much time together. He understands the situation. So why am I on edge?

"How's the date going?" Sarah asks, dropping down into the seat next to David. "Are your siblings totally in love?"

David's face has taken on the bland, distant expression he

wears at school like a fencing mask. I hadn't realized it was gone until it reappeared.

"This is disgusting," he says, and for a second I think he's talking about Sarah's question but then I realize he's tapping on the soda can.

Although I wouldn't rule out a double meaning.

"So don't drink it," I say.

"I wasn't planning to." His tone is adversarial. We were friends a minute ago. We're not now.

"Can we see the date in action?" Sarah asks.

"It's not very exciting," I say.

"Please?"

"Fine. Just don't expect fireworks."

She gets up, and I lead her and James out of the kitchen and down the hallway. David follows a few steps behind the rest of us, hands jammed in his pockets.

In the family room, Mom and Ron are hovering over Ivy and Ethan.

"Is it a good movie?" Mom asks.

"Not really," Ivy says.

"I like it," Ethan says.

"I'm sure Ivy's enjoying it too," Mom says.

"No, I'm not," Ivy says.

Mom laughs like it was a joke.

Ron says, "Can you please pause the TV while we're talking to you, Ivy? That's the polite thing to do."

"Okay." She picks up the remote and stops the movie but stays slumped on the sofa.

"Hi, Ivy!" Sarah says, and moves deeper into the room. "How are you doing? We came over to see your sister. Who's your friend?"

"Ethan," Ivy says.

"Introduce everyone, Ivy," Ron says. "You know how to do that."

"I just did," she says, her eyes darting around the room, taking in all the faces looking down at her, watching her every move. I don't blame her for looking a little terrified. She and Ethan are like two bugs that are about to be pinned to a card and cataloged.

"Come on, you know how to do this right," Ron tells her. "Stand up. You too, Ethan. And now you say, 'Ron, this is Ethan, Ethan, this is Ron.' That's the right way to introduce people, isn't it?"

They're quietly doing what he told them to do — they're both standing up, and Ivy's repeating his words, and Ethan's shaking first Ron's hand and then Mom's, and then Sarah's and James's — and I'm the only person (well, maybe David, too) who can see how Ivy's chin is down and her hand is slapping quietly against her thigh and how Ethan's eyes are more evasive and more troubled than I've ever seen them before.

All the comfort and peace of the afternoon are gone.

"Can we get you guys anything?" asks Sarah, all smiles and curly hair and knowing winks. "Chloe makes really good popcorn . . ."

"We already have snacks," Ethan says, and points to the table.

"How about some carrots?" Ron says. Ivy shakes her head at that, and Ron says, "No, thank you?" like he's prompting her, so she says, "No, thank you," and her hand pumps faster at her side.

"We don't mean to interrupt," Mom says. "You two should finish your movie and then maybe we can all have an early dinner together?" She turns to James. "That reminds me— I've been meaning to thank you for all the meals your parents have treated Chloe to. I think if she could trade our family for yours, she would."

"Well, my parents would trade me for her, so it's even," James says easily. He's so good at this make-the-parents-happy kind of thing. Meanwhile David stayed behind in the hallway, where he's staring down at his phone, ignoring the rest of us.

"Let's go back to the kitchen," I say and start us moving back in that direction. I want everyone to leave Ivy and Ethan alone.

I pass David, who backs up against the hallway wall to make room as we go by. "You coming?"

"I think I'll go see how the movie ends." He slips past the others, moving away from the rest of us and into the family room.

TWENTY

"OH, MY GOD, this is amazing," says Sarah once we're back in the kitchen. "Ethan is so cute! If Ivy doesn't want him, I'm going to ask him out."

"So will you stay for dinner?" Mom's nailing the hostess role right now. There was a time when she would have crawled to her room to curl up in a fetal position at the ring of the doorbell. And here she is, smiling, welcoming, social. Progress.

"I have to be home for dinner," Sarah says. "Sorry."

"How about you, James?"

"I should probably check with my mom first."

"Yes, of course. I'm thrilled to hear that you check with your parents before making plans. I'm not always sure Chloe does." She laughs, and Ron adds, "I'm pretty sure she *doesn't.*"

I need to get away from them both before I lose it. I say to my friends, "Let's go to my room."

Once we're safely behind a closed door, Sarah asks me what's wrong. "You're being weird." she adds.

"No, I'm not."

She looks to James for corroboration.

"Yeah, you're in a bad mood," he says.

"It's just . . ." I sit on the edge of my bed and pull my knees up to my chest. "I'm working really hard on this Ethan and Ivy thing and then everyone just descends on them like they're mating pandas in a zoo or something."

"Oh, please." Sarah sits down on my desk chair. "They barely even noticed us. And we told you we were coming."

"I didn't think you were serious."

"We thought it would be fun to drop by. Sorry if it annoyed you." But her tone isn't apologetic. It's pissy.

"Maybe she's mad because we interrupted something between her and David," James says.

"Yes," I say. "That's exactly what's going on here: I'm furious because David Fields was just about to tell me who his biggest crush is, and I had my fingers crossed that he was going to say *me,* and that's when you guys walked in and ruined everything. I'm sorry this had to be the way you found out I've lost interest in you, James, but what can I say? David is twice the man you are. I mean, that body . . . and then there's his radiant personality—"

"Okay, okay." James holds up a hand. "Sarcasm noted."

"Good. Because you're being ridiculous. You know why I have to hang out with him. Ivy isn't ready to be alone with Ethan."

"That explains why *you* have to be here," Sarah says. "Doesn't explain why David does."

"Same deal with his brother."

"So he says. I mean, the guy probably has no social life—I bet he came just to hang out with you."

"Well, it's what he told me," I say irritably. "Feel free to ask him if he was lying or not."

"See?" Sarah says. "You're in a bad mood."

The three of us are watching music videos on my laptop when Ivy comes in and informs us that Ethan and David left as soon as the movie ended.

I say, "You should have told me. I would have said good-bye."

"It's okay. They didn't care."

Sarah's parents tell her she has to come home, and James says he'll drive her. I get the sense he doesn't particularly want to stay alone for dinner with my family, so I don't push him to come back.

Mom's annoyed that she ordered a lot of pizza and now only the four of us are eating. "At least James and Sarah explained why *they* had to go, and of course I don't blame Ethan for not communicating. But that brother of his . . . Not only did he completely ignore the fact I'd invited them to dinner—no response one way or the other—but he didn't even say good-bye, so I thought they were still here when I placed the order."

"I actually thought *he* was the autistic one," Ron says. "I mean, when we first walked in, before we met the other one. He seems to have his own social difficulties."

It's lovely the way he talks about autistic people in front of Ivy—like there's something wrong with them. She's chewing away at her pizza, and I can't tell whether or not she's bothered by what he said.

"Well, maybe he's on the spectrum too," Mom says, picking up her own slice with a sigh. "It can run in families, you know."

Ron doesn't like pizza because it's "all carbs," so he put together a salad for his own dinner, which he washes down now with several glasses of red wine.

Mom keeps fretting about all the leftover pizza she's going to have to deal with, but when Ivy reaches for a third slice, Ron puts out a hand to stop her. "Don't you think you've had enough?"

"No, I'm still hungry." She puts the slice on her plate.

He takes a long sip of his wine. "Ethan's pretty thin. You don't want to be heavier than your boyfriend, do you?"

"I don't think he's my boyfriend." Ivy looks at me. "Is he?"

"I don't know," I say. "He's not *not* your boyfriend. And I want another slice of pizza too." I'm lying. I don't really want it—I just don't want Ron to make Ivy feel bad about having one. I take a couple of bites just to make my point.

Ivy turns very quiet, and later, when we're alone in our room, she says, "I don't think Ethan's my boyfriend. We don't kiss like you and James do."

"Do you want to? Because I think he'd be up for it."

"Would I know if I wanted to?"

The question kind of blows my mind. You can't assume anything with Ivy. Finally I say, "I think so. I did. I really, really wanted to, pretty much every time I kissed a guy. I mean, it was scary the first time—"

"The first time with James? Or the first time kissing

anyone? Because you had a lot of boyfriends before James. There was Juan and Brian and—"

I cut her off before she can finish the whole recitation. "Yeah, yeah, I know. The first kiss with any guy is always scary, I think. But the *first* first kiss is the scariest. Even when you want to do it, it's terrifying."

"So why do it?"

"Because at some point, the wanting is stronger than the terror."

"Do you think you'll marry James?"

"Marry him? Ivy, I'm *seventeen*."

"I know. You're three and a half years younger than me. I'll turn twenty-one before you turn eighteen, and then I'll be four years older than you, but only for five months. Do you think you'll marry James when you're older?"

"Nah. I'll probably go out with tons of guys before I get married, if I even ever get married."

"I don't think I'll marry Ethan either. I'm old enough to get married, but I don't want to marry him."

"No one's expecting you guys to get married, Ives. This is just about having someone to do fun things with. That's good, right?"

"Yeah, I guess."

"So relax," I say.

TWENTY-ONE

TV at our house on Friday?

It's Wednesday night. I'm lying on my bed doing homework. The text is from David. He adds, Ethan's idea

Ivy or both of us?

Up to you

We still don't talk to each other at school. We do this nodding thing when we pass, and we don't attack each other's comments in English class anymore . . . but we don't talk.

I ask Ivy what she thinks about going to Ethan's house. She says, "Only if you go too."

"Come on, Ives. You can't always be dragging your sister along wherever you go."

"Just this time."

"And then you'll go out with Ethan by yourself?"

"I don't know. Maybe."

"Seriously, I can't keep going with you. It's getting weird for me."

"Why?"

"I think it's starting to bother James that David and I spend so much time together."

"Why?"

"Because James is my boyfriend. Which you know."

"Does he think you want David to be your boyfriend?"

"God, no!"

"Then why is it weird?"

I fling my hand out. "It just *is*. Guys don't like their girl-friends to hang out with other people when they could be with them."

"Why not? Why does it matter?"

"Look, what if Ethan said to you, 'You shouldn't always be with—'" I stop because I can't think of an example.

"With Diana?" she suggests.

"What if he said, 'You're spending all this time with Diana instead of with me, and that hurts my feelings'? You'd feel a little bad, right?"

She shakes her head. "You should be with who you want to be with. If I wanted to be with Diana more than I wanted to be with him, then I would be."

"I mean, obviously no one should ever tell you who you can and can't be with. I'm just saying that if it bothered him, you'd feel bad."

"But why *would* it bother him?"

"Because it's less time that he gets to be with you."

"That would be okay," she says. "Are you worried that James won't let you come on Friday?"

"It's not a question of whether or not he'll *let* me—"

"Okay, good," she says. "Then you can come."

. . .

As I drive up to the Fields family home in Westwood, I'm surprised that it's so normal-looking—just a midsize stucco house with a neat lawn, like millions of other houses in LA. I'm not sure what I expected it to look like—dark and mysterious? Dilapidated? Surrounded by fog? It just seems impossible that someone as tortured as David could come from an unremarkable middle-class home.

It's just a house, and whoever answers the door is just a woman, not a ghoul or a monster or a witch. She's tall and thin and has chin-length brown hair that's slightly layered, and her makeup and clothing are neat and unremarkable.

"Yes?" she says with a wary smile, opening the door a few inches. Not someone who likes unannounced visitors—there's a small NO SOLICITORS sign next to the door.

"Hi," I say. "I'm Chloe. And this is Ivy." She's standing behind me, holding back a little, like she always does, waiting for me to take the lead and do the talking for us both.

"Can I help you?"

"We're here to see David and Ethan? They know we're coming."

"Oh!" The woman steps back. "Sorry. The boys never tell me anything, and we get the strangest people at our door sometimes. I have a little one, so I have to be extra careful. I'm Margot Fields. Come on in."

She shouts up to the boys and then invites us into a very clean and organized kitchen, where a chubby baby in a blue romper and a bib sits in a highchair playing with a spoon.

There's some kind of food smeared all over his face and on the tray in front of him, but he seems happy.

"It's Caleb's dinner time," Mrs. Fields tells us. "We were just eating mashed bananas, weren't we, my love?"

The baby bangs his spoon on the tray and makes a *ba-ba-ba* sound.

"That's right!" his mother says delightedly. "Bananas! You see David's friends, sweetie? These are David's friends."

"I'm not David's friend," Ivy says. "I'm Ethan's friend. Chloe is David's friend. They go to school together."

"Is that right?" Mrs. Fields says. She studies Ivy, assessing the stretch pants and the ponytail and the averted gaze. "And do you go to school with Ethan?"

"Yes."

"Ah," she says like now she understands something. "Can you two gals excuse me for a second? The boys must not have heard me. Let me see where they are." She leaves the kitchen, and we can hear her calling up the stairs for the boys.

The baby stares at us and mouths the back of the spoon.

"I think it threw up," Ivy whispers to me, clutching at my arm. "There's throw-up on its chin."

"That's just the bananas."

She retches audibly and takes a few steps back. She has a very low tolerance for disgusting things, and is phobic about vomit.

Mrs. Fields returns in time to see the dry retching. "Are you okay?" she asks anxiously. "You're not sick, are you? We have to be careful with a baby in the house." She puts her body between Caleb and Ivy, like that would stop germs from spreading.

"Is that throw-up on its face?" Ivy says.

"Excuse me?"

"I already told you it's just food," I say impatiently.

"This?" Mrs. Fields says, swiping the baby's chin. "That's just banana."

Ivy retches again.

"Maybe you should go home," Mrs. Fields says. "Babies shouldn't be exposed to germs."

"She's not sick," I say as David enters.

"Who's not sick?" he asks.

"Ivy."

"Who said she was?"

No one answers him. His stepmother says, "Where's your brother?"

"Bathroom."

"Does he know his friend is here?"

"Are you sure it's bananas?" Ivy asks me. "Because if someone throws up, people who are nearby breathe in molecules of the vomit and then they throw up a day later."

"No one in this room is sick!" I say.

"I'm not sick, but I'm not well," David says.

A man comes into the kitchen, and Mrs. Fields says, "Oh, Kevin. Look! The boys have guests." She gives a little laugh. "Too bad for them the Browns canceled on us at the last minute. Looks like we accidentally crashed their little party."

Mr. Fields is around the same height as his sons but

significantly heavier. He shakes my hand and then holds his out to Ivy, who hesitates a couple of seconds before taking it. She's not being rude; it just takes her a moment to process social niceties and remember what she's expected to do with them.

"Nice to meet you both," he says. He's got the boys' gray-ish-brownish-greenish eyes but they've receded deep into a lined face. He looks like he's a lot older than his wife.

There's a pounding of steps in the hall, and Ethan bursts in. "I'm sorry!" he says. "I'm really, really sorry. I wanted to open the door for you, but I was in the bathroom. It took me longer than I wanted it to. I'm sorry."

"No worries," I say.

"Hi," he says to Ivy. He tentatively strokes her arm. "I'm glad you came to my house."

She just nods.

"Why don't you kiss her on the cheek?" his father says with a jovial wink. "I bet she'd like that, wouldn't you, Ivy?"

"Don't encourage that kind of thing," his wife says with a tight smile. "The slower, the better."

Ethan looks confused and a little concerned. "Should I kiss her?" he asks David.

"Nah, man, you're good," his brother says. "Let's show the girls around the house."

"You'll stay downstairs, right?" Mrs. Fields says. "I think that's best. And doors have to remain open."

"Why?" Ivy asks.

"Oh, you know . . ." An uncomfortable little laugh. "Boys and girls together . . ."

Ivy waits for the rest of the explanation, but it doesn't come.

Instead, the boys' stepmother turns to me and says, "Oh, you're a good person to ask—I'm always trying to take advantage of people with experience . . ."

"Experience?"

She waves her hand toward Ivy. "You know . . . Have your parents ever said anything about your sister's vaccination experience? Do they feel this"—another hand wave—"was connected to that? I'm terrified of getting Caleb vaccinated. With my husband's family history and all . . . I just don't want to take any unnecessary risks. I assume Ivy was vaccinated?"

"Yeah, of course. We both were."

She considers this. Then dismisses it. "Well, back then they didn't know as much about the connection . . ."

"There *isn't* a connection," David says impatiently. "How many times do I have to tell you? The original study used falsified data."

"Maybe," she says stiffly. "Maybe not. A lot of very smart people say the medical industry is part of the deception."

"He's right," I say. "Vaccinations don't cause autism, and it's dangerous not to vaccinate kids. They'll end up getting the measles or something like that."

"Better measles than autism," Mrs. Fields says darkly.

"But measles is a disease," Ivy says. "People get really sick if they get the measles. Why is that better than autism?"

"It's not," David and I say at the exact same time.

"Oh, gosh!" Mrs. Fields says. "I didn't mean it like that at all! I just want to make the right decision here. Caleb is my first child, and there's just so much to think about . . ." She brushes the back of her hand against his cheek and gazes brightly around the room. "You all understand."

There's an awkward pause.

"Can we watch TV?" Ivy asks. Her hands are fluttering anxiously at her sides. "Chloe said we were coming over to watch TV."

"Yeah," Ethan says. "Come on." He steers her out of the room.

David and I start to follow them. Mrs. Fields says from behind us, "We'll be upstairs. Please keep the noise down. I'm putting Caleb to bed soon."

"We'll be quiet," David says.

"But not too quiet," she says with a little nervous laugh. "I don't want anything going on that Chloe and Ivy's mother might not approve of."

"You really don't have to worry about that," David says, and we leave the kitchen.

TWENTY-TWO

I CAN'T BELIEVE SHE'S an antivaxxer," I say as David and I linger in their formal, white-on-white living room. There are double doors at the other end of it that open onto a wood-paneled family room, and I can see Ethan and Ivy settling down on the sofa in there, TV remote already in Ethan's hand. "I thought all rational people had given that one up."

"Emphasis on *rational*. Margot was always nervous and a little nuts, and I wasn't thrilled that my dad married her, but we got along okay at first. Then she got pregnant and went off the deep end. We so much as cough, and we're banished for the rest of the week so we don't infect the baby."

"Oh, yeah, I saw a bit of that."

"Mostly, though, she's terrified that Caleb will be autistic —anytime he, like, gazes off into the distance or something, she freaks out, even though it usually just means he's pissing his diaper. She asks everyone we meet about the vaccination stuff." He glances around. "Hey, want to just sit in here? I don't really feel like watching TV."

"Yeah, me neither." I sit on a super-hard armchair and have to squirm my butt around to find a position that's comfortable. David sits on the end of the sofa closest to my chair. "I hate when people talk about how awful autism is when Ethan and Ivy are right there."

"I know. When she says stuff like that, I wish Ethan would blow up at her, but he's too nice—he just shuts down. Sometimes it drives me crazy that he doesn't get mad or fight back ever. I've even yelled at him for being too nice." He runs his fingers through his hair. "Charming of me, right? To tear into him because he's a better human being than I am? Meanwhile, I have no trouble losing my temper with anyone and everyone—including him."

"Me too with Ivy," I say. "So many times. Once, in middle school, she got worked up about something in front of one of my friends, and I told her that if she didn't learn to control herself, I wouldn't let her hang out with me anymore." I stare down at my fingers, spreading them out wide on the arm of the upholstered chair. "I was so mean." I've never told anyone about this before. It's kind of a relief to confess.

"Siblings say stuff like that to each other all the time."

It's sort of amazing—David Fields is trying to comfort me. Who knew he had it in him?

"And let's be honest," he says. "Ivy and Ethan can both be incredibly annoying."

"True." Our eyes meet, and I see . . . understanding. I've always felt like I had to make other people see the *good* in Ivy because they're so quick to judge her, but since I know David already gets it, I can be honest with him. "But they don't mean to be. I hate how annoyed and impatient I can get with her."

"You shouldn't hate yourself for that," he says.

"Yeah? What *should* I hate myself for?"

"I'll make a list," he says with a smile that makes it a joke, not an insult.

"There isn't enough ink in the world . . ."

"I'll use a spreadsheet."

There's a moment of silence.

"They're pretty quiet in there." I nod toward the family room.

"They're both champion watchers," David says. "It's their superpower."

"Too bad they can't make a career out of that."

He leans toward me and whispers, "Ethan's planning to make a move tonight."

"What kind of move?"

"First holding hands and then, if that goes well, a kiss on the mouth. We discussed it. Made a plan of action."

"With diagrams?"

"I considered it. But I'm pretty sure he knows where the hands and lips are, and I warned him to stay away from all other areas."

"Did you tell him to stop holding hands if there's a sweat situation? That's important."

"I didn't think of that."

"What kind of love guru are you?"

"Believe me," he says, "I'm well aware it's the blind leading the blind here."

I wonder what his romantic history is. If he even has a

romantic history. He stays so far apart from everyone at school that it's hard to believe he's ever made a real connection there. But people have summer flings and stuff like that, right?

I try to picture David flirting with a cute, nameless girl, but it's too weird a thought. He'd have to let his guard down, and he never does that. Except for now, I guess. And a couple of other times alone with me.

My phone buzzes on the coffee table in front of me, where I'd tossed it when I sat down. I glance at it and laugh.

"What's so funny?" David asks.

"It's from Ivy. She wants me to join them in there." But I don't get up.

"Texting is the greatest invention ever," David says idly. He doesn't seem to be in any hurry to get up either. "For a sociopath like me, it's the gift that keeps on giving. I once had a friend who always called me on the phone."

"Not a friend anymore?"

"Goes without saying."

"And yet I said it."

"Some people just can't help stating the obvious."

"Some people don't know how to make polite conversation."

"Yeah," he says. "That would be me."

"You do okay when you want to." My phone buzzes again. Ivy: Where are you? I ignore it.

"You know what we should do?" David says. "The next date, we should just leave Ivy and Ethan at one of our houses and go somewhere else together. Not too far away, just not *there.* I think it would help your sister get used to not always having you there without making a big deal out of it."

"Yeah? Where would we go?"

"I don't know," he says. "Wherever you like."

I have the strangest feeling that David Fields is sort of asking me out on a date. And an even stranger feeling that I don't mind.

But then I quickly tell myself that's not what he means, because he knows I have a boyfriend. A great boyfriend. The best.

Ivy calls from the doorway to the family room before I have to respond. She's gotten up from the sofa to check on us. "Why are you guys sitting in here?"

Ethan comes up behind her. He puts his hands on her shoulders and gently squeezes. The last couple of times they've been together, he's been reaching out to her a lot, clearly eager to get his hands on her in some way—but it's more sweet than pervy.

"We're just talking," I say.

"It's so dark." She moves toward us, and Ethan's hands drop off her shoulders, but as he follows her, he keeps reaching out to touch her back or arm. "Why don't you turn on the lights? Is it so you can make out?"

"Oh, for God's sake, Ivy," I say. It's funny, but it's also embarrassing. "Do we *look* like we're making out? We're not even sitting together."

"It's just that when you and James make out, you leave the lights off like this."

"Who's James?" asks Ethan.

"Chloe's boyfriend," Ivy says.

"Chloe's big, strong, athletic boyfriend," David says. "Which is why there's no danger of me making out with your sister, Ivy. We were just too lazy to turn on the light."

"Let's go back in the TV room," Ethan says to Ivy. He tugs at her arm and then runs his fingers down to her wrist. "Come on. I like when it's just us two in there. And I want to finish the show."

"But you guys will come in too?" Ivy says to me. "Since you're not making out?"

"Yeah," David says. "So long as we don't suddenly start making out in the next few minutes, we'll be in soon."

"Okay." She lets Ethan take her hand in his and lead her back into the family room.

"That wasn't awkward at all," David says.

"Sorry."

"It's fine. I have a high tolerance for embarrassing situations. I mean—" He gestures at himself. "I'd have to, right?"

I don't know what to say to that, so I just shrug. He's okay. There's nothing actually wrong with the way he looks or even the way he acts when we're hanging out together. It's just that he can be so weird and standoffish at school.

He says, "Ethan seems pretty happy whenever he's with your sister."

"I am so proud of myself." I give a little bounce in the chair. "I mean, I saw Ethan and was, like, *This is the perfect guy for Ivy.* I am brilliant."

"I'd pat you on the back, but you're doing a good enough job of that on your own. Plus, you start off patting someone's back in a dark room, and you know what that leads to—"

"What?"

"Ask Ivy," he says. "She's figured it all out."

We eventually make our way to the family room, where we watch the end of Ivy and Ethan's show with them—although I'm really watching Ivy and Ethan, not the show. They're more interesting. He's sitting all squished up next to her on the sofa, much closer than the space requires.

His thigh is tight against hers, his fingers constantly creeping toward her arm in the desire to touch her somehow, somewhere . . .

I know that feeling. I've felt it myself, on those first early dates with James and a couple other boys—that aching, itching desire to touch, to feel, to bond, to give in to desire. And I've sat next to boys who've given it off like smoke from a fire, who've pulsated with so much need, so much yearning, that you can practically feel the heat rising off of them.

Maybe Ethan can't put it into words. Maybe he can't even completely understand what he's feeling, but he's definitely in love or lust or whatever you want to call it with my sister. Serious skin hunger has set in. Mom would probably be alarmed, but why shouldn't he feel physical desire for the girl he likes? I mean, so long as he doesn't push himself on her in any way.

What about her? I study my sister. She's mostly just staring open-mouthed at the television, but then I see her glance down at Ethan's hand and there's something in the way she looks away again quickly—I can't tell whether it's nervousness or excitement or uncertainty or *what*—that makes me think she's aware of his thirst on some level that might not even be conscious.

So, yeah, he's a step ahead . . . but maybe she's not *too* far behind?

As we're saying goodbye, Ethan leans forward, grabs Ivy by the upper arms, leans in, and plants a big, wet, juicy one right on her mouth.

Part of me wants to cheer him on, and the other part wants to say, *Whoa there, Dude. Make sure the lady wants it.* But I'd be the first to admit that, in this case, it's a little hard to know what the lady wants.

Ivy steps back as soon as she can and wipes her mouth on her shirt—not deliberately or insultingly, just like there's saliva on it and she wants to get it off.

I glance at David. He looks anxious. I flash a smile that's more reassuring than I feel. I want this to work so badly. For Ivy's sake. And for Ethan's.

And, oddly, a tiny bit for my own. I'm kind of enjoying having someone all in with me on this project—David wants this to succeed as much as I do. If Eth-vy (Iv-an?) doesn't work out, I'm back on my own.

And that sounds so lonely.

TWENTY-THREE

As flies to wanton boys are we to the gods; they kill us for their sport," Ms. Campanelli recites at school a few days later. "Anyone know what that's from?"

Jana instantly says, "Shakespeare. *King Lear.*" And checks to see if people are impressed with her.

Spoiler: they're not.

Except maybe for Camp, who beams. "Right! And what's he saying? Because I think it relates to what we're talking about here." We started off the day with Salinger's story "Teddy," and somehow that got us onto the subject of religion, which led to the current discussion of polytheism.

Jana says, "It means the gods torture us for fun just like boys do with bugs."

"That's right," Camp says. "It's sort of an early precursor to chaos theory, when you think about it—there are no guarantees that just because you're a good person, things will go well for you. Some god might just be in the mood to mess around with your life."

"It's sort of the opposite of a real religion, then," says Sarah.

"Interesting," says Ms. Campanelli.

David lifts his head to look up from his computer screen. "What's the difference between a 'real' and a 'not real' religion?" he asks Sarah.

"You know what I mean."

"No, I don't. Enlighten me. What makes one religion more real than another?"

"I just meant, like, you know, the Jewish-Christian stuff. What we all believe."

"We all?" he repeats.

She waves her hand and says again, only more irritably, "You know what I mean."

"Yeah," James says, turning in his seat to glare at David. Almost like he's been waiting for an excuse to do that. "Don't pretend you don't understand her just to make her feel bad."

"He's not," I say, and both James and Sarah swivel to stare at me. "There are tons of other religions. And there've been, like, *thousands,* since humans have started keeping records. And for all you guys know, people in this room could be Buddhists or Zoroastrians or Mormons or atheists. I mean, you can't just assume that everyone believes what you believe or say that your religion is more 'real' than other people's."

"I didn't!" Sarah says. "You're totally putting words in my mouth!"

"Everyone, relax." Ms. Campanelli holds up her hands. "Your choice of adjective *was* a little unfortunate, Sarah."

Sarah's mouth hinges open in the universal sign of *this is so unfair!*

"But," Camp continues, "I also agree that we all knew what you meant, so let's move on. I want to talk about Teddy's parents—do you think they love him or not?"

Jana is of course already answering the question by the time I'm sliding back down in my seat, my heart pounding in a way it usually doesn't when I speak up in class. David catches my eye. He looks grateful . . . and confused. He didn't expect me to defend him.

I shrug and look away, and now it's James's turn to catch my eye. He also looks a little confused. But not at all grateful.

Later that day, I have lunch with James and Sarah as usual. Neither of them mentions English class, but they laugh more at each other's jokes than at mine—it's a subtle thing, but I don't think I'm imagining it.

Afterward, James splits off, and Sarah and I head to our next class together.

That's when she says, "So what's going on between you and David?"

I groan. "Nothing. How many times do I have to tell you?"

"You've always said that he's a jerk, but suddenly today you're all *David's right* in class."

"Because he *was* right—you shouldn't have said some religions are real and others aren't."

"Oh, please. Everyone knew what I meant. You would never have taken his side before."

"What are you implying?"

"Nothing. But just so you know, James is feeling really weird about you right now."

I have a sudden desire to stab Sarah in the throat with a pen. Too bad mine are all felt tips and wouldn't do more than leave a dot of black on her skin. "Did he say something to you? Or are you just spinning your own little web of insanity?"

"I don't want to betray his confidence," she says loftily, hugging her books against her chest. "So I probably shouldn't say anything else. But just be aware that he's noticing."

"Noticing what?"

"How you and David are suddenly besties . . . and maybe more."

I could still throttle her, right? You don't need a sharp pen to throttle someone. Or do you? What the hell *is* throttling, anyway? "Are you serious?" I say. "You guys know what the situation is — that this is all about Ivy and Ethan. And if James has a problem with that, he can tell me himself. And if you say stupid things like your religion is more 'real' than other people's, then I'm going to call you on it."

"Fine," she says angrily, and we walk in silence to class and don't speak to each other for the rest of the day.

That evening, Ivy shows me a text from Ethan.

Your very hot. Can I see you soon?

"Nice." I hand the phone back to her. "So are you going to see him again?"

"Do you think I should?"

164

"Absolutely. I like that boy."

"Okay," she says. "But can I also do something with Diana this weekend?"

I shrug. "Ask Mom."

"I want you to take me."

Apparently all of this chauffeuring and chaperoning of her and Ethan has made her more dependent on me, which is ironic, given that my original goal was to make her *less* dependent. "I do have a life of my own, you know."

"You take me to see Ethan."

"That's different."

"Why?"

"Just because it is."

She gazes silently past my shoulder at the wall behind me.

I sigh. "Fine. I'll drive you if I don't have other plans, but there's no way I'm taking you all the way to Alhambra or wherever she lives. We can meet near school or something."

"I'll ask. I got her cell phone number — it was my idea." She sounds proud, and maybe she should — I don't think she's ever planned a get-together with a friend before. Maybe this whole Ethan thing really *has* motivated her to be more social, which would be sort of amazing and great. "I'll text her."

"You do that," I say with a yawn.

When I enter the cafeteria on Tuesday, I spot David sitting alone at a table as usual, eating pasta and keeping his eyes on his laptop screen. As I watch, a piece of penne falls out of his mouth and onto his keyboard, and he just picks it up and sticks it back in his mouth, then swipes at the keys with a napkin.

He glances up and our eyes meet. He raises his hand with a gesture that seems like maybe he's beckoning, so I come over. "Hey," I say. "What's up?"

"We have to see our grandparents on Saturday. Can you guys do something on Sunday?"

"I think so." I idly swing my lunch bag from my fingertips. "Let me find out what Jeannie and Ron's plans are." I prefer to call my mother by her first name when I'm talking to other people. I'm sure there's some deep psychological reason why. "If they're going out, Ethan and Ivy can hang out at our house together. If they're not . . ." I stop. "Your house isn't any better, is it? I'm running out of ideas. Everything seems potentially disastrous."

"Not everything," David says. "There's always the Roller Derby. They couldn't possibly draw attention to themselves there."

"Or pro wrestling . . ."

"Or we could take a different approach," he says. "Send them off to high tea at a snobby hotel. Like tearing off the Band-Aid all at once — just get the worst over with and then nothing else can possibly feel as bad. Are you just going to stand there, or are you going to sit down and eat with me? Or does the very fact I even suggested it demonstrate my ignorance of the school social hierarchy and its unwritten rules?"

"D, all of the above," I say, and plop down on a bench

across from him after only a fraction of a second of hesitation. I wasn't planning on eating with him—I always eat with Sarah or James or both of them and whatever other friends are around. But it's ridiculous to stand there clutching my lunch and talking. Not just ridiculous—kind of rude, like he's not worthy of total lunch commitment. "But now you have to close your laptop. Unwritten rule number one of eating lunch with another human being is that you have to pretend to want to talk to them."

"I'd rather look at you anyway," he says, and closes the screen and shoves the laptop away from him.

I was unwrapping my bagel, but I stop and stare at him. "Was that, like, a compliment? Or some sort of . . . I don't know . . . *pleasantry?*"

"Yes," he says, flushing and looking away. "It was a pleasantry. A misguided attempt to make social conversation. And now that you've made me feel stupid for saying it, and ruined the word *pleasantry* for future generations, you have successfully convinced me never to say anything nice to anyone ever again."

"You can't blame me for being surprised." I take a big bite of my bagel. I didn't have time to toast it, and I didn't put enough cream cheese on it, so it's basically a big dry bite of stale bread. I drop it back down in disgust—it's not worth eating.

David tears a chocolate chip cookie in half. "Want some?" He holds a piece out to me. The chocolate glistens, and the brown-buttery inside looks like it will be chewy, which is how I like my cookies. I can't think of a single reason to refuse. So I reach for it.

"Thanks." We chew together for a companionable moment. "That was really good," I say after I've swallowed.

"I know." He balls up the wrap it came in. "It was a pretty big sacrifice on my part to give you half. I'm already regretting it."

"I'll make it up to you someday, somehow. This, I swear."

"How about giving me your firstborn child?"

"Okay, but when climate change has destroyed life as we know it and we're all fighting to survive, you can't favor your natural children over my poor little loaner."

He laughs, and I notice a couple of other kids turning to look at us. I guess the sound of David Fields laughing is unfamiliar enough to draw attention. His laugh is unexpectedly warm—I've heard it a few times now, but its richness still surprises me.

"Someone's been reading too much dystopian fiction," he says.

"Yeah, don't get me started on the zombie apocalypse."

"What's to get started on? All you need is an axe and you're good."

"You need some chain too."

"For what?"

I roll my eyes. "To chain up your loved ones when they get bitten. Duh."

"Why even bother fighting? Why not just give in and all

become zombies? Nothing would change—most of the kids here would already tear out each other's flesh if it meant they had a better chance of getting into Stanford."

"Yeah, but their parents would never let them eat any old brains—they'd have to be *organic.*"

We go on like this for a while, and then, since English is next, we walk over to class together, stopping by each other's lockers to pick up our books.

Inside the classroom, we separate automatically to go to our normal seats—his by the wall, mine near Sarah and James. He's got his laptop open before I've even made it across the room.

"We missed you at lunch," Sarah says as I slide into my seat.

"Sorry. I got into a conversation."

James says, "We noticed."

Camp calls for attention, so we can't talk more, but after class is over and we're standing up, I say to James, "You're not going to start being all possessive, are you?"

"You can talk to whoever you want; just don't take me for granted."

"I never have," I say. "I never would." I raise myself up on tiptoes to give him a reassuring quick kiss, but he grabs me and presses me tightly against him and turns it into something that's dramatic enough to inspire a couple of kids to clap and whoop as they're leaving the classroom. I get the sense he's sort of marking his territory, but what the hell—it feels good from where I'm standing.

"Lovely," says Camp, as we walk past her together. "You guys give my heart hope. So long as two beautiful young people can still walk hand in hand, there's good in the world."

"We're beautiful," I say to James outside her classroom.

"Yes," he says. "Yes, we are." He squeezes my hand and kisses me fiercely and then we say goodbye and go to our separate classes. I pass David huddled against the wall, checking something on his phone, but he doesn't look up as I go by, and I decide to just keep walking.

TWENTY-FOUR

Ivy WAKES UP super early on Saturday morning and immediately starts talking to herself in little whispers that I can't quite make out but are just audible enough to wake me up.

I'm tired and want to sleep more. James and I stayed up late the night before, first at a friend's party, and then watching scary movies at his house and stalling until the rest of his family went to bed, so we could have some time alone.

All evening long, I felt some weird unspoken pressure to reassure him that everything was good between us, flirting with him like he was a new conquest and not my longtime boyfriend. He seemed to enjoy being freshly seduced. And I enjoyed the hours I spent at his house entwined with his muscular body—I have to remember to appreciate it more and as often as possible.

But right now I'm tired, so I hoarsely beg Ivy to either leave the room or stop whispering. She stomps out of the room, making it clear she's hurt that I would imply she was bothering me, and I go back to sleep for a couple of hours. When I finally come downstairs, she's not in the kitchen, but Mom and Ron are at the table drinking post-workout protein shakes. I stumble past them on my way to the coffee maker.

They're wearing matching outfits — black sweatpants and white T-shirts. I hope it was accidental. If they're going to start dressing like twinsies, shoot me now.

"You have fun last night?" Mom asks. "You got home late."

"Can't talk," I croak. "Need coffee."

Ron says, "A run would perk you up more than coffee. Why don't you try that first?"'

"Great idea. I'll do that."

There's a pause while they try to figure out if I'm being serious or sarcastic.

Here's a hint: I'm being sarcastic.

"Where's Ivy?" I ask, yawning as I pour milk into my coffee.

"Where do you think?" Ron says. "Watching TV." He turns to Mom. "That's why she can't lose weight, you know. She spends all her free time sitting in front of the TV. You have to get her to move more."

"I know," Mom says. "You're right. I just don't know how to make that happen. She doesn't like exercising."

I leave the room with my mug before he can launch into a lecture.

Anyway, he's wrong — Ivy *is* moving. Even though the TV's on, she's not watching it: she's wandering around the family room with a jerking, half-skip sort of a gait, muttering to herself, her hands fluttering at her sides, occasionally slapping against her legs.

She doesn't hear me the first time I say her name. I repeat it more loudly, and she jumps in the air and whips around, ending in a terrified crouch. She's still in her pajamas—flannel ones with a sushi design. (Another Mom pick—Ivy hates sushi.)

"You scared me," she says accusingly.

"Sorry. I didn't mean to. What's going on?"

"Nothing. I'm just watching TV."

I perch on the arm of the sofa and take a sip of coffee. "Is something worrying you?"

"No."

"You sure?"

"I'm okay. We have to go meet Diana soon."

"Not for another, like, three hours."

"I don't want to be late."

"We won't be."

"You say that sometimes and then we are."

"Hey, I'm doing you a favor driving you. Don't make me regret it."

"Okay." There's a pause. "You should probably go shower," she says.

My mother suggests that the family all eat lunch together, so I suddenly "remember" that I promised Ivy we'd grab some burgers at In-N-Out before meeting up with Diana. Ron won't touch fast food, and Mom won't either anymore, although back in pre-Ron days, dinner for the three of us was often just a greasy bag of takeout from almost anywhere.

I miss those meals.

Ivy's really out of it at lunch for some reason—she's so distracted she can't even make the limited conversation she's usually capable of—so I spend the meal texting other people. James and I go back and forth about which movie we want to see that night, and then David sends me a text that says You figure out Sunday yet?

Mom and Ron will be home

So not your house?

yeah

Movie? E and I could go to one and we could go to another

And suddenly I'm discussing what movie to see with *both* James and David. If my life were a sitcom, I'd accidentally make plans to see the same movie at the same time with both of them, and end up running back and forth, pretending to be going to the bathroom and buying popcorn and doing stuff like that so I could keep switching from one seat to the other, and hilarity would, of course, ensue.

Ivy suddenly shrieks, and I look up from my phone.

"What?"

"Look!" She lifts up her hand, and there's ketchup smeared all over the fabric at the wrist of the floaty top I gave her for her birthday and told her to wear on her first date with Ethan. "It's ruined!" she says.

"Just go into the bathroom and rinse it off."

"What if it doesn't come out?" Her voice is too high and loud and upset. People are looking at us.

"Well, then you don't ever have to wear that top again. That should make you happy." I'm hoping a joke will defuse the situation, but her face screws up in distress.

"You said it's nicer than my other tops! You said I should wear it when I want to look nice! I don't want it to be ruined!"

"Calm down. All you have to do is wash it off. Do you want me to help you?"

"No! I can do it!" She gets up and runs to the bathroom with her arm held up and away from her body like it's bleeding or about to fall off or something. More people look at her. One young guy whispers something to his date, and they both laugh. I glare at them, but they don't notice.

Ivy's gone long enough for me to wonder if I need to go in after her, but I really don't want to. When she does return, she happily informs me that the ketchup came out. She doesn't seem to mind that her sleeve is visibly soaked from the wrist to the elbow — so much so that water is dripping from it and pooling on the table. I hand her a few napkins and suggest she sop it up a bit. She blots at her sleeve carelessly, then goes back to eating her lunch.

Diana is pretty much the way I remembered her — very skinny with incredibly pale skin that's pitted here and there with acne scars. Her dirty blondish hair is pulled into a long, narrow braid down her back, and she's in overalls again. She mutters a low, toneless "hi" to Ivy's much more enthusiastic greeting.

Diana's mother is an older, more polished version of her daughter — gaunt, with a long, pale face and hair pulled back in a ponytail and no overalls (thank God), just plain black slacks and a button-down shirt. She greets us both warmly, and when the girls go to look at the boba tea menu on the wall, she says to me, "You're such a nice sister—Diana's brother would never offer to chauffeur her around."

"Thanks for coming in our direction."

"I'd drive a hundred miles to get Diana together with a friend. Except I can't drive her at all during the week, because I work. But on the weekends, I'd do anything to get her out and being social."

"My mom feels the same way." Actually, it's more me than Mom, but this sounds more normal.

She says, "I can keep an eye on them if you have something you'd rather do—I brought a book and was just going to wait here."

I check with Ivy, whose response to my "do you mind if I leave?" is an impatient wave of her hand and a "no, just go, I'm busy." She turns back to Diana, and I hear her telling her that the green dragon tea is best and also that she has enough money to pay for *both* of them. "I just want water," Diana is saying as I leave. "I don't like tea."

I wander in and out of a bunch of stores around Westwood Village, idly looking through racks of clothing and occasionally trying on stuff. I buy a black dress on sale at Brandy Melville, a candle at Urban Outfitters, and mascara at Target.

I drop the stuff off at the car, feed the meter, and decide it's time to head back to the boba shop. Ivy hasn't texted me, which is great. I wish she could be as mellow about hanging out with Ethan as she is with Diana, but it's not surprising that she finds a date more stressful than just hanging with a friend.

As soon as I enter the place, Ivy spots me. "Chloe! It's too soon. Go away."

"Nice to see you, too."

"We want more time here."

"I don't," Diana says. "I'm a little bored."

I have to hide a laugh. I can't decide if the world would be a better or worse place if everyone was as honest and literal as these two. Better in some ways, I guess, but maybe a little harsh?

Diana's mother was sitting at a table reading by herself, but she gets up and comes over. "So what do we think?" she asks. "Do you girls want to do something else before we head home?"

"Can Diana come back to my house?" Ivy asks. "We live close."

"It's okay with me," Diana's mom says. Her daughter just shrugs.

We make a plan: I'll drive the girls to our house while Diana's mother runs an errand, and she'll pick Diana up in an hour. I give her our address and lead the two friends to the car.

When I glance back, Ivy is walking so close to Diana that their arms keep bumping. Ivy has mild spatial issues — she doesn't always seem to know exactly where her body *is*. Still, it's weird that it keeps happening.

"My sister is younger than I am, but she drives and I don't," she tells Diana as they climb into the back seat of the car.

"You're both going to sit back there?" I say over my shoulder. "I feel like a chauffeur."

"We want to sit together," Ivy says. She scoots over to the middle seat, so she's right next to Diana.

Diana says she once drove her father's car in a parking lot, but it was scary and he yelled at her a lot, and now she isn't sure she wants to learn how to drive. Ivy says she thinks Diana would probably be very good at driving a car and that she, Ivy, will probably learn to drive when she's twenty-five, which is the first time I've heard anything about that.

I glance in the rearview mirror when we're stopped at a light. It seems so crazy the way Ivy is sitting all smushed up against Diana's side when there's plenty of space to spread to. But also kind of sweet. Maybe this is the beginning of a beautiful friendship . . .

Too bad Diana doesn't live closer, though.

At home, Ron's car is gone, and Mom must have gone out with him, because she's not around. I go upstairs and do some homework while I listen to music.

Eventually I get a text from Diana's mom saying she'll be here in five minutes, so I go downstairs to tell the girls. I follow the sound of the TV to the family room and peer around the doorway.

They're sitting on the sofa together. Diana's staring at the set, her mouth slightly open, totally absorbed by whatever they're watching. But Ivy isn't. Ivy's staring at Diana. Like she's some kind of miracle.

While I'm watching, she shifts her leg ever so slightly so it's right against Diana's, then puts out her hand and gently strokes an index finger along Diana's lower arm. Diana doesn't seem to notice, just shifts her arm a little without taking her eyes off the screen. Ivy lets her head fall back on the cushion and rolls it toward her friend, like she wants to rest her head on Diana's shoulder—only she doesn't. She just huddles close like that—as close as she can be without their heads actually touching. Her eyes slide sideways so she can still see Diana's face.

I watch Ivy watching Diana watching TV, and something's nagging at me—Ivy's reminding me of something, something I was just thinking about, and I can't remember what it is, and that bugs me, and I'm standing there . . . and then I realize what it is, and I actually grab at the side of the doorway to steady myself because my legs feel suddenly wobbly as two words explode in my head, bright and shiny, my own internal neon sign:

SKIN HUNGER.

TWENTY-FIVE

DIANA'S MOTHER IS IN A RUSH and steers Diana quickly to the front door, reminding her to thank us for having her over. "I know," Diana says irritably, the way I would have at the age of eleven. But she's over seventeen (how much over, I don't know), and Ivy's twenty. They're not little kids.

Physically, they're adults.

Ivy throws her arms around Diana, who stiffens and waits, expressionless, for the hug to end. But then she does say, "Thank you for having me over."

"Can we do it again?" Ivy asks eagerly as she steps back. Her hand lingers on Diana's arm.

"I don't want to get boba tea again," Diana says. "I don't like bumps in my drinks."

"We can do something else."

"We just need to figure out the logistics," Diana's mom says, flashing a tired smile at me. "I wish we lived closer."

Ivy says, "Can we do something tomorrow?"

"Sorry," Diana's mother says. "This was our only free time all weekend."

"We have plans tomorrow too," I remind Ivy. "With

Ethan." And then I feel a weird blast of anxiety. Ethan. What if I've been making a horrible mistake? Have I been?

"Okay. But soon?"

"Absolutely," says Diana's mother, and follows after her daughter, who has already headed down the walkway toward their car.

I close the front door and trail after Ivy, who's on her way into the kitchen, where she opens the refrigerator and pulls out a carton of milk. "That was really fun," she says, putting it on the counter and getting a glass out of the cabinet. "I want to see her again. And again."

I study her as she pours, frowning in concentration, her tongue thrust out.

She's careful. Doesn't spill a drop.

I say, "You really like Diana, huh?"

She puts the milk carton on the table and takes a sip from the glass. "Yeah."

"Can I ask you something?"

She shrugs, raises the glass to her lips again, swallows.

"If you were stranded on a desert island—all alone there—would you rather have Ethan or Diana come keep you company for however long you were stuck there?"

"Diana," she says instantly.

"Even if you were stuck there forever?"

"Yeah. Why?" She gulps some more milk. When she puts the glass down, she has two white wings at the corners of her mouth.

"I guess I just didn't realize how much you liked her."

"I like her a lot."

Does Ivy just adore and admire Diana in a best-friend kind of way? Or is there something else going on here?

Even though Ivy is over three years older than me, from the time I could talk, I felt like I needed to tell her what to do, what to think, what emotions to express. There's a home video of me at age four, ordering seven-year-old Ivy to tell Mom she loves her because it's Mother's Day and that's what you're supposed to say on Mother's Day. Ivy turns to Mom and obediently repeats "I love you" with almost no intonation. Mom makes a big fuss over it and slathers her with hugs and kisses, which Ivy endures.

The point is, I've always helped Ivy express the emotions I was sure she was feeling and just couldn't put into words. I've been assuming that she *does* feel something for Ethan—affection, attraction, maybe even lust or love—and I've been trying to guide her responses to him.

But right now I'm confused. I'm not sure *what* she's feeling, for him or for Diana. I want to ask her more questions and I also want to run away from the whole complicated mess.

She finishes her milk and leaves the kitchen.

I come up to our room a little while later. Ivy's circling the rug, whispering to herself and gently weaving her hands through the air. I sit at my desk and open my laptop.

"Chloe?" she says, approaching me.

"What?"

"Do you want to kiss Sarah?"

Wow. She's definitely thinking *thoughts*. "Not really. I mean, we hug when we haven't seen each other for a while . . . But I don't want to kiss her on the lips or anything like that. Why?"

She thumps her hands softly against her hips. "I don't know. I just wondered."

"Is something worrying you?"

She shakes her head, but it's pretty clear she's feeling anxious.

"Is it something to do with Diana?" I ask.

"Don't be mad at me," she says. "But I think I want to kiss her."

"Why would I be mad about that?"

"You don't want to kiss Sarah, and she's your best friend, and I want to kiss Diana, and she's my best friend. Do you think that's bad?"

"No, of course not."

"Why don't you want to kiss Sarah the way you kiss James?"

"Is that how you want to kiss Diana? Like I kiss James?"

Ivy hesitates and then whispers, "Yes."

I'm tempted to run away from this conversation—it's so heavy, and shouldn't this be Mom's job?—but Ivy needs me to stay in it with her. "Are you—" I stop. "Do you—" I stop again. Then: "You know how sometimes guys marry guys and women marry women?"

"Yeah. That's because they're gay."

"Right."

"And that's okay," Ivy says, like she's memorized it. "Boys can love boys, and girls can love girls. And sometimes people are bisexual and love both."

"Right," I say again.

We're silent. I watch her. She stares at the wall and bumps her palms rhythmically against her legs—more thoughtfully now than nervously.

"Chloe?"

"Yeah?"

"You're not gay, right?"

"I don't think so. I like kissing boys."

"I don't. I mean, I've never really kissed a boy or a girl, but I didn't like it when Ethan kissed me." A pause. "Chloe?"

I'm pretty sure I know where this is leading, and I feel a strange mixture of elation and confusion and shock—and a tiny edge of hysteria. "Yes, Ivy?"

"Could I be gay?"

I keep my voice matter-of-fact. "Yeah. I mean, anyone can be gay. Do you think maybe you are?"

"I don't know." Poor Ivy—she's so used to taking her cues from other people. And we've—*I've*—been leading her in a completely different direction, automatically assuming something that might have been totally wrong.

I say slowly, "If you'd rather kiss Diana than Ethan, it could mean that you're gay. Or that you're bisexual and you just happen to like that particular girl more than that particular boy."

"I do like Diana more than Ethan."

"Right, but . . ." How do I help her figure all this out? "Have you ever wanted to kiss a boy? Or hug him super close?"

She thinks. Shakes her head.

"Any girls other than Diana?"

She thinks some more. "I don't know. Maybe. There was this girl back in my old school. I liked the way she had wings on her eyes."

"Wings on her eyes? You mean eyeliner?"

"Yeah! But it went up like wings. I liked to look at her eyes a lot. She was really pretty." There's a pause. "Chloe?"

"Yeah?"

"I think maybe I'm gay."

My first thought is, *Oh, crap, this is going to make her life harder.* And then I realize that Ivy already feels isolated most of the time. This won't really change anything much.

Plus . . . she likes someone! Someone in her class. Someone who's also on the autistic spectrum. Wasn't that what I wanted for her all along?

"Do you think Diana likes you as much as you like her?" I ask.

Her hands thump a little faster. "I don't know."

I hadn't gotten the vibe from Diana that she wanted to be as close to Ivy as Ivy wanted to be to her, but maybe Diana's just not all that into being touched—a lot of autistic people aren't. That wouldn't necessarily mean she's not in love with Ivy.

She wears overalls a lot, right? Maybe that's a good sign?

Okay. Now I'm being ridiculous.

How amazing would it be, though, if Diana felt the same way about Ivy that Ivy feels about her? She could be the friend, confidante, and companion that Ivy will need after I go to college. Maybe they could even get a small apartment together in a couple of years and live happily ever after with a terrier named Eleanor Roosevelt and a cat named Sappho —

Ivy breaks into my daydream. "Chloe? Should I text Diana to say I'm gay and ask her if she is?"

"Umm . . ." *Why are you asking* me? *I'm seventeen and don't know anything about what to do when you're autistic and gay.* But Ivy expects me to guide her, like I always do. She still trusts me, even though it's starting to look like I've been leading her in the wrong direction all this time. I say, "Maybe don't rush into it yet? This was the first time you guys have even gotten together outside of school. Maybe wait until you've spent more time together."

"Can I tell Ethan?"

Ethan. Oh, God.

I remember how he kept reaching out for her the last time we were all together, and I feel terrible. I'm convinced he really likes her, which means he's about to have his heart broken — because of me. Two people simply falling in and out of love, that's no one's fault. But I'd deliberately pushed the two of them together. Over and over again. Even when Ivy seemed uncertain about it, I slammed them together.

"Why aren't you answering me?" she says.

"Sorry. I was trying to figure out what you should do. I don't want him to be hurt." On the plus side, he can't take it too personally, right? She wouldn't have fallen in love with *any* guy.

"I could text him," she says, and picks up her phone, just as the door to the garage opens and Mom calls out, "Come help with the groceries, girls."

"Hold off on texting," I say, tugging Ivy toward the garage. "Let me talk to David first and see what he thinks."

"Okay."

We pass Mom and Ron. They're both lugging full bags. "There are a few more in the trunk," Mom says.

"Guess what?" Ivy says to her. "I'm gay!" She continues on into the garage.

Mom stares after her, then swings her head in my direction. "Chloe?"

"Yeah, uh . . . hold on. I'll explain in a sec."

Ivy and I grab the rest of the bags and join Mom and Ron in the kitchen. Mom asks Ivy to repeat what she just said.

"I'm gay."

"What makes you say that?"

"I like Diana more than Ethan."

"Oh, that doesn't mean you're gay," Mom says with a relieved laugh. "I like a lot of women more than a lot of men, but I'm not gay."

Ivy's brow furrows. "Chloe says I might be."

Mom turns to me. "Chloe? What's going on?"

"She thinks she's being funny," Ron says.

I shoot a brief glare at him and say to Mom, "Ivy's trying to figure some stuff out. That's what's going on."

"You must have put the idea into her head," Ron says.

"I think we're all jumping to conclusions here," Mom says. "Let's just slow down. What about Ethan, Ivy? You've been spending so much time with him, and I thought . . ."

"He's okay," Ivy says. "But—" She stops and looks to me for help.

"She'd rather kiss Diana than him," I say.

"Did she *tell* you that?" Ron asks. "Or was it your idea?"

I say to Mom, "Can we please just discuss this with the family?"

"This *is* the family," she says. "Ron is part of our family."

"Yours, maybe. Not mine."

She breathes in sharply. "That's a horrible thing to say! Apologize to him right now, Chloe."

"Are you kidding me? He accuses me of all sorts of things, and that's fine? But I just ask to speak to you alone, and *I* have to apologize?" God, I'm sick of this.

Mom crosses her arms. "Apologize or I'm sending you to your room. You're acting like a child."

"Jesus, Mom! All you think about these days is your precious husband. You've completely stopped caring about me and Ivy!"

"That's it!" Ron grabs my arm. "You can be rude to me,

but I won't allow you to be rude to your mother. You're going to your room if I have to drag you there."

"Let go of me!" I shove at his hand and spin away. "Don't touch me! Don't you ever touch me!"

Ivy puts her hands over her ears. "Stop it! Don't! Don't fight!"

"It's okay, Ivy," I say, warily keeping an eye on Ron as I circle around to her. "It's okay. Ron's being a homophobic dick, but otherwise everything's fine."

"I am not homophobic!" he spits out furiously. "That's not what this is about! I have a ton of gay friends, and if I truly believed that Ivy was gay, I'd be fine with it! But what I'm not fine with is you bullying both her and your mother into believing something just for your own personal amusement!"

"You're insane! Totally batshit crazy. Why would I ever make this up?"

"Because—" He stops, his face red, as he flails about for a reason. "Because you like to make trouble!"

"I don't think Chloe's doing this to be difficult," Mom says unhappily. "But I do think she's rushing to conclusions—and she's definitely not being very mature right now—"

I throw my hands up in the air. "You're both unbelievable! This is a waste of time. Come on, Ivy. Let's go upstairs." She follows me out, her palms still plastered over her ears, her face taut with anxiety.

"Why is everyone so angry?" she asks once we're in our room with the door shut. "Is it because I'm gay?"

"No. It's because Ron hates me and wants to make Mom hate me too." I'm pacing around the room, too upset to settle down.

Ivy perches on the edge of her bed, her fingers fluttering above the quilt as she watches me anxiously. "Does he hate me too?"

"No. No one could ever hate you. I'm the hateful one."

"I probably shouldn't have told them I was gay," she says morosely. "Mom got upset, and so did Ron."

"Only because they think it was my idea."

"What was your idea?"

"That you're gay."

"How could that be your idea? Isn't it just how I am?"

"Right."

"I'm confused," she says.

"Join the club."

"What club?"

Sometimes I feel really lonely. This is one of those times.

TWENTY-SIX

I HAVE TO FIGURE OUT how to tell Ethan, so I text David, hoping he'll be able to help me.

can you meet me for coffee or something tomorrow morning?

Just me?

Yeah

sure name the place/time

So I do, and we agree to meet at the Starbucks on Montana and Fifteenth at ten.

Mom comes into my room when Ivy's in the bathroom —she must have been waiting to talk to me alone. She sits on the edge of my bed and says in a low voice, "Is this for real, Chloe?"

"I think so." I'm still a little pissed at her for not defending me more—and a lot pissed at her for marrying Ron in the first place—but I really need to talk to someone about this, and she's all I've got.

"I've been thinking about it, and it actually kind of makes sense to me," she says. "Even though I never for a second considered it before. There are things about her . . ."

"I know."

We sit in silence for a moment. Then Mom says, "Do you think I need to do anything?"

"In what sense?"

"I don't know . . . Put her in therapy? Introduce her to more gay people? There's my friend Patricia's brother—he's gay. I could ask her if he would talk to Ivy."

"I think that might confuse her more."

"I just feel like I should do *something*."

"I don't think we have to do anything right now," I say. "Except maybe try not to be so heteronormative about everything."

She squints at me. "Am I supposed to know what that means?"

I shake my head. "Forget it. I'm just saying we should try to let Ivy know we're okay with this and that it's no big deal. She thought you guys were mad at her."

"Oh, poor baby," Mom says. "I'll make sure she knows I'm not—of course I'm not—but I feel so worried for her."

"Well, don't."

"I can't help it."

"Can't you?" I say, and then Ivy comes back in.

Mom gets up and gives her a hug. "I love you," she says. "You're the best girl ever."

"Thank you," Ivy says. "You're not mad I'm gay?"

"Not at all!"

"Is Ron mad?"

"No," Mom says. "No one's mad about this. I promise."

There are tears in her eyes as she steps back. Ivy doesn't notice them, but I do. And I know it's not because of Ivy's sexual orientation. It's because Mom can't ever adequately explain to Ivy all the complicated nuances of her worries, fears, and hopes for her. Neither of us can.

James can tell from my texts that I'm dealing with something major at home, and so he just shows up at the door half an hour later and tells me he's taking me out for an ice cream break.

He's so nice. I'm lucky to be with someone who's always so nice.

Over a hot fudge sundae, I tell him the whole story, and he says, "Holy shit!" and laughs.

"It's not funny."

"Sorry. But it's a little funny, right? I mean, there you are, wondering why she's not falling in love more quickly with David Fields's brother, and meanwhile she's *gay*." He laughs again. "Are you sure, though? How does she know?"

"What do you mean? How does anyone know?"

"Yeah, but this is Ivy—she can be a little confused about stuff. And it's not like she's ever said anything about it before."

"I saw her with Diana," I say. "I know what lust looks like."

"Glad to hear it." His hand reaches under the table and slides along my thigh.

I move my leg impatiently away. I don't even know why. I just don't want to be touched right now.

James sits back and folds his arms over his chest. "What's going on with you, Chloe?"

"Nothing. I just don't feel like being groped in a public place, that's all."

"So let's go somewhere private."

"Maybe in a little while."

"Your enthusiasm is overwhelming."

"Sorry," I say, only I don't feel sorry. I feel annoyed. And I don't know why. "I'm just tired, I guess."

There's a pause. James unfolds his arms, sits forward, sits back again, moves his legs restlessly, and glances around the ice cream shop. There are a few other people there, mostly couples and parents with small kids. For a while, we're the only ones at a table who aren't talking to each other.

When James does speak again, his voice is quiet. "What are we doing?"

"Eating a hot fudge sundae? Or is this a trick question?"

"I'm serious, Chloe. What's going on with us? I feel like at some point we switched from being together because it was fun to just being together out of habit. But neither of us wants to admit it."

"Wow." I stare at the dish of ice cream. I feel sick to my stomach.

The problem is, he's not wrong.

There's another silence.

"That's it?" he says. "You're not going to argue with me? Or say anything?"

"I love you a lot," I say, but it sounds forced. I don't know why. I *do* love him, and I've said so plenty of times before. The first time we kissed was pretty much the happiest moment of my life. He's been an amazing boyfriend, loyal and supportive and kind. I feel panicky at the thought of losing him.

But I also know he's right, that lately I've been spending way too much time convincing myself I feel closer to him than I actually do.

"Nothing's changed," I say. "Everything's fine."

"Really?"

I stick my spoon in the ice cream and leave it there, like a flag sticking up. "I mean, I know I've been a little distracted lately because of the Ivy stuff. I've had a lot on my mind . . . And having to process that she's probably gay—"

"You only just found that out today."

"I know. But if I seem a little out of it tonight, that's why. It's not because of you or anything to do with us."

"It's not just tonight. It's been, like, every day for the last month. Sarah says she's noticed it too."

"When did she tell you that?"

"I don't know. Recently."

I feel stung. They were complaining about me to each other. "That's really weird. She hasn't said anything to me, and I'm supposed to be her best friend."

"Well, you've been 'distracted' lately."

"I *have* been. I'm not lying about that."

"Sorry if I'm not crazy about being the last item on your list of priorities."

"Yeah," I say. "It must suck for you to not always be first. You must not know how to handle that."

"What's that supposed to mean?"

"Just that your entire family treats you like you're some kind of crown prince. The world revolves around you, and you get whatever you want whenever you want it. So when I just need a little time to myself, a little headspace, you can't deal with that." Wow. I hadn't even known I felt that way until the words came out. But I do.

"And she goes right for the personal attack. Nice."

"I'm not attacking you! I'm just saying that most guys would understand if sometimes I need to help my sister—"

"Most guys? Or David Fields?"

"Are you serious? That again? You know what the situation is, that we both—"

"You ate lunch with him! I was waiting for you, and you just sat down and ate with him! Don't pretend that's about *Ivy*."

"Yeah," I say. "What a betrayal. I actually talked to a male human being who wasn't you. I totally forgot that when you go out with someone, you're supposed to cut off all communications with the opposite sex. Next thing you know, I'll forget to keep my chastity belt locked whenever we're apart."

"Sure that hasn't happened already?"

I stare at him. "Jesus. What are you accusing me of exactly?"

"I don't know," he says. "Maybe you should tell me."

I breathe in sharply. "Wow. I guess the part of the relationship where we trust each other is officially over."

"Just that part?" he says softly.

And, like that, we break up.

James drives me home—he would never leave me stranded—but we don't say anything in the car, and when I get out, all I say is a stony "Thanks for the ride," and all he says is a cold "You're welcome." I slam the door shut and run inside and upstairs to my room, where I throw myself on my bed and burst into tears.

Ivy was curled up with her iPad, but now she sits up. "What's wrong, Chloe?"

I roll onto my back. Tears run down my temples and into my hair. I can feel them sliding along my scalp. "James and I broke up."

"Is your heart broken?"

Trust Ivy to say something that makes me almost want to laugh, even though I'm in pain. "A little bit, I guess."

"Maybe if you told him you were sad, he'd want to get back together."

I shake my head, and a tear slips into my right ear. "I don't want us to."

"You don't? Why are you crying, then?"

"It's just sad." I turn onto my side so I can look at her. "He's really great, and I really love him, but I think we want different things from each other right now."

"What do you want from him?"

"I don't know. Just for him to be supportive, I guess."

"He's not supportive?"

"Sometimes. But he was feeling like I didn't care enough about him."

"Did you?"

"Did I what?"

"Care enough about him?"

"I thought so."

"I still don't understand why you broke up," she says, a little plaintively. "It doesn't sound like anything was that bad."

"It's complicated." I roll back and look at the ceiling. My tears have stopped. Now I just feel tired. "People are complicated."

"If Diana and I went out, I would never break up with her."

"You say that now, but things change. You might meet someone you like even better."

"Is that what happened? Did James meet someone he liked better than you?"

"I don't think so." But that makes me wonder. Could he have?

Nah. He wasn't planning to break up with me tonight—everything was fine until suddenly it wasn't.

"I thought maybe you guys would get married," Ivy says. "People sometimes marry their high school boyfriends."

"Not often, though."

"Mom and Dad met in college."

"Yeah, that happens more often."

"If you want to cry more, you can. I don't mind."

"Thanks. Is it okay if I stop talking now?"

"Do you want me to stop talking too?"

"Maybe."

"Okay," she says. "But I'll come sit with you."

"That would be nice."

So she comes over to my bed and sits down on the edge. I lie there, my arm over my forehead, too tired to move. She pats my leg a couple of times, not saying anything, just keeping me silent company until I tell her I'm going to get ready for bed and then she goes back to hers.

Getting ready for bed and actually falling asleep—two very different things. The first is easy. The second . . . not so much. Not when your day has left you reeling.

My thoughts don't even know where to land. I can't decide which is the more unsettling thing—that James and I have just broken up or that Ivy's gay and I hadn't noticed.

I'm sad that James and I aren't boyfriend and girlfriend anymore—my tears were real—but I'm not devastated. I even feel maybe a tiny bit of relief mixed in with the sadness. He's right: things have been moving in a weird direction with us for a while. Lately I've been finding myself more and more irritated by things he says. I'm hurt that he could say goodbye to me this easily, and I'm scared about losing my constant companion, and my ego is going to miss having the best-looking guy in our school at my beck and call . . . but I don't feel like I've lost the Great Love of My Life. I'll date a lot of other guys, and some of them may even understand what it's like to want to do whatever you can to help your sibling, because they'll feel the same way about theirs. Like David does.

Of course, my imaginary future boyfriends won't be like David in other ways, because . . . David.

And that brings me back to Ethan and Ivy.

Ugh. What a mess I've made.

TWENTY-SEVEN

DAVID AND I walk up to the Starbucks at the exact same moment. We say hi, and David opens the door. "After you," he says with a gesture.

"Wow. When did you become domesticated?"

"I've always known the conventions. I just don't always choose to follow them."

While we wait in line to order, I notice that he's dressed more nicely than usual, in a button-down shirt and jeans that look reasonably new. "You just come from church?" I ask.

"I don't go to church. Why? Did you?"

"No. It's just that I'm wearing sweats, and you look kind of nice."

"Not really," he says. "And I like your sweats."

"Yeah, they're my good sweats." It's a joke, but it's also sort of true: they're soft and heather-brown and tapered, and if you could marry an article of clothing, I'd probably propose to them today. I'm wearing an equally cozy sweater—it's blue and fuzzy, and sometimes when I'm wearing it, I stroke my own arm. I haven't showered yet today—I finally fell asleep around two in the morning and lingered in bed as late as I could—so I pulled my unwashed hair into a sloppy topknot before leaving the house. I definitely don't look like I came from church. Or from anywhere other than my bed, actually.

David keeps shifting from one foot to the other. He sticks his hands into his pockets, rattles his change, glances around . . . He seems uneasy, and it *is* a little weird, just the two of us out together. I keep waiting for Ivy and Ethan to show up.

"I want a morning bun," I say, more to break the silence than for any other reason.

"You should get one, then."

"Should I, though?"

"What's the downside?"

"I feel sick afterward?"

"Life's short. Take a chance."

He puts his order in with mine and pays with his phone app before I can hand over any cash.

The indoor tables are all occupied by unshaven guys writing movie dialogue on their MacBook Airs, so we sit outside. It's a beautiful LA morning, still cool enough that the hot coffee feels good and so does the sun on our shoulders.

"So," David says, leaning back in his chair and idly watching me as I take the warm morning bun out of its bag. "What's up? Are we here to do some more plotting?"

I push the pastry toward him. "Want some?"

He nods and we both tear off pieces.

"You're not answering my question."

"I know. It's just . . ." I drop my piece of bun back on top of the bag. "I have something to tell you. And it's kind of big. And it's also kind of weird."

He sits up straight. "What is it?"

"It's about Ivy."

"Oh." His body relaxes. I wonder what he was thinking —what else would it be about? "What about her?"

"I sort of realized something. I mean, *she* did." I take a deep breath. "You see, she had this friend over—this girl named Diana—and she was really into her and didn't want her to go and kept sitting really close to her . . ." I stop.

"What?"

"Ivy's gay," I say. "I mean, I think she is. I mean, she *is*. I think." I shake my head. "Sorry. I sound insane. But she *is* gay, I'm pretty sure. I think she's in love with her friend."

His mouth drops open. "Are you serious?"

"I think maybe that's why things weren't moving along with Ethan. I kept thinking she just needed some time—I mean, I really thought she liked him—but then when I saw her with Diana . . . There was just something else there, something I hadn't seen before."

He just stares at me.

So I keep going. "And then we talked about it, and Ivy figured some stuff out for herself, and what she figured out is that she's gay. So I guess she and Ethan probably can't work out romantically. But they can still be friends, right?" When he doesn't respond, I repeat, "Right?"

"I don't know."

I wait.

Nothing.

I peer at him. "So . . . you're angry?"

He shrugs, glances away.

"I didn't do this on *purpose*," I say. "I wouldn't have set her and Ethan up if I'd known."

"I never said you would have."

"You haven't said anything at all."

He tugs at his hair. He speaks slowly. "Ethan woke me up early this morning, worried because the movie he wanted to take Ivy to had gotten a very high rating on Rotten Tomatoes, and he was convinced it would sell out. He didn't want to get there and not be able to get tickets, but he didn't want to buy the tickets online in case Ivy preferred to see a different movie. He also wasn't sure if he should wear a sweater or just a nice shirt on their date and needed me awake so he could talk to someone about all that."

"I know he's incredibly sweet," I say. "You don't have to convince me. And I could tell he liked Ivy—"

"Likes."

"Likes her. But you know better than anyone else how bad they both can be at letting us know what they're thinking and feeling. I had no idea how Ivy felt about Diana until I saw them together."

"But it was your idea to set her and Ethan up. It was your idea to push them together over and over again. So the fact that Ethan is totally one hundred percent in love with your sister, who's never going to feel the same way in return—who never *could* feel the same way in return . . ." He trails off, shakes his head, and says, "Maybe you didn't *mean* to hurt him, but I don't see how that helps him right now."

"I'm know. I'm sorry. I made a mistake. But—"

He abruptly pushes his chair back and rises to his feet. "So I guess we should cancel today's date?"

"We don't have to." I stand up too. "They could still get together as friends. So long as Ethan knows what's going on."

"How is he going to find out?"

"Maybe we could all talk together this afternoon?" My heart is pounding nervously. I want David to tell me he's not mad and that I haven't done anything wrong. But his face is cold and shut down. "Instead of going to the movies or just canceling? If Ivy can tell Ethan how much she does like him —just not as a boyfriend—maybe they can hold on to their friendship."

"Yeah," David says. "That always works out so well, doesn't it? 'I don't like you *that* way, just as a friend.'"

"If it's sincere—"

"Would it be? Does Ivy actually care? Or is that something else you're projecting on her?"

"I think she's really had fun going out with him. I have too. I'd like—" I stop. But then I go ahead and say it. I don't have a lot to lose at this point. "I'd like us all to keep doing stuff together. If you guys want to too. It's been really nice for me."

"Yeah?" His gaze flickers across my face, but evades my eyes. "Nice, how? Why?"

"It's been amazing being able to talk to someone about Ivy —someone who gets it." It's the easiest way to answer the question, and it's true. But it's not the whole answer. Even when we weren't talking about Ivy and Ethan, I was starting to like hanging out with David.

"Join a support group," he says, and turns away.

"Wait! What about this afternoon?"

"I'll bring Ethan over at three," he says over his shoulder. "You guys can tell him what you need to tell him. Let's just get it over with." And he walks away before I can say anything else.

Which is fine, because I have nothing else to say.

It's funny: the night before, after James broke up with me, even though I cried, I kind of felt okay deep down, like the right thing had happened, like it was inevitable. But now, as I drive home, totally dry-eyed and outwardly calm, I feel awful inside, all the way through — even my bones and my intestines ache.

I wish I could go back in time. I wouldn't try to push Ethan and Ivy together.

Except if I hadn't done that, I wouldn't have gotten to know David, and I've really liked getting to know him. He's crazy and angry and surly, but he's also smart and funny and challenging in a good way. James is kind and charming and helpful to everyone. David . . . David's not nice to very many people. But he'd sit and talk to me like I was actually a human being, and it felt like I'd broken through some barrier other people couldn't get past. It felt meaningful, like I was someone special.

I hope Ethan will be fine with everything, and then maybe David will be fine with everything, and then maybe we'll all be friends again, and maybe Diana will decide she's in love with Ivy, and Ethan will find someone else to be in love with, and David and I will be able to get together and talk about how great it is that Ivy and Ethan are friends with each other and in love with other people . . . and then unicorns will spread rainbows all over the sky, and flying pigs will play in them, and we'll all live together and have dogs named Eleanor Roosevelt and cats named Sappho.

TWENTY-EIGHT

You have to be kind of tactful when you talk to Ethan," I tell Ivy over lunch.

Mom and Ron are out, so she and I are eating grilled cheese sandwiches by ourselves. I burned one side of them, but I don't care, because I don't have much of an appetite at the moment. Ivy complained about the burned taste but is managing to eat hers anyway.

I go on. "Don't just say, 'I'm gay and don't want to go out with you.' Tell him you really like him as a friend; you just can't be his girlfriend. Make sure he doesn't take it personally, that he knows you wouldn't like *any* guy that way."

"You should probably tell him."

"No, you should."

"I don't want to."

"Well, neither do I." I get up to clear my plate. "And I already had to tell David, so this one's on you."

"Why can't David just tell him, then?"

"He doesn't want to either."

"But—"

"It's your job to tell him. You're the one who's gay."

"See? You always make it sound like a bad thing."

Great. Now I feel even cruddier.

When I open the door to Ethan at three, he's alone. I ask him where his brother is, and he points to their car and says, "He didn't want to come in. He said we're not going to see a movie today because Ivy wants to have a talk instead. I like movies better than talks, though." He's wearing a button-down shirt and a belt. His hair is combed. He looks like someone who is trying to look extra nice because he's going on a date with a girl he likes, and it wrecks me.

I lead him to the kitchen, where Ivy is sitting with her iPad. "Hi," she says. "Do you want some popcorn?"

"No, thank you," Ethan says. "But you should have some if you want to."

Ethan and I sit and watch as Ivy gets the bag of popcorn out of the pantry and comes back to the table with it. She sits down, opens the bag, and starts eating popcorn.

"I wanted to see a movie," Ethan tells her. "But David said you wanted to talk."

"Chloe wanted to talk, not me."

"I just thought you two *should* talk," I say. "Ivy, tell Ethan what's going on — what you realized yesterday."

"Okay." There are bits of popcorn shell on her lips. I catch her eye and make a wiping gesture toward my own lips. She stares at me blankly before turning back to Ethan. "Chloe wants me to tell you that I'm gay."

Ethan blinks several times rapidly. "What do you mean?"

Ivy waves her hand; grains of salt fly from her fingers. "Being gay means you like your own type of people, so girls like girls, and boys like boys."

"I know what gay means," he says impatiently. "I'm not stupid. But you're not gay."

"Yes, I am."

He shakes his head. "No, because you're going out with me, and I'm a guy."

"I don't want to go out with you."

There's blunt . . . and then there's cruel. I quickly cut in. "She likes you a lot as a friend—she's just saying that she doesn't think you guys should date."

"I want to go out with Diana and not with you," Ivy adds.

"Diana from school?" Ethan hugs himself and starts rocking back and forth in the chair. "You like her more than me?"

Ivy just nods, so I say, "Not *more*, just in a different way."

Ethan turns to me, his eyes confused and anxious. "Are Ivy and I still going out?"

"Maybe not romantically? But you can still do stuff as friends."

"Like Chloe and David," Ivy says. "Chloe has a boyfriend, but she still talks to David. Except she doesn't have a boyfriend anymore. They broke up."

"Why?" Ethan asks.

"Sometimes things don't work out," I say. "Even when two people like each other." I'm trying to make a point here.

"I'm not Ivy's boyfriend anymore?" he says, his voice high and strained.

"Just my friend," Ivy says.

Ethan starts rocking faster. "Diana's not very nice. She always tells me I talk too much."

"You do," Ivy says.

"No, he doesn't!" I say. "You're great company, Ethan."

"I wish you didn't like Diana more than me," he says to Ivy.

"It's probably because I'm gay."

"You guys can totally stay friends," I say. "That's even better—I mean, boyfriends and girlfriends break up all the time, but friends can stay friends forever, right?" I can feel sweat tickling under my armpits and beading at my temples. I'm so stressed right now.

"Are you and James going to stay friends?" Ivy asks me.

"Definitely."

"Then I guess we can too," she tells Ethan.

"Can I go to the bathroom?" he asks.

It's kind of a relief when he leaves the room.

"You could have been nicer to him," I hiss at Ivy as soon as he's out of earshot.

"Why wasn't I nice?"

"You kept talking about how much more you like Diana. That probably hurt his feelings."

"Really? But it's just true." She crunches some more popcorn and turns on her iPad.

I look at my phone. Sarah just texted me.

did you and James really break up??

yeah — after you told him I was acting weird

i didn't say that

He said you did, more or less

Are you seriously blaming me for your break up?

Am I blaming her? I stop to think about it. She was a little too quick to agree with James that I was being a bad girlfriend, a little too eager to commiserate with him — at least according to what he told me. She could have stuck up for me more. But would that really have changed anything? We were doomed anyway.

So I write: **sorry just upset and taking it out on you**

that's ok. i get it.

and just so you know, I totally defended you

Ivy says, "Are you mad at me?"

I look up. "What? Why?"

"You just looked a little annoyed about something."

"It's not because of you. I got a text."

"Who from?"

"Sarah."

"Are you mad at *her?*"

"Not really."

It's way too much work to try to untangle the different emotions I'm feeling right now so I can describe them all to Ivy. Like . . . I'm pretty sure Sarah *didn't* really defend me to James, but I'll never know for sure, and maybe it doesn't matter, anyway. So I feel mildly betrayed but not actually upset—and that's not really something I can decipher for Ivy. Right and wrong, she can get. Good guy, bad guy, truth, lies—those I can explain to her. But this is all too complicated, too messy, too unclear. She'll want to know if she should be mad at Sarah or not. And it's just not that simple.

My phone vibrates. I look at it. Sarah again.

now that you're free . . . anyone else interesting to you?

it's been like five minutes!

i just thought

I wait and then finally text **what?**

nothing

The word just lies there. She doesn't write any more, and I don't want to ask her again.

I check my Instagram feed and then decide I need a snack. I'm tense and bored—prime grazing conditions.

I search through the refrigerator and pantry and, as usual since Ron moved in, don't find anything satisfactory in the junk food department (even the popcorn Ivy's been eating is some super health food low-fat, low-salt kind that's not worth wasting my time on). I'm about to wander back to the table empty-handed when the doorbell rings, so I head into the hallway instead.

It's David. He doesn't greet me, just says, "Ethan didn't answer my last couple of texts. I wanted to make sure he's okay."

"He's fine." I gesture inside. "Come in."

He hesitates a moment, glancing down the walkway at his car like he just wants to go back there, but then he steps inside the foyer. "How'd he take the news?"

"Fine." I lead him down the hall. "I mean, he wasn't thrilled, but I think he's okay."

We walk into the kitchen. David says, "Hey, Ivy. Where's Ethan?"

Ivy looks up from her iPad. "He went to the bathroom. It takes him a long time."

"Not always."

There's a pause. David's got his hands jammed into his pockets, and he's not meeting my eyes.

"Do you want something to eat or drink?" I ask.

"I'm okay." He checks his watch, then leans back against the counter.

"I'm gay," Ivy tells him.

"So I've heard."

Her mouth curves down at the corners. "Are you mad at me?"

"No, of course not," he says impatiently. "Why would I be mad at you?"

"Then are you mad at Chloe?"

A slight pause. "No."

"You *seem* mad," she says. "For some reason, people always seem mad when I say I'm gay and then they say they're not mad."

"I promise I'm not mad at you, Ivy."

"Ivy's right," I say. "You do seem mad."

"Well, I'm not."

"Maybe if you said that less angrily?" I suggest.

He shoots me a look, then checks his watch again. "I'm going to see what's taking Ethan so long. Where's the bathroom?"

"This way." I lead him out of the kitchen and down the hallway. "Are you going to admit you're acting strange?"

He doesn't answer right away. Then he says slowly, "I'm just a little bummed, I guess."

"For Ethan?"

"Yeah. For me too."

"What do you mean?"

"It's been nice. Hanging out with you and Ivy. It's pathetic, but it's probably the most social I've been in years."

"We'll still hang out."

"Will we? You sure you won't feel like there are better ways to spend your time?"

"I'm not sure there are."

"Wow," he says. "That's the nicest thing anyone's ever said to me."

"I believe that. You don't exactly bring out people's softer side."

"I know."

"Still—" I say, and stop.

"What?"

I don't know how to put it in words. I only know that I like being alone with David in this hallway and that something about this moment seems filled with possibility and hope. "If you want to hang out, I'm totally up for it," I say finally.

He waits a moment, but when I don't say anything else, he says, "Sounds good," and his light, almost indifferent tone makes everything normal again. Which is both a relief and a loss.

"That's the bathroom," I say, gesturing at the door.

He knocks. "Ethan? You okay in there?"

There's no response.

David bangs on the door more loudly. "Ethan? Hello?"

Nothing.

He turns the doorknob. "It's not locked." He raises his voice. "Ethan? I'm coming in. Say something if you don't want me to." There's no response, so he opens the door slowly and peers around it. Then he shoves it completely open. "He's not in here."

"Oops—sorry! It's the closest one, but he must have gone upstairs." We retreat and go up to the second floor. Ethan's not in the hallway bathroom. "He must be in my mom's."

"This way?" David races ahead toward the master bedroom. As soon as we enter, we can see that their bathroom is empty. "Shit," he says.

"He's got to be around here somewhere."

We run around the house, calling Ethan's name, but there's no answer. When I'm in the kitchen, Ivy asks what's going on, and I tell her. She just shrugs, unconcerned.

"Is there a back way out of the house?" David asks me when we meet up in the hallway.

"Yeah, but it only goes to the yard—"

"Show me."

The back door is unlocked. We go outside and call some more. That's when we both notice:

The side gate is wide open.

TWENTY-NINE

WE GO BACK INSIDE and into the kitchen.

"How long ago did he say he was going to the bathroom?" David asks.

"It's been a while."

"Twenty-seven minutes," says Ivy.

"Jesus Christ!" David says to me. "Twenty-seven minutes? Why didn't you check on him sooner? No one goes to the bathroom for that long."

"Sometimes people do," Ivy says.

"I didn't really think about it," I say. "I'm sorry. I should have checked." The truth was, I'd been relieved to have Ethan out of the room because I was feeling so guilty about everything. I was in no rush for him to return.

"I should have come in with him. I just—" David stops and shakes his head. "I was an idiot." He moves toward the doorway. "I'm going to drive around and look for him. If he texts either of you or shows up, let me know immediately, and don't let him out of your sight again." He disappears into the hallway and the front door slams a second later.

"David was upset," Ivy says.

"Yeah. He's worried about Ethan."

"It'll be okay," she says, and I'm just about to snap at her that that's a ridiculous thing to say and she doesn't know that at all, and then I remember that it's what she hears from us all the time when *she's* worried — "it will be okay; everything will be okay" — so why wouldn't she parrot it back at me when I'm more worried than she is?

I try Ethan's phone number again and again, every ten minutes for the next couple of hours. No response. And no news from David.

When Mom and Ron come home, Mom takes one look at me and says, "What's wrong?"

Ivy says, "Ethan came over and went to the bathroom and didn't come back, and his brother couldn't find him."

Not surprisingly, Mom's confused. "He couldn't find him in the bathroom?"

"He wasn't *in* the bathroom," I say. "He snuck out of the house. He runs away when he gets upset."

"Where does he go?"

"If they knew that, it wouldn't be running away, would it?" I know it's not fair to get snarky with her, but I need an outlet for all my pent-up anxiety. It's awful waiting and not being able to *do* anything about the situation.

"So they haven't found him yet?"

"Not as far as we know." I instinctively check my cell phone for the millionth time, even though I have it on vibrate *and* the volume is way up high, so there's no way I'd miss a text.

"Do you want us to help look for him?" Ron asks.

I'm surprised — I'd have expected Ron to be all *not our*

problem about this. "Let me ask David." I send a text: should we drive around too?

He writes back: Can't hurt. Maybe by ocean—he likes it there like, Pali Park

Mom and I head out, leaving Ron and Ivy to wait in the house just in case Ethan comes back or is hiding somewhere on our property. Ron says he'll have dinner waiting for us when we return.

Mom drives while I peer out my open window, scanning the sidewalks and grass. Ethan was wearing a white shirt and jeans, so every time I see that combination on a skinny young man—or a couple of times on a girl with short hair—my hope rises, only to be crushed when I get a closer look.

I feel sick inside, scared for Ethan, sad for David, angry at myself for letting this happen.

I can't stop thinking about how vulnerable Ethan is—how childlike in so many ways. But other people won't look at him and think that. They'll see a young man—and an odd one, at that—so no one's going to go up to him and offer to help, the way they would if a little kid was lost. Anything could happen to him. Anything.

The world is such a mean and big and judgmental place. And Ethan, like Ivy, has no guile, no social awareness, no ability to see beyond what people say to what they may be thinking or scheming. Which makes him an easy target.

And Ivy too. She's safe at home right now. But that can't always be true. There are going to be times when she has to be out on her own. She can't just hide at home for the rest of her life, because that's not a life. But being out in the world is dangerous for someone like her, because . . . people.

I want to protect Ivy and Ethan, and I also want them to be independent, and right now it feels like those two things can't coexist, and I feel hopeless.

The sun is setting, and it's getting harder and harder to see clearly.

"Not him?" Mom says when I curse after about the fifteenth disappointment.

"Yeah, it *was,* but I didn't want to bother you by mentioning it."

"Sorry," she says humbly. "That was a stupid question."

I feel bad. "No, that was mean of me. Sorry. I'm just so worried."

"They'll find him eventually. And he's not a toddler — he can take care of himself."

"Up to a point."

"Up to a point."

I say slowly, "How do you think Ivy would do if she were out there on her own?"

"I was thinking about that too. I'm grateful she isn't the running-away type."

"Yeah. She never even wants to go out without us. But that could change, right? What if she starts wanting to do stuff by herself? She told Diana she's going to learn to drive —"

"I don't see that happening," Mom says. "I mean, that's terrifying."

"But she *said* it. So she likes the idea of it. She needs to get better at doing stuff, Mom — like buying things and finding her way around and dealing with strangers. If she doesn't . . ."

"Don't. Please, Chloe. I can't think about that right now. I'm stressed enough already."

I spot another pair of jeans with a white shirt on the sidewalk. Another Not-Ethan.

We're both silent for a moment.

Mom brakes at a red light. "Should I turn on Pico or stay by the ocean?"

"Let's just head home — I can't see anything anymore anyway." I check my phone. I'd kill for a simple Found him. But there's nothing.

I finally get a text from David around eight, an hour after I excused myself from a dinner of microwaved vegetable lasagna that I couldn't even pretend to eat.

Dad and M found out, just called the police

you okay?

No response.

I throw my phone down on my bed with a loud curse.

"What's wrong?" Ivy asks.

"I'm worried about Ethan."

"He'll be fine. He's eighteen. That's old enough to vote."

"You don't understand."

"Yes, I do!"

"You don't even understand what you don't understand."

She's silent. I glance over at her. Her lip is thrust out, and her brows are drawn together.

"I'm sorry," I say wearily. "I didn't mean that. I'm just really stressed right now."

"You think you're so much smarter than me."

"I don't."

"Yes, you do. You're my little sister, you know. You're younger than I am by forty-three months."

"I know."

"I'm going to text Diana. I'd rather talk to her."

"You do that."

She curls up again with her iPad, and I hear her tip-tapping on it.

I could use someone to talk to too—I feel like I'm losing my mind with all this waiting. But James and I are broken up, and if I call her, Sarah will want to talk about *that*, and Mom comes as a package deal with Ron.

I stare at my phone. *Text me,* I order David silently.

My phone stays dark and quiet.

So much for telepathic communication.

After another half an hour of staring uncomprehendingly at words on a page, pretending to do homework, I finally break down and text him again.

please tell me they found him

Nothing.

I stay up until one without hearing anything else from David. Even after I go to bed, I keep picturing Ethan out in the dark, scared and hungry and alone—or worse, cornered by brutal faceless people who want to hurt him. What ability does he have to defend himself against anything threatening? To navigate a city's streets alone? He can't even deal with a chili pepper.

I doze off finally but then wake up an hour later, my heart pounding, terrified that something's wrong with Ivy, who — I sit up and check — is snoring peacefully in her bed. Why am I worried about her? She's not the one who's wandering the streets alone.

And then I realize I was dreaming about her, only I can't remember any details, just that something very bad was happening to her and I couldn't stop it, and even though the dream has vanished, I can't get rid of the sick fear it left in its wake.

No more texts when I get up the next morning, and no David in school that day, either. I'm desperate for information. I can't sit still. I feel like a million tiny bugs are crawling all over my skin, and it's hard to breathe. I have no idea what anyone's saying in any of my classes, and I can't focus on the quiz I have to take in AP bio. Not that I care. School seems meaningless today.

What if they never find Ethan? What if he's been beaten up? Or locked up in some maniac's shed? Or killed?

There are too many awful possibilities, and the longer he's gone, the more the worst seems possible.

At lunch, I sit with a bunch of kids, who talk about how hard the quiz was, like getting As in school actually matters. I barely pay attention, just keep checking my phone to make sure I haven't missed a text.

When we walk out of the cafeteria, Sarah says, "You okay?"

"Yeah. Just some stuff going on at home." I don't think I should tell her about Ethan. David probably doesn't want people to know—he's a pretty private guy. And I don't want anyone pestering him for information. Except me, of course.

"Is that why you were ignoring James?"

"I wasn't." James was at the same table, but we were sitting far apart and couldn't really talk.

"He kept trying to say hi to you, and you totally ignored him."

"I honestly didn't hear him."

"I'd better tell him that. He looked hurt, and I want you guys to get along. You're my two closest friends. It's no fun if you're fighting."

"We're not fighting! Seriously. I want us to be friends too."

"Well, then maybe you should try not to ignore him," she says. "You could join the conversation now and then too, you know. You were pretty spacy at lunch."

"Sorry." I'm too tired to argue or defend myself—and it all seems so ridiculously petty that I don't want to, anyway.

I text David when I get home. I can't wait any longer. any news?

My phone vibrates a minute later.

no

Shit

And there the conversation ends.

My mom calls from the car on her way back from picking up Ivy. "You hear anything about Ethan?"

"Just that there's no news."

"Oh, God. I hope he's okay."

She's on Bluetooth, so I can hear Ivy say, "Why wouldn't he be?"

Mom just sighs and tells me they'll be home soon.

When she puts dinner on the table, I'm not hungry. I just want to lie on my bed and try to distract myself with videos. I tell Mom I'm skipping dinner, and Ron starts to object, but Mom actually shushes him for once and lets me escape.

Ivy comes up to our room when they're done eating.

"Are you sick?" she asks.

"I don't feel great."

"We had chicken Marsala. I didn't like the mushrooms, so Mom said I could scrape them off. It was okay then, but I don't want her to make it again. The mashed potatoes were good, though. It was all from Trader Joe's. I like their macaroni and cheese better."

"Yeah, it's good stuff," I say dully.

Nothing from David all evening long. I'm so tired by this point that I fall asleep on my bed fully dressed. I wake up a couple of hours later and wiggle out of my jeans, but I can't get back to sleep.

Fears for Ethan and fears for Ivy circle around my mind, chasing each other, tormenting me.

I'm brushing my teeth the next morning when my phone vibrates. I snatch at it eagerly.

He's home

I'm so relieved I lean over the sink and close my eyes for a second. Then I drop my toothbrush and punch out a text: is he okay? who found him? where was he?

And David texts back . . . nothing.

I get to English early, hoping David will be there and I'll have a chance to talk to him, but he doesn't show up until Camp has already started the class. She nods at him as he slips through the door—she's not the kind of teacher to give a kid a rough time for being a couple of minutes late—and keeps talking.

I try to catch his eye, but he just opens his laptop and stares at the screen. His face is pale except for dark-purple bruise-like circles under his eyes.

Class ends, and I'm on my feet and in front of his desk before he's even closed his computer. He looks up at me, expressionless.

"What happened?" I say. "Is he okay? Where did they find him?"

"I don't really feel like talking about it now." He closes his computer and slips it and his schoolbooks under his arm as he stands up.

"When, then?"

He shrugs and walks away from me.

I follow him out into the hallway and grab his arm. People are turning to look at us. Maybe I should care, but I don't —I just want to know about Ethan. "Please! Just tell me what happened, and I'll leave you alone. It's all I've been thinking about. I need to know."

He turns to me, lowers his voice. "Fine. The police got a call from someone who found Ethan stumbling around on the beach in Santa Monica in the middle of the night. He was soaked from head to toe, and his shoes and shirt were missing, and he was shaking. He said he had been hanging out with people on the beach, but no one was there. It sounds like maybe some kids dared him to go swimming or actually threw him in the ocean or something, but he can't seem to explain it clearly. He said they were all fooling around together and that they were friends, but he also seems scared of them and said he didn't want them to come back." David's voice is a monotone, but it's the monotone of someone who's fighting to stay in control of his emotions. "Because the police brought him in, he keeps asking if he's going to go to jail and doesn't believe us when we say no. He screams and tries to hide when he hears loud noises. I wanted to stay home with him today, but my father said I wasn't allowed to miss another day of school. So I'm here."

"Oh, God, David, I'm so sorry. But at least he's home now."

"Not for long."

"What do you mean?"

"They're going to send him away to some kind of institution. Just like Margot's always wanted."

"Oh, no. They can't."

"Can't they?"

"This is all my fault. I'm so sorry."

His eyes scan my face for a moment, like he's thinking about that.

I'm hoping he'll say no, it's not my fault. But he doesn't.

"I've got to get to my next class." He walks away, his shoulders hunched forward, his head down.

I watch him go. Kids are swirling and talking and laughing all around me, busily leaving one class and heading to the next, but all I see is David's retreating back. And I have the strangest feeling about that back—as slumped over and defeated and round-shouldered as it is. Like it's something precious to me. Of all the backs in this school, this is the only one that I want to go walking up to and put my arms around. I want to console him, and I want him to console me.

I can't believe I feel that way—it's ridiculous and embarrassing. David was, not that long ago—only a few weeks, really—the last guy in the entire school I wanted anywhere near me. And now it's almost unbearable that he's walking away from me like we have nothing to do with each other. I could help him. I know I could. If he'd let me.

But David cares about his brother the way I care about Ivy —fiercely and entirely. And now Ethan's going to be sent away because he ran, and he ran because Ivy broke his heart, and Ivy broke his heart because I didn't know she was gay and kept pushing them together.

And I know that as much as David likes me—and he *does* like me—or at least he did until two days ago—he won't be able to look at me again without seeing the cause of Ethan's being sent away. David will ache for his brother every single day. And I'll be the person who made him ache.

We can't be friends. Not if Ethan gets sent away.

"Chloe? Why are you just standing here?"

I turn. It's Sarah.

"I don't know," I say. "I'm really out of it today." I'm trying to sound like myself, but it's hard. I'm too depressed to pretend to be all lighthearted and carefree right now. Usually I can pull it off. But not right now.

"That's what you said yesterday."

"Yeah, I know. I'm just a little overwhelmed by life, I guess."

She pats my arm gently. "Do you want me to speak to James for you? I really think he'd be open to talking things out."

"Thanks," I say. "But I'm okay." If I weren't so on edge, I might actually laugh — it's almost funny how wrong she is about what's upsetting me.

THIRTY

MOM AND IVY get home around five. Before I can even greet them, Ivy runs past me, her face red and unhappy. I can hear her heavy footsteps thumping rapidly up the stairs.

"What's going on?" I ask Mom.

"I have no idea. She wouldn't say a word in the car, but something was obviously upsetting her. She kept muttering to herself and, you know . . ." She mimes hitting her hip with the ball of her right hand.

"I'll see if I can get anything out of her."

"Thanks." Mom drops into a chair. "I was just too exhausted to try. I'm going to rest for a minute and try to figure out something for dinner tonight."

"It's an exciting life you lead." I start to head out of the kitchen. "Oh, wait—I didn't tell you about Ethan. The police found him."

"Oh, thank God," Mom says fervently. "Is he okay?"

"Sort of?" I tell her what David said, and she shivers.

"What a nightmare. If Ivy were out there on her own, for any reason . . . She's such an innocent. It's terrifying."

"We need to work on her independence," I say. "Start making her do more and more stuff on her own and make sure she learns to find her way safely home from anywhere without us. So this never happens to her."

"We should," Mom says with a weary sigh. "Someday."

I find Ivy in our bedroom, walking in circles on the rug, one hand hammering and hammering against her thigh, the other weaving through the air in spirals. She suddenly slaps hard at her forehead.

"Don't do that!" I go to her and take both her hands in mine and squeeze them tightly. "What's going on? Why are you upset?"

"I'm not upset." Her eyes dart around the room blindly.

"Yeah, right. And I'm not Chloe."

"You're being sarcastic."

"Tell me what's wrong. I might be able to help."

She pulls her hands away, shaking her head.

"Come on. Tell me. If you want me to keep it a secret, I will."

She hesitates, her body trembling with tension, and then she drops her head and whispers, "Diana doesn't like me."

Oh, crap. "Why do you say that? You guys had fun together the other day."

Ivy shakes her head. "She doesn't like me the way I like her."

"How do you know?"

"I tried to kiss her."

"Wow." I sit down on the edge of my bed. "You move fast."

She flutters her hands anxiously. "Do you think I shouldn't have done that?"

"I don't know. What led up to it?"

"What do you mean?"

"What made you decide to kiss her?"

"I wanted to." Her hands are back to their repetitive motions.

"But where were you when it happened? What were you doing?"

"It was break. We were outside. We were just walking around the yard. I said she was pretty and she said thank you and then I held her hand and then we walked like that and then we stopped because we were at the fence and then I tried to kiss her on the cheek but she moved away and said don't do that."

"Maybe she's just not into kissing?"

She flails her arms. "But I said I liked her and we should go out like you and James used to go out. And she said we can't because we're both girls. So I said, yes you can if you're gay and I'm gay. And she said that gay people aren't normal and could we go back to the main yard now. And she wouldn't hold my hand anymore. I tried but she wouldn't let me."

"Oh, Ivy, I'm sorry." I get up and put my arms around her. She averts her head but doesn't push me away. "It hurts to be rejected. I know."

"How do you know?"

"I've had my own rejections."

"Did I do something wrong?"

"I don't know. I mean . . . I might not have rushed into a kiss quite that quickly."

She twists away from me.

"But it doesn't really matter," I say. "I don't think you and Diana were meant to be, anyway."

"Meant to be what?"

"Together. If she's not gay, she's probably not going to feel comfortable going out with a girl, even one she likes a lot."

"She could be bisexual."

"It doesn't sound like she is."

"Maybe she just doesn't like me."

"I'm sure she does, Ivy. How could she not?"

"She said gay people aren't normal."

"Well, that's just wrong. Not to mention mean."

Ivy sinks down on her bed and huddles her arms and legs together like she's trying to shrink down to nothing. "It's not fair. I love her, but she doesn't love me."

"It happens a lot. Listen to the radio — every song is about that."

"This is *real*."

"I know. I'm just saying that it happens to everyone at some point."

"I want to be with her all the time, but I can't be. Maybe we can get together sometimes, but not the way I want to be together always."

"I'm so sorry, Ives. That just sucks."

"It feels so bad," she says. "So bad."

I sit next to her. "I know. It's the worst feeling in the world, wanting to be with someone and knowing you can't."

"Yeah," she says.

I say slowly, "And the worst part is that you know there's nothing you can do to force them to want to be with you — that it's the one thing in your life that you can't just *make* happen, no matter how much you want it to and no matter how hard you try."

"Huh?" she says.

"Never mind," I say. "I was just thinking out loud."

David doesn't talk to me in English class the next day, just stares at his laptop and ignores everyone, including Ms. Campanelli, who occasionally glances at him hopefully when people say stupid things. But she gets no help from him.

At lunch, I bring my tray to David's table and ask if I can join him. He says, "Feel free to sit here, but I'm about to leave," and starts to load his dishes on his tray. So I go sit with some other friends, and I notice from there that David has stopped cleaning his place and gone back to doing whatever he was doing on his laptop. So he was lying about leaving to get rid of me. Which hurts.

James comes and joins our group. This time I make sure I smile and wave at him, so he won't think I'm ignoring him again. He waves back and flashes an uncomfortable — but not angry — smile. Sarah arrives at the table and takes the seat across from him. They start talking, but they're at the other end of the table, so I can't hear what they're talking about.

Other conversations wash over me. Jana complains about an unfair grade; Lambert says his grandparents are giving him an old car they don't use, and he's annoyed that they expect him to pay something toward it; Caroline Penner whines about how she can't go to a Coldplay concert that weekend because her little sister is performing in her school play and her parents are making her go to that instead.

Every kid in that cafeteria is only thinking about himself.

Except no. There's one person in the room who cares about someone other than himself, and I feel more connected to him than anyone else in the room.

But he won't even look at me.

THIRTY-ONE

OVER DINNER ON WEDNESDAY, Ivy says, "Can I bring cupcakes to school on Friday? I said I'd bring cupcakes. It's Ethan's goodbye party." She adds, a little wistfully, "Diana likes vanilla cupcakes but not chocolate. But I like chocolate."

"Sure," Mom says. "I'll buy some tomorrow—I can get half vanilla, half chocolate so—"

"Hold on," I say. "A goodbye party for Ethan? Where's he going? Did he say?"

"To sleep-away school," Ivy says. "He won't live at home anymore."

"Fuck."

Ron says, "Hey, hey—watch the language, Chloe."

"What's wrong?" Mom asks me.

"David told me this might happen." I push my plate away. I'm not hungry anymore. "And it's all my fault."

"Why is it your fault?"

"Because I let him run away."

Ivy says, "Ethan tried to run away from school today too, but the security guard stopped him. Ethan was crying and hitting his head a lot and had to go sit with Kimberly in the Self Management Room. He's never had to go to the Self

Management Room before, but Ajay has to go almost every day."

Mom reaches out and touches my hand. "It's not the end of the world," she says gently. "It probably *is* safer for him at a boarding school."

"But there's no way they're sending him to a *good* place. I mean, come on, it's been, like, three days, and they're already shipping him off? They must have just grabbed at the first school they saw. And he won't have David to watch out for him anymore. And David won't have him." My voice breaks, even though I'm trying hard not to let it. "The two brothers are everything to each other. And their stepmother doesn't care."

"Where's their biological mother?" Mom asks. "Why isn't she getting involved?"

"She totally abandoned them and started another family. Which is basically what their father's done too, except at least he lets them live with him."

"Those poor boys. It all sounds very complicated."

"Yes," Ron says, and I raise my head to glare at him. He's going to tell us all about how hard it is to parent difficult kids and how I'm being unfair to Ethan's stepmother, and then I'm going to lose it, I'm just going to *lose* it, and it'll end with both of us screaming at each other.

There will be blood.

Only that's not what Ron says. What he says is, "It's complicated, but that doesn't excuse sending the boy away. When that woman married their father, she made a commitment not just to him, but to his sons. And shipping Ethan off makes it sound like she's not honoring that commitment."

I stare at him, open-mouthed.

Mom says, "Yes, of course, you're right about that."

And I find my voice enough to say, "Yeah."

I've never told Ron he was right before.

He's never *been* right before.

"It's something I've thought a lot about," he says. "I take my responsibility to you girls very seriously."

Mom says, "But we don't know all the details. I don't think we should judge the stepmother too quickly—she may feel like she really doesn't have any choice."

"I wonder if it would help if I tried talking to her," Ron says.

"Really?" I say. "You'd do that?" Has he gone crazy? Have I?

"She might listen to me. We have parallel situations. I know exactly what it's like to be the stepparent of a kid who—" He glances at Ivy and doesn't finish his sentence. "Anyway, maybe she'd listen to me if I said I understand where she's coming from but I really think she should reconsider her decision. If you give me her phone number—although maybe it would be better to go in person?" He appeals to Mom. "Do you think she'd be more likely to listen if I went to their house?"

"Maybe," she says. "But—"

He cuts her off. "I say let's do it. What have we got to lose?"

"Really?" I'm stunned. "You'd really do that?"

"Of course," Ron says, and does that peacocky thing to try to impress us, stretching up his neck and rounding his shoulders with his musculature.

"Cool," I say. "Let's go."

Less than an hour later, we're all in the car heading to the Fieldses' house.

I don't know if we'll actually be able to help at all, but I'm glad we're doing something to try.

Ivy wanted to come with us. I'm not sure she completely understands what kind of a visit this is going to be, just that we're all going over to Ethan's house to talk about him, and she doesn't want to be left out.

"I go to school with Ethan," she pointed out when we were getting ready to leave. "He's *my* friend. So I should be there."

I let Mom and Ron lead the way up the stone path to their front door. It's oddly comforting to follow them and for once not have to be the one in charge.

Mr. Fields answers the door and responds to my mother's cheery "Hello!" by silently pointing to the NO SOLICITORS sign.

Seriously?

I step forward before he can shut the door on us. "Hey, Mr. Fields, remember me? We met the other day. I'm David's friend, and my sister goes to school with Ethan."

"And we're their parents." Mom holds out her hand. "I'm Jeannie, and this is my husband, Ron."

"Nice to meet you." Mr. Fields shakes their hands. "Forgive

me—I didn't know you were coming. No one tells me anything around here." He turns his head and shouts down the hallway. "Margot? We have guests."

She comes out of the dining room, a cloth napkin balled in her hand. "Guests?"

David's behind her. His eyes open wide with surprise when he sees us all filing in.

"So sorry to just drop in like this," my mother says.

Mrs. Fields eyes her warily. "I'm afraid I'm confused . . ."

Mom explains who we are again, and recognition dawns on Mrs. Fields's face. "Oh, yes, I remember you girls," she says. "I believe you had something to do with our scare this week."

"I'm really sorry," I say. "I feel terrible about that."

"To be fair to you, Ethan was supposed to be under his brother's supervision at the time." She glares accusingly at David. "But the good news is that Ethan is safely upstairs right now, and this whole awful incident has helped us make some difficult decisions." She turns back to Mom and Ron with a brittle smile. "So . . . to what do we owe the honor of this visit?"

"Actually," Ron says, "we're here to talk about those difficult decisions you just mentioned."

She blinks rapidly. "I'm sorry?"

"Maybe we could all sit down?" And, with a flick of his fingers through his dyed hair, Ron marches right into their living room. His unwarranted self-confidence is actually kind of useful right now.

Mrs. Fields watches him go, gestures at her husband to follow Ron, then runs back into the dining room.

David comes over and whispers to me, "What the hell's going on?"

"We're here to help. If we can."

"Ethan's *my* friend," Ivy says. "That's why *I'm* here."

"Where is he?" I ask David.

"Margot's been making him stay in his room when he's not at school. She said we can't take any chances on him running away again."

"That sucks."

"Yeah — although I think he kind of likes it. He gets to be on the computer all the time. His favorite thing."

Mrs. Fields emerges with the baby in her arms, and we follow her to the living room, where Ron and Mom have planted themselves side by side on the sofa. The Fieldses exchange slightly pained looks, but it's clear their guests aren't leaving anytime soon, so they sit down too — Mister on an armchair, Missus settling herself on a chair with the baby on her lap. There's some mushy stuff on his face again.

"That's probably not throw-up," Ivy whispers to me. "It looks like it could be, but it's probably not, right?"

"Definitely not. It looks like mashed carrots."

Ivy retches a tiny bit, but quietly enough that I'm the only one who hears.

"All right," Mrs. Fields says, while David, Ivy, and I find places to stand behind the sofa. "So what have you come to say?"

Mom speaks. "So my girls tell me that Ethan is being sent away from home? They're a little concerned about it, and we thought maybe we could learn more about your thought process."

Mrs. Fields says, "I don't understand why this would be any business of yours. I've never even met you before."

"Our kids are so close," Mom says. "My girls just adore your boys."

"Adore?" David repeats skeptically in my ear.

"Her word, not mine," I whisper. But then I grin at him. He misses it—he's back to watching the conversation.

"How nice," Mrs. Fields says, crushing her baby against her chest like she needs to protect him against us—or maybe wants him to protect *her*. "At any rate, yes, it's true—Ethan is going to boarding school. He's really excited to be trying something new."

"No, he isn't. He said he's sad he's going." Ivy's hands are fluttering at her sides, but she's speaking up, which I know is hard for her around people she doesn't know. "At school. I was there. He said he doesn't want to go. He said he wasn't crying, but Diana said he was. And his face was wet, so I think he was too. He was lying, I guess."

There's a pause. Mrs. Fields says uncomfortably, "Saying goodbye to your friends is always difficult, but that doesn't mean—"

David cuts her off. "Ivy's right: he wants to stay home. And you know it."

"He'll feel differently once he sees where he's going."

"I doubt it. What do we even know about this place?"

"It comes highly recommended."

"By whom?" he says. "The National Association of Parents Who Want to Get Rid of Their Children?"

"David!" says his father. "You're out of line. Your stepmother and I worked hard to find the right place—"

"How much work could it have been? It's only been a few days."

"We had to move quickly," Mrs. Fields says. "We can't continue to have the kind of crazy situations that bring the police into our lives." She kisses the top of Caleb's head. "I want a healthy home life for all of us."

Ron says, "Can I just say something?"

She doesn't give him permission, just waits, a cold smile frozen on her face.

He says, "You know, you and I . . . we're kind of the same."

"Excuse me?"

"We both married into families that were already dealing with some pretty heavy stuff." He glances at me, his eyebrows raised. "It's not always easy—I'd be the first to admit that."

"You've never had to deal with boys," Mrs. Fields says.

"Trust me, girls aren't exactly a walk in the park. And I'm not saying we're right out of a Norman Rockwell picture or anything, but when I married Jeannie, her kids became mine. I want what's best for them, and I always will."

"Are you implying that I don't feel the same way about my husband's children?"

"Of course not. I'm just saying—"

She cuts him off. "I assume David asked you all to come here tonight. I know he's not happy about this decision but—"

"He didn't ask us!" I say. "He didn't even know we were coming."

"No?" She purses her lips.

Oh, great. She blames David for our intrusion.

"I know we messed up that day," I say, looking back and forth between her and her husband. "All of us kids. David should have come in with Ethan, and I should have noticed he was missing, and Ethan shouldn't have run away. We screwed up, and the whole thing must have been really awful and scary for you. But overall, hasn't Ethan been doing great? I mean, he's happy at school, and he's totally sweet and tries really hard . . . Why give up on how well he's doing because of one bad day? If you let Ethan stay, we'll all do whatever we can to help. Like, I could watch him when David can't."

"Thank you," Mrs. Fields says. The baby squirms, and she stands up and bounces him on her hip. "But we've made our decision. I really don't see the point of all this."

I turn to Mr. Fields. "You can always send him to school later, right? Keep him at home now but send him away if something else goes wrong? Can't you give him one more chance?"

David steps forward. "Dad. Please. Listen to Chloe." His hands are in fists at his side—not in a threatening way, just like he's squeezing something that isn't there. "Punish me, if you want to. Ground me, take my car away, whatever. I screwed up. But don't punish Ethan. Don't send him away."

"It's not a punishment," Mr. Fields says. He rises heavily

to his feet. "It's a school. A good school that will be the right fit for Ethan. It's just not working here at home for him, or for us." He looks around the room. "I'm sure you all mean well, but I'm not thrilled about being ambushed by strangers."

"We just care a lot about Ethan," I say.

"Not as much as we do," he says. "Now it's time for us to finish our dinner." And he leads us all back to the front door.

In the car, Mom says, "I think we planted seeds of doubt. Maybe they'll take root?"

I don't even call her out on the stupid metaphor. Her optimism is just *sad*. There's no way Mrs. Fields will change her mind—it's clear she's decided the safety of her baby is in some way dependent upon Ethan's being exiled. It doesn't make any sense, but her husband doesn't seem to care that it doesn't. He's just going to do what she wants.

I lean my head back, stare up into the darkness at the top of the car, and listen to Mom and Ron talk.

Inside the house, I'm about to head up to my room when I stop. "Hey, Mom? Ron? Thanks for trying."

"Did Chloe just thank us for something?" Ron asks my mom. "Pinch me, I'm dreaming."

"You're welcome," Mom says, rushing over to give me a hug. "I'm sorry it didn't help more."

"*I* told them Ethan was sad to be leaving," Ivy points out.

"It's good you said that," I tell her.

"I know he's sad now," Mom says. "But maybe he'll end up liking the school. The father said it was a good one."

"What else is he going to say? That he's throwing his son to the wolves?"

"I'm sure he cares about his son."

"I'm not."

Ron says, "The important thing is that you girls know this would never happen to you — we would never send you away anywhere you didn't want to go."

Maybe Ivy and I didn't exactly win the lottery in the stepparent department — Ron manages to annoy me with every word out of his mouth — but I guess we could have done worse. He may criticize and try to change us, but he's never once made either of us feel like our home isn't our home or that he wishes we were gone. And that's something.

Actually, after this last hour, I'm willing to admit that it's a lot.

THIRTY-TWO

I CAN'T BRING MYSELF to get in touch with David — until he confirms the worst, I can still hold on to some hope that maybe his father and stepmother have changed their minds.

But I'm pretty sure that if there were good news, he'd text me . . . and I don't get a text.

The next day, I see him in the hallway at school. He keeps moving past me, until I grab at his sleeve to stop him. "Hold on — what happened after we left?"

"What do you think?" He jerks his arm away.

"Oh, shit," I say. "They didn't change their minds."

"Big surprise." He keeps going.

I want to yell after him that he's not being fair, that he has no right to treat me like I'm one of the villains here, that I'm in pain too, that he hasn't even acknowledged that my entire family trooped over to his house last night to try to help.

But we're in a crowded hallway and he's moving fast, so I just let him walk away without saying any of that.

At lunch, Sarah and James are already sitting together with a couple of other kids when I enter the cafeteria. Sarah catches my eye and pats the seat next to her. I take it, and she starts telling me about how she and James are making plans to see a movie, and do I want to go with them on Saturday?

I feel like I'm underwater and she's talking to me from up above, her face flattening and widening and receding, her voice faint and distant. I can barely process what she's saying.

She's waiting for a response, so I say, "Yeah, maybe. I'm not sure."

"Was that a yes or a no?"

"Sorry. I just haven't thought about the weekend. There's so much to deal with right now . . ."

"I know," she says generously. "I have, like, three tests tomorrow, which isn't even supposed to be legal."

"History's the one that worries me," James says.

"Want to study after school?" Sarah asks him.

"I have practice, but after that?"

She turns to me. "How about you, Chloe?"

"I'd like to, but I think Mom wanted me available to pick up Ivy today." Not entirely true, but sometimes she does ask at the last minute, so it's not a total lie either.

"No worries," Sarah says, and James echoes her.

I really do appreciate how nice they're both being. James could have turned into a dick when we broke up. I haven't been talking as much to Sarah lately, and she could hold that against me. But instead they're both working hard to keep our friendship intact. It's not their fault that all I can think about is what's going to happen to Ethan and that right now I can't even remember what it's like to care about a history test.

Maybe they're a little relieved I said no. Certainly they

don't seem to mind. They start talking about what might be on the test, and I eat bits of my bagel and sort of listen and sort of let my mind wander.

David doesn't ever show up in the cafeteria. I know because I'm watching for him.

I'm sitting in my room that evening, listening to Adele, trying to do homework, and wishing Ivy would go to another room if she's going to keep walking in circles. She's driving me crazy, not because she's doing anything wrong or unusual, just because I'm one big exposed nerve and everything she says or does is like a guitar pick twanging it.

I get a text and check it. It's from David.

I'm in front of your house

I'm stunned. He's never just shown up before.

My fingers fly as I text back.

be right out

I jump out of bed and shove my feet into flip-flops. I'm wearing cropped sweats and a T-shirt—my pajamas. I look sloppy, but I'm not indecent.

"Where are you going?" Ivy asks, pausing in the middle of a circuit.

"To see a friend." I'm out the door and down the stairs before she can ask me anything else. I'm relieved that Mom and Ron are in their room with the door closed and the TV way up high, so I'm spared from having to answer any of *their* questions.

David's car is pulled up to the curb. I open the passenger door and peer inside.

"Get in," he says.

I slide in and close the door. "What's up?"

He's gripping the top of the steering wheel tightly with both hands and staring at his knuckles. "They took him away today. While I was in school."

"That's awful."

I can't tell if he's even heard me or not. He keeps pressing his lips together and swallowing, and I know that trick —it's to keep yourself from crying. I've used it plenty of times myself.

"I didn't even get to say goodbye to him. They told me they weren't leaving until tomorrow and then I got home and they were gone and he was gone and I tried calling him and *she* answered his phone and said, 'You've been so negative about this whole thing that we decided it would be easier for Ethan if you two didn't have a big goodbye.'"

"That's so wrong."

"She won't even let me talk to him. Not even *talk* to him."

"What about visiting? Can you visit him? Where is it?"

"A couple hours north on the 101."

"That's drivable," I say. "We could go. We could go and bring him back."

He shakes his head. "They have security at this place — my stepmother kept talking about that, about how protected he'd be there, how he wouldn't be able to run away. Even if they let me in, they won't let me take him away from there — not without my parents' permission."

"We should visit anyway — at least he'll know you wanted to say goodbye, and we can see how bad it is."

"Yeah." He takes a deep, shuddering breath. "Sorry to bother you," he says, still not looking at me. "I just had to talk to someone."

"I'm glad you came." We're silent for a moment. Then I say, "Please, can we be friends? I know I screwed up. But I had no idea Ivy was gay, or I never would have set them up. And I know I should have watched Ethan more carefully, but I really thought he was just in the bathroom. I'm so sorry for every stupid thing I did, but I care about you both so much, and I can't stand to have you hate me when everything else already feels so sad."

"I don't hate you," he says. "And I don't blame you for that stuff either."

"You've kind of been giving off that vibe. At school today —"

"I was scared I'd break down if I talked to you. I was barely holding it together, and a friendly face was pretty much the worst thing right at that moment."

"Oh. So we can be friends?"

"Of course. We *are* friends. I'm here, aren't I?"

"Yeah."

We sit there a moment.

And then he says, "All I can think about is him being in a room somewhere . . . alone and scared and —" His hands go up to his face, and he makes the saddest sound I think I've ever heard—a moan of pure grief. His shoulders start shaking, and even though his face is covered, I can hear his sobs.

There's only one thing I can do and I do it. I wrap my arms tightly around his shoulders and pull him to me. He drops his hands and buries his face in my neck. I can feel his tears on my skin, hot where they're fresh, cooler where they've already slipped down and dampened his cheeks and chin.

I hold him while he cries.

His sobs gradually slow down. He stays a few more moments in the crook of my neck and then suddenly and abruptly pulls away and sits back in the driver's seat, wiping his eyes and nose on his sleeve.

"I'm sorry," he says thickly. "I'm really sorry about that."

"You think I mind?"

He doesn't answer that. "I should go. It's late."

"Just sit for a second. Make sure you're okay."

"I'm fine." He takes a long, shuddering breath and rubs hard at his face, like he's scrubbing it clean. "Today's been rough, that's all. But I'm fine. I don't have to keep you here any longer. I don't even know why I bothered you."

"Because you knew I'd understand. Because if this had happened to Ivy, I'd be a basket case. I'm in this with you, Fields, and you'd better not try to shut me out." I pull on his sleeve. "Look at me."

He does. At least, I think he does—he turns toward me —but it's so dark in the car that his eyes are just black holes.

"Somehow you've become the person I'm closest to in the

world right now," I say. "I don't know why or how, because you're kind of a dick."

This gets something that's almost a laugh out of him.

"And you don't exactly welcome people into your life," I say. "You've shoved me away every chance you've gotten. But I don't care. I need you in my life because you're the only person who gets me—and you need me in your life for the same reason. And this whole Ethan thing is scary and sad and wrong, and some of it's my fault, but not on purpose, and you know that, and that's why you're going to forgive me and let me help you help Ethan. We'll rescue him together, and maybe we'll figure out Ivy's future together, too."

"Okay."

I wait. He doesn't say anything else.

"Okay?" I repeat. "That's it? That's all I get for my beautiful speech?"

"Okay, *Chloe?*"

"I was right. You *are* a dick." I reach for the door.

He grabs my hand. "I was kidding."

I turn back to him with a grin. "I know. So was I."

He squeezes my fingers so hard it's painful. "Thank you. For coming to my house and being nice to me tonight and for saying you want to be my friend."

"I don't just *want* to be your friend. I *am* your friend, whether you like it or not." I squeeze his fingers back, just as hard. "You're not dealing with all this shit alone, you know. I'm in it with you, all the way."

"I'm beginning to get that feeling." He's not letting go of

my hand, and I'm okay with that. "Want to hear something really screwed up?"

"Sure."

"Don't judge me for this, okay? I think part of the reason I was upset that your sister was gay was because it meant I didn't have an excuse to hang out with you anymore."

"I'm reporting you to GLAAD," I say. "And you were wrong. We're hanging out right now."

"How about tomorrow? Any chance we'll be hanging out then?"

"A very good chance. If you ask nicely."

"Will you please meet me after school tomorrow?"

"You didn't actually have to ask nicely. I was going to say yes anyway."

THIRTY-THREE

CAMPANELLI'S ON FIRE the next day, fluffing up her hair and shoving up her sleeves—an adorably dowdy little ball of energy and enthusiasm. She plunges right in when class starts. "'For Esmé—With Love and Squalor' is my favorite story in the collection—that's why I saved it for last. We all know what happens in the story, but what would you say it's *about?*"

"How bad war is," Jana says instantly, without bothering to raise her hand.

"Okay, good," Camp says. "Salinger is definitely not in favor of the war."

"What an insight," David mutters, and Camp looks over at him.

"You have something to add, David? Something constructive?"

"Anything would be more constructive than 'war is bad.'"

"Shut up," Jana says, swiveling so she can glare at him over her shoulder. "War *is* bad."

"Well, duh."

"Don't *duh* people in my classroom, please," Camp says.

"Sorry," David says. "I just think there's more going on here than just the obvious."

"And that would be . . . ?"

He says, "This is a story about a girl who saves a guy by proving there's still some good in the world."

After school, we walk together to a coffee shop, where we get lattes and talk. We've had plenty of deep conversations, but it's like a layer of thick scar tissue has been peeled off or something — we never knew for sure before if we were actually friends or just two people who were stuck spending time together.

Now we know.

David has gotten more information about Ethan. He won't be able to talk to him for at least a week — the school doesn't let students call home until they've settled in — and he can't visit for an entire month.

"They think it'll help him adjust," he says. "Seems just mean to me."

"We'll plan a visit for the earliest possible date."

"You'll really go with me?"

"Whether you want me to or not."

"I'm okay with it," he says, and flashes a brief smile that's warmer than his words. "The weird thing is that I couldn't be doing this if he were home, you know? Just hanging out with you here. I'd have to be rushing off to make sure I was home before he was. It's not fair that I get to be sitting here talking to you and he's stuck in some awful place all by himself."

"We'll visit him as soon as we can. And if he hates it there, we'll get him out. Somehow."

"I admire your optimism," he says dryly.

"Yeah, well, most of the time, it's all I've got."

"Let's talk about something else," he says, shifting in his seat. "Distract me — if I keep thinking about this when I can't do anything about it, I'll drive myself crazy."

"Okay." I tell him about Ivy and Diana — how Ivy is in love with her, but she doesn't seem to feel the same way.

"That sucks," he says. "It's like the eternal triangle, isn't it? Ethan likes her, she likes Diana . . . Who does Diana like?"

"No idea. Probably no one. She's not the most social creature I've ever met."

"But boys?"

"I think so. I mean, odds are good, right? So now all I have to do is find a lesbian with autism who lives nearby and is roughly Ivy's age and who's available."

"Tinder?"

"*Swipe right, Ivy, swipe right* — Yeah, no." I flick at the plastic top to my cup. "I'll keep trying to help her make friends, but if nothing works out . . . There are a lot of good colleges nearby, right? I'll just stay close enough to be able to drop by a lot and make sure she leaves the house now and then."

"Yeah, I was going to commute to somewhere local so I could keep living with Ethan. I still will if he comes home."

"Don't you feel like we're living in a different world from everyone else at school? All anyone else ever thinks about is getting into the best college they can afford." I wind my fingers around my cup, seeking out the warmth. "And if I weren't worried about Ivy, I'd totally be like that — I mean, I work hard at school. I want to get a huge scholarship and go somewhere amazing just as much as everyone else. But if I *only* thought about that . . . if I just stopped caring about what's going to happen to Ivy . . . I'd end up hating myself."

David's mouth opens like he sort of wants to say something, but then he doesn't. I glance up, and he's just sitting there looking at me. His eyes are such a cool color — a mixture of brown and gray with tiny flecks of yellow ringing the pupils. How could I ever have thought they were colorless and uninteresting?

I squirm under his steady gaze. "You'd tell me if I had something on my face, right?"

"You have, like, this beautiful face on your face."

I feel my cheeks turn hot. I give a shaky laugh. "Don't turn into someone who gives compliments. I won't know you anymore."

"Don't worry," he says, flushing. Which is kind of adorable. "That one just slipped out. It won't happen again."

I study him for a moment, and feel my heart suddenly speed up. It feels like maybe there's more that needs to be said. I take a deep breath and look down at the table. "You know, when I said I'd be your friend whether you wanted me to or not, I wasn't being entirely honest."

His chin jerks up. "What do you mean?"

"You're kind of an arrogant asshole, and it wasn't that long ago that I couldn't even stand being in the same room as you, but you're the only person I know who cares as much about his brother as I do about my sister." There's a drop of coffee on the table. I touch it lightly with the tip of my finger, and it turns into a tiny flat puddle. "And I don't know whether that's a good reason to start to like someone, but apparently it was enough for me, because I did. So . . ." I have to swallow to be able to get the words past my swelling throat. Even so, they're barely more than a whisper. "I was kind of hoping we could be more than friends."

There's silence. A dull, agonizing thud of a silence.

"Crap," I say. "That was a mistake, wasn't it? Saying that out loud?" I shove my coffee cup away and get to my feet. "Sorry. I'm going to pretend I didn't say that, and if you're a decent human being, you will too. Let's go."

"Hold on," David says, jumping up and grabbing my arm. I twist away, still too embarrassed to even look at him, but he doesn't let go. "Don't say something like that and then run! I mean, you don't say to someone, 'You just won the lottery,' and then get mad because they need a second to process the news."

"Is it like that? Like winning the lottery?" My voice is still not much more than a whisper. I don't seem to have the breath for talking normally, what with my heart knocking away inside my chest the way it is.

"Kind of," he says.

There's a pause. We're both frozen in place. "Say something nice, okay?" I plead. "I need you to be nice right now."

"I just said you were beautiful, like, two minutes ago."

"I need more. I feel all vulnerable right now."

"Well, now you're just being a pain." His hand is still on my arm; he slides it down and wraps his fingers around my wrist.

"Someone needs to teach you how to be human," I say. "You're not all that good at it. But you will be."

"Because you'll teach me?"

"Or die trying. Probably that."

The coffee shop door opens, and a couple of kids from our school walk in. They're not friends or anything, but they know us enough to wave . . . and to react to the fact that David and I are there together, apparently holding hands.

I don't care that they can see us, but David says, "Let's go somewhere we can talk."

Mom and Ivy won't be back for a while, so I suggest we walk to my house. It's over a mile, but it's a beautiful day—not too hot—and it feels good to stroll side by side, our hands linked, the sun warming the tops of our heads. I feel too overwhelmed to talk much, and he's pretty quiet too.

We reach my house. I let us in, then close the door and turn to face him.

"What now?" he asks, nervously shifting from foot to foot. "You should know that this is all new to me. I've never had a girlfriend. Or even gone on a date."

"I'm shocked. I'm not shocked." I heave an exaggerated sigh. "Clearly I'm going to have to do all the work here." I lead him into the living room and push him down so he's on the sofa. "The first thing you should do is sit very close to me." I sit down so that our legs are touching, side by side. "Then you should say something nice."

"Again?" He rolls his eyes. "Jesus. How many times am I supposed to compliment you in one afternoon?"

"Just do it."

"Last night I didn't think I could ever feel happy again. Turns out I was wrong."

I let that sink in for a moment.

"Was that okay?" he asks.

"Yeah. Pretty good, actually." We don't say anything for a moment, and I think of Ethan, sitting next to Ivy, wanting to touch her and hold her and kiss her, and I think of Ivy sitting next to Diana, wanting to touch her and hold her and kiss her, and it occurs to me that maybe the greatest thing in the world is sitting next to someone you want to touch and hold and kiss, who actually wants to touch and hold and kiss you *back*.

"What are you thinking about?" David asks me.

"Skin hunger."

"Huh?"

I answer by turning toward him, taking hold of his arms, pulling him toward me and pressing my mouth against his.

He's not a great kisser, but that's just lack of experience.

So I give him a crash course.

And he improves quickly.

THIRTY-FOUR

I'm GLAD OUR GARAGE DOOR is noisy, because it gives us time to separate and enter the kitchen just as Ivy and Mom do.

"What are you doing here?" Ivy asks David.

His lips look a little swollen and darkened. I hope I'm the only one who notices that. He says, "Just hanging with your sister," and drops into a chair.

"Where's Ethan?"

"He's gone," David says. "He went to boarding school."

"That's what I thought," she says. "Why are you here?"

"David's my friend, too," I say. "Not just Ethan's brother."

"How's Ethan doing?" Mom asks him.

"I wish I knew. I can't communicate with him for a while. They want him to get settled in first."

"I guess that makes sense," she says uncertainly.

"Not really."

"I'm sorry we couldn't help more."

"You were really great," he says. "Coming over and talking to my father and stepmother . . . I'm sorry I wasn't more grateful at the time. I've just been a little overwhelmed by the whole thing."

She shakes her head. "You have nothing to apologize for."

It occurs to me that, for all her flaws, my mother is a Very Nice Person. I go over to her and give her a hug.

"What's that for?" she asks.

"I don't know. Just felt like it."

"Someone's in a good mood," she says, and her gaze flits over to David and then back to me, eyebrows slightly raised. So maybe she *did* notice his lips. And mine? I probe them gently. Yeah, they're swollen.

Ivy says to David, "Why can't you talk to Ethan? Why does he have to get settled first?"

Mom says, "I think the teachers are probably worried he'll get homesick if he talks to his family too soon."

Ivy turns to her. "But if he gets homesick, he should go home."

"Sometimes you have to get past the homesickness. I'm sure that's what they're hoping will happen—that even if he feels homesick at the beginning, he'll get more comfortable over time."

"I wouldn't get homesick if *I* went away."

"Says the girl who's never spent a night away from home," I say. It's only a slight exaggeration—we've gone on a couple of road trips, but she's always shared a room with me and Mom, and she's also always hated it. She's never been on a sleepover by herself.

I touch David's arm. "Hey, now that my mom's home, I can use her car. Want me to drive you home?"

"I need to go back to school. I left my backpack there."

"I could drive you to school and then home . . ."

"If you insist."

I go with him to retrieve his backpack. The hallway's deserted, so he and I steal a kiss against the row of lockers. Then I push him away. "I thought you were morally opposed to PDAs."

"Yeah, they're gross," he says, and leans in again.

I hold him off with the palms of my hands against his chest. "I'd hate for you to have to do something that makes you uncomfortable."

"I'll survive."

"Come on," I say, and shove him toward the exit. "Let's go. But admit you were wrong about that whole kissing in public thing. It's not such a crime."

"It is when I'm not the one kissing you."

"Were you jealous of James? Even back then?"

"I don't know," he says. "Not exactly. And you guys *were* pretty annoying. I was sincerely disgusted by you—"

"Thanks."

"But I'll admit that if I'd been standing where he was standing, I'd probably have had a different view of the whole thing."

"The funny thing is, he was jealous of *you* for a while there."

He snorts. "I seriously doubt that your ex has ever been the slightest bit jealous of me. Look at him. And look at me."

"I'm not comparing you two—"

"Because I'd lose."

"Well, yeah, but only in looks and personality."

Now it's his turn to thank me sarcastically.

I say, more seriously, "James knew I shared something with you that he couldn't. Not that he *wanted* to. But still."

"You mean Ivy and Ethan?"

"Yeah. He didn't get why I cared so much about her. To be fair, I don't think he's all that into his own siblings. He's kind of self-centered. In the most likable way possible."

"Is that why you broke up?"

"A little bit. And maybe a little bit because I was starting to like another guy."

"Yeah? Who?"

"Don't be an idiot."

He shakes his head somberly. "It's going to take me a while to really absorb this. Girls like you don't like boys like me."

"There aren't other girls like me," I say. "I'm unique. And don't you forget it."

We decide to make an In-N-Out run—David's in no hurry to get home. "It's too weird to be there without Ethan. He's been my constant companion pretty much my whole life."

But he has an AP physics test to study for, and I have a paper to write, so after we eat, I drop him at his house and go home.

No one's downstairs. I go up to my room and find Ivy on her bed, playing on her iPad.

"We had dinner without you," she says as soon as I walk in. "It was chicken and peas. Mom said you went to In-N-Out with David. Why didn't you take me?"

"Sorry. I will next time."

"Are you and David going to be boyfriend and girlfriend?"

"I think so."

"You said that wouldn't happen."

"Believe me, Ives— no one's more surprised than I am that I was wrong about that."

"Everyone makes mistakes," she says, which is another thing we've told her so many times that she recites it mechanically. "Don't feel bad about being wrong. But I want to go to In-N-Out with you next time."

"Okay. What are you watching?"

"A funny cat video."

I'm not a fan of cat videos, but I feel like hanging out with my sister right now, so I curl up next to her on her bed and we watch it together, laughing at the exact same moments.

THIRTY-FIVE

I HAVE TO TELL SARAH about me and David or she'll be hurt I didn't. So I invite her to go out for frozen yogurt later that evening. She's up for it—the great thing about Sarah is that she's always up for ditching homework and doing something fun—and we meet up at, ironically, the same fro-yo place where David and I brought our siblings for their first "date." It's hard not to cringe as I walk in and remember how certain I was that I was doing something brilliant that day.

It's pretty unfair that I got a boyfriend out of all those dates and Ivy didn't.

On the other hand, she doesn't *want* a boyfriend and probably never will.

Sarah's a few minutes late, so I text with David until she shows up, and then we get our frozen yogurt and sit down with it.

We talk about some minor stuff and then she sits back and regards me thoughtfully. "Hey, Chloe? Would you tell me if it bothered you that James and I spend time together? Because you're both my friends, and I don't want to lose either of you."

"I don't mind at all. I think it's great."

"Okay." She seems a little dubious. "But we'd always rather you joined us, just so you know. I mean, yeah, it's a little weird still for James, but he told me he really does want to stay friends with you."

"I'm glad he has you to talk to. Seriously. And I'm glad *I* have you to talk to, because I have something important to tell you."

"Is it that you're going out with David Fields?"

I stare at her, my spoon frozen in midair on its way to my mouth. "Oh, my God. How did you know?"

"Oh, please." She waves her hand dismissively. "I'm not an idiot, Chloe. I notice things. Plus Brandon Seltzer's brother saw you guys at Starbucks today making out, and it's kind of already gotten around."

"We weren't making out!" I amend that. "Well, not at Starbucks anyway."

"Ugh. David Fields? Really?" Then she covers her mouth. "I'm sorry! I shouldn't judge. It's your life. And I know you guys have the whole sibling thing going on. And you did say he's different when you're alone . . ."

"He is." I lean forward, eager to make her see that this is a really good thing. "He's kind of great, actually. I mean, I know I thought he was awful, and I don't blame you for thinking that too, because he likes to pretend to be the worst, but he isn't, not really. He loves his brother, and he's a good human being. He's just a little damaged."

"Well, who isn't?" Sarah says gaily.

"Exactly."

We smile at each other in mutual understanding before digging into our frozen yogurt.

But then I look up again. "Oh, wait—does James know? About me and David?"

"No idea. I haven't said anything to him. But someone else might have. You want me to tell him?"

"That would be amazing. Do you mind?"

"That's what I'm here for," she says. "That and to tell you that Jana hooked up with some random guy from Harvard-Westlake at Brandon's party last week who turned out to have a girlfriend who's Helena Saperstein's cousin. You missed all the excitement."

"Tell me," I say fervently. There's nothing I want more right now than to hear some juicy gossip that's not about *me*. "Tell me."

Ethan is finally allowed to call home, but Mr. and Mrs. Fields won't let David talk to him. "We can't trust you to stay upbeat," their stepmother says.

"She's probably right," I point out when David calls me afterward, upset. "Even when things are good, you're not exactly 'upbeat.'"

"I wouldn't have upset him," he says irritably. "I just want to know how he's doing, but all *they* asked him was whether he needed more underwear. They couldn't get off the phone fast enough."

"They'll let you talk to him eventually, right?"

"They said when he calls next week I can talk, but only for a minute or two."

After that second call, he drives over to my house and texts me from his car so I can come out and we can talk in private.

"How was it?" I ask as soon as I'm in the car with him.

"Confusing."

"Why? How did he sound?"

David rubs his forehead. "He's just so bad on the phone. It's impossible to get a real conversation going. I asked him how he was doing, but all he said was 'fine.' And then he talked for a while about the movies they've been showing."

"Did he sound happy or sad about them?"

"He was annoyed they showed a Disney movie because — and I'm quoting — 'those are for little kids.' But he liked that they showed a Clint Eastwood movie."

"He doesn't *sound* miserable."

"I don't know. It's not like he would ever say, 'I'm unhappy here, take me home.' I mean, if he could express what he was feeling and ask for help, he wouldn't *need* to run away. Running away has always been how he lets us know he's unhappy. And he can't run away from there. They've got him locked up tight."

"When can we visit?"

"That's the one good thing. I called the school when my parents weren't around and asked when Ethan can have visitors, and they said I can come up next weekend."

"Yay!" I say. "And I can come too?"

He grins. "I didn't ask whether I could bring you, because I didn't want them to say no. But you're coming with me."

"Damn right I am."

David is tense during the long drive up to the boarding school. He doesn't talk much, and when he does, it's more snarling than talking.

"Can we stop for a cup of coffee?" I ask after we've been on the road for a while.

"I want to get there before lunch," he says. "Why didn't you have some before I picked you up?"

"I did. I just wanted more. But it's fine."

We drive for another ten minutes. I poke around on Instagram and Twitter, figuring it's better to amuse myself than to try to get civil conversation out of him right now. Then he exits the freeway and pulls in at a Starbucks.

"I thought we weren't stopping."

"You wanted coffee."

"But I don't want to make us late."

"It's fine." He gets out of the car, and I follow him inside. We get in line. He nudges my shoulder with his. "I'm sorry," he says. "I'm really glad you're with me today. But I won't relax until I see him."

"I know," I say, and I do. "I'm not mad. I totally get it." I'm worried, too — what happens if the place is awful and Ethan's really unhappy? It's easy to say we'll rescue him. It's another thing to do it. And what if the place is only moderately bad, and Ethan is okay but would rather be home? Do we leave him there, drive away, try to forget that he wants to come with us?

The caffeine was a bad idea—it only makes me more nervous.

THIRTY-SIX

W ELCOME TO PRISON," David mutters as we stop at the gate guard booth.

The guard does carefully check both our IDs before giving us visitor passes, but none of this is all that different from what I went through at Ivy and Ethan's high school. And once we drive in, the place is a lot prettier than a prison — not that I've ever actually *been* to a prison, but I assume most of them don't have nearly so much in the way of trees and paths and low buildings and sunlight.

We park where the guard told us to, in a space marked VIS-ITOR in front of the main administration building. Neither of us says a word as we get out of the car and walk inside, where there are lots of sofas and chairs and big windows looking out on more of the campus.

The woman sitting at the front desk is tall and thin and looks like something out of a Roald Dahl book illustration — all spiky hair and spiky limbs and spiky eyebrows. She does not give me a warm feeling, and my heart sinks.

David explains why we're here.

"Visiting hours aren't until eleven on Saturdays," she says. Spikily.

I glance at my watch. We're only, like, twelve minutes early.

David points that out, and she says coldly, "I'll see what I can do. Have a seat." She waves toward the sofa as she picks up the phone and presses a button or two.

We ignore the sofa and wander toward the windows. I lean against the frame and watch David as he gazes out at the buildings and fields. A few weeks ago, I'd probably have said his face was expressionless, but I can read him a lot better now: there's tension in his cheek and in the slight tuck of his bottom lip under his teeth and in the line between his eyes. He's right on the edge, and a single word might make him explode. So I stay quiet.

It feels like forever before we hear someone come in from a side door. We both whip around, but it's not Ethan. It's a young man, probably about twenty-five or so. His dark hair is already receding from his forehead, and he's slightly sweaty around the temples, but he has a nice smile. He's wearing sweatpants, a T-shirt, and sneakers.

"You guys are here to see Ethan Fields?" he says.

"Yeah," David says. "I'm his brother, and this is my friend Chloe. Where is he?"

"He's just finishing up an activity. I'll walk you over to him, but I'd like to talk for a second first."

"Can't I just go see my brother?" David's voice is barely civil, but the man doesn't seem bothered by that. His voice stays calm. "I'll be fast, I promise. Please." He indicates the sofa, and I promptly walk over and sit down and glare at David until he reluctantly does the same.

The guy takes a chair facing us. He leans forward and clasps his hands between his legs. "I'm Sammy. I'm one of Ethan's primary helpers."

"Helpers?" David repeats.

"We offer support in the life skills areas—getting up, getting dressed, going through the day's routines—"

"Ethan doesn't need help with any of that."

"Believe me, I know. He's amazing. He makes my job easy. But he's still technically under my care a lot of the time, and I want to fill you in before you see him. First of all, he's doing great. He fits right in and already has lots of friends. He's attentive in school and joins in a lot of activities with a good spirit. He's been a wonderful addition here."

David says, "You wouldn't exactly tell us if he were miserable."

Sammy says calmly, "I would tell you if I had concerns, and I don't. I'm not saying life here is sunshine and daisies every single minute. Ethan did have a rough first week. He seemed to feel he was sent here because he had misbehaved, and we had to convince him that this is a school, not a punishment."

"Don't kid yourself," David says. "My parents definitely sent him here as a punishment."

"What makes you say that?"

"Never mind. When you say the week was rough, how rough?"

"He tried to run away a couple of times. He couldn't get past the gate, so his safety was never in question, but he got pretty upset when he was stopped."

Even though Sammy couldn't sound more matter-of-fact, his simple words tear at me. Ethan desperately wanted to go home and couldn't. At my side, David shifts restlessly, and I know he's feeling it too.

"But that was only at the very beginning," Sammy says. "He actually settled in faster than most. He's pretty content here — except when someone puts on a movie or TV show that he doesn't approve of. He has strong feelings about entertainment — I'm sure you know that." He smiles at David, who doesn't smile back. "But we're working with him on expressing his opinion *once* and then letting it go. He's learning. He's not there yet, but he's learning."

"Great," David says. "Can I see him now?"

Sammy holds up his hand. "Just one more thing. Ethan is really starting to feel comfortable here, but it's early days still, and it wouldn't take a lot for him to feel unsettled again. Please try to be positive. Even if you believe he's being punished in some way by being sent here — and I'm not sure you're right about that — I'd ask you not to communicate that sentiment to him."

"Okay," David says, standing up. "If he's as happy as you say, I'll try to keep him feeling that way. But he's not a baby or an idiot — if he tells me he's miserable, I'm not going to try to convince him he's not."

Sammy stands up too. "Just be aware that if he tells you he's miserable, it may be because you represent home to him and he's still thinking that's where he belongs, and not because anything is going wrong here."

"Or," David says, "it may be because he's actually miserable."

"I'm with him every day," Sammy says, and for the first time, his voice sounds a little tight. "I promise you he's not."

"How about you actually let me talk to him, and I'll judge for myself?"

Sammy hesitates, glancing at me. I flash my *Love Me!* smile at him. I don't actually disagree with what David's saying, but, man, he needs to learn not to alienate people who could help him.

"We can't wait to see him!" I say, all bouncy hair, white teeth, and adorability. "We've missed him a lot!"

"All right, then!" Sammy responds to my smile with one of his own. "Come on."

He holds the side door open for us, and we tromp through and then across a sunlit patch of grass to a path that takes us past a group of students who are attempting some tai chi exercises, past a couple of small buildings, past another group working in a garden, and eventually to the walkway of a long, low building, where Sammy leads us inside. "Arts and crafts," he says as we enter.

There are a couple of looms and a few potter's wheels, baskets of yarn and thread, a row of sewing machines, several big tables where students are working, and shelves all around them filled with art supplies and paper. I'm still gazing around, taking it all in, when David suddenly runs over to one of the tables and throws his arms around Ethan, who's sitting there drawing with a few other people.

Ethan twists around so he can look at his brother. "Hi, David. What are you doing here?"

"I came to visit you!"

"I'm doing art," Ethan says. "I'm not done yet. I have art from ten thirty to eleven thirty on Saturdays." He spots me. "Hi, Chloe! Did you come with David?"

"Yes! It's so good to see you." I bend down to hug him.

He looks a little different to me, maybe because he's wearing sweatpants and flip-flops, and I've only seen him in jeans and sneakers before. Everyone seems to wear sweatpants and flip-flops at this place.

"Where's Ivy?" he asks, peering around me like she might be hiding behind somewhere.

"She's not here. Sorry."

Sammy says, "Hey, Ethan—how about you introduce all your friends to your brother and Chloe?"

"Okay." Ethan flaps his hand at each of his table companions in turn. "This is Julia, and this is Emily, and this is also Ethan. They call me Ethan F and him Ethan W because my last name is Fields and his is Wilson."

We say hi to the others, who say hi back, except for the other Ethan—Sammy has to ask him several times to look up and acknowledge us.

Our Ethan says to us, "Julia is one of my best friends, and Ethan and I live in the same room, but I don't usually hang out with Emily. I don't know why she's sitting with us right now."

I say, "It's nice to meet you all."

Julia has dark skin and black curly hair and square glasses

and a sort of hipster, intellectual look that may not be intentional but totally works for her. She stares at us openly, her scrutiny a little too intense to be comfortable. Emily is chubby and fair, and seems a little shy. The other Ethan has long reddish hair and an even redder beard and has already gone back to his drawing, which, I can see now, is really *good*—a detailed pen-and-ink drawing of an octopus.

"Can we take Ethan to go talk alone somewhere?" David asks Sammy.

"Sure," Sammy says. "So long as you stay on campus."

"We can't take him out to lunch?"

Sammy shakes his head. "Sorry, guys, but we only give off-campus permission to adult relatives."

"I'm eighteen," David says.

"You'd have to be over twenty-one."

"I promise you we're responsible."

"I'm sure you are."

There's a short silence. David heaves an irritated sigh and turns to his brother. "Come on, Ethan—you can show us around the school."

"What about my drawing? I'm not done."

Sammy says, "I'll hold on to it for you. You can finish it later."

"Don't throw it out."

"Of course not."

But Ethan won't leave until he's watched Sammy put the drawing on an "unfinished work" shelf. Only then will he let us take him away.

THIRTY-SEVEN

ONCE WE'RE OUTSIDE, David lowers his voice. "So what's it like here, Ethan? Really?"

"I don't know. Okay, I guess. Except Nicholas keeps putting on *Bones*. He says it's a good show, but it's not. It's boring."

"But how are the people? Like Sammy and the other helpers?"

"Sammy's nice," Ethan says. "He gives a lot of high-fives. Joe doesn't give high-fives, but he does give fist bumps. Joe's my other helper."

"What about the teachers? Are they nice to you?"

"Pretty nice," Ethan says, drawing out the first word a little dubiously. "They give a *lot* of homework, except we do it in study hall and we don't ever go home, so I don't know why they call it homework. I like creative writing and Spanish, but I don't like math as much. I'm writing a play in creative writing. It's about a police detective whose wife is killed by a thief."

"That sounds super cool," I say.

Ethan looks pleased. "Yes. The teacher said maybe we'll actually put it on, with actors and everything. I would be the writer and the director. If we do, will you come see it?"

"Of course!"

"And Ivy?"

"Sure. I bet she'd love to see it."

"Is she still gay?"

"Yeah, I think so."

There's a pause. "That's okay," he says after a moment. "It's not her fault."

"Yeah, it's not really a fault kind of situation."

David points to a bench on the grass and says, "Let's sit here." The two brothers sit down together, and I take a couple of photos of them with my phone, then say I need to use the bathroom—I just want them to have a few minutes alone.

The campus feels both busy and peaceful as I wander back toward the main administration building, where I'd noticed a ladies' room. Along the way, I do notice a couple of people who are screaming or rocking or crying—but only a couple, and there's always an aide soothing or calming or just sitting with them.

I stop still at one point because for a split second I think I see Ivy, waiting for a turn at handball, and I have a crazy moment of thinking, *Did Mom bring her here?* And then I realize it's not Ivy. Of course it's not Ivy. It's just that this girl is dressed like her and is moving her hands the way Ivy does when she's anxious, pumping them at her sides just like Ivy does. That one gesture conjured up Ivy for me.

What if Ivy did come here? Not as a visitor but as a student?

That thought tints everything I see on my way to the

bathroom and back to the bench. Would she like it here? Would she be in that group of girls on the bench over there, who aren't exactly laughing and chatting, but who seem to be sort of enjoying being together anyway? Or would she be alone with a caregiver, like the dark-haired young man near the tetherball pole, who's clearly upset about something and having trouble calming down?

Ivy doesn't usually like being outside, always wants to get back into the house if we try to get her to go for a walk or even just into the backyard. Would that change if she were here? Would she enjoy this beautiful afternoon, this pretty place? Or would she find some corner to sit in, where she'd hug herself and moan and miss her home?

I don't know. I can't picture her here, but a few hours ago, I couldn't picture Ethan here either.

He's talking loudly to David when I approach.

". . . And so I said we shouldn't watch *The Amazing Spider-Man,* because the first *Spider-Man* is better, but Nicholas said *The Amazing Spider-Man* is better. I got kind of mad and used a pretty bad curse word, and Joe said I couldn't see the movie if I didn't calm down and apologize, and I said I didn't care if I didn't see the movie since it was *The Amazing Spider-Man,* so I went back to my room. Julia told me afterward that she thought *The Amazing Spider-Man* was stupid but that Nicholas wouldn't admit it."

I say, "So is Nicholas your nemesis?"

"He's my friend," Ethan says seriously. "We do a lot together, but I don't like him that much."

"That sums up my entire middle-school social life."

"Come on." David stands up. "I want to see your dorm room."

"Okay." Ethan gets up too. As he moves into the lead, I whisper to David, "Well? What do you think?"

"I don't know."

"He seems pretty good."

"Maybe they told him that if he complained, they'd lock him in his room or stop feeding him or something."

I roll my eyes. "This isn't a Dickens novel, David."

"I never said it was." He strides forward impatiently, so I have to scramble to keep up.

On the front step of the dorm building, which is a couple of stories tall and more blocky than the other buildings we've been in, Ethan reaches inside his shirt and pulls out a key card attached to a lanyard around his neck.

"Only the people who live here can go in," he says as he expertly waves it in front of a sensor. "But it's okay for you to come in, because you're with me. You can't come in without me, though."

"Got it," David says.

"Same for my room," Ethan says, leading us through the hallway. "You can only come in if I take you. It's the same key." He heads up a flight of stairs, and we follow. "These are the stairs I usually take. There are other ones, but they're farther away. And there's an elevator, but it's only for people who can't walk up the stairs. When I'm tired, I think I should get to take the elevator, but Sammy and Joe won't let me."

"Why won't they let you?" David says. "That's weird."

"I know," Ethan says. "Really weird."

"They probably just think it's faster and easier to take the stairs," I say. We reach the top. "Which one's your room?"

"The second door on the right-hand side, coming from these stairs, and the third door on the left-hand side, coming from the other stairs."

"Let's see it."

"Okay, but it's weird being here now. Usually we're not allowed to be in the dorms during school hours." He pulls out his keycard again.

"What if you're sick?" David asks.

"Then you go to the infirmary. There's a nurse and three beds. I met the nurse last week because I got a splinter in my finger. It hurt so much. It hurt as much as getting stabbed with a knife." He pushes the door open. "This is my room. I share it with Nicholas and Ethan W and Jonathan, but Jonathan went home this weekend because his grandmother died."

"Oh, poor Jonathan," I say.

"She was ninety-two years old. She was born in 1925, which was between the two world wars. Jonathan said she was supposed to die last year, but she didn't, and his parents had to cancel their summer vacation, so his mother was annoyed."

I laugh.

"That wasn't a joke. Why are you laughing?"

"I'm just so happy to see you?" I offer guiltily.

David has been circling around the room, checking everything out with a worried frown on his face. "So this is your bed?" He points to the top mattress on one of the bunks.

"Yeah. Don't you see my blanket from home?"

"That's how I knew. You like being on the top?"

"No!" Ethan says. "I hate it. If you need to go to the bathroom, you have to climb down in the dark, and it's hard to find the places to put your feet. I wanted to be on the bottom, but Ethan W already had the bottom and said I couldn't have it."

"You're kidding me," David says. "That sucks."

"Someone has to take the top bunk," I say. "And Ethan's the new guy, so—"

"That's exactly why he should have a decent place to sleep. I'll make them change this before we leave." David continues to prowl the room. "What about your clothes? Where do you keep those?"

"I get half of the drawers." Ethan points to one of two plain wooden dressers. "The bottom ones. And Ethan W gets the ones on top."

"That's not fair either!" David slams his palm on the top of the dresser. Ethan flinches. "It's harder to get stuff in and out of the bottom drawers. You have the worst of both worlds. The least they could do is give the people in the top bunks the top drawers."

"I didn't think about that," Ethan says nervously. "I should have. The top should go with the top. No one told me that before."

"Because it's not an actual rule," I say. "Most people don't care which drawers they get. I know I don't—Ivy has the top ones in our room, and I don't care."

"It's a fairness thing," David says. "They're treating Ethan like a second-class citizen." He turns back to his brother. "What happens with your dirty clothes?"

"I have a hamper in the closet. Mine is blue. Ethan W's is green, and Jonathan's is red, and Nicholas's is yellow. Nicholas keeps putting his clothes in mine, though. He says that means I have to wash them for him."

"You don't," I say. "He's just teasing. Are there laundry machines in the building? Do they help you do it, or are you on your own?"

"I do my laundry on Mondays," Ethan says. "Sammy helps. I separate the whites from the darker colors. You use hot water for the whites and—"

"Hold on," David says. "What was that about Nicholas trying to make you do his laundry? Is he bullying you? You shouldn't have to share a room with a bully." He grabs Ethan's arm. "You have to tell me honestly right now, while we're alone—"

"Chloe's here."

"She doesn't count."

"Much appreciated," I say.

He gazes intently at his brother. "Tell me if you hate it here, Ethan. Because if you do, I'll take you home right now."

"I could go home?"

"Yes. Right now. If that's what you want."

"But Dad said I couldn't go home. So did Sammy. I cried at the beginning a lot and kept asking, but he said no."

"Oh, Ethan," I say. "That sounds really scary."

"Yes, it was."

"Is it still as scary?"

He hesitates, glancing sideways at David, whose face is taut with tension. "I'm not sure," Ethan whispers.

"You don't have to decide now," I say quickly, before David can speak. "Maybe you should stay for a little while longer and see how you feel? You can always come home another day if you decide that's what you want."

"That's a good idea," Ethan says with relief. "It's Saturday, and they always have french fries and milk shakes on Saturday nights."

"We can get you fries and milk shakes," David says. "If that's all that's keeping you here."

I say, "Hey, Ethan, I need to talk to David out in the hallway for a second. Do you mind? We'll be right back."

"Why?" Ethan asks.

"Because he's my boyfriend."

"Oh. You probably want to kiss."

"You'll never know," I say gaily. But I'm anything but cheerful once I've pulled David out of the room and far enough down the hallway so Ethan can't hear us. "Stop it," I say. "Just stop it."

"Stop what?"

"You know what. You're *trying* to make Ethan hate being here."

"Why the hell would I do that?"

"I have no idea. I've been wondering the same thing."

"You don't know Ethan the way I do. He lets people push him around and take advantage of him. No one's looking out for him here—"

"Are you kidding me? Sammy's amazing—he's totally on top of everything. And people here seem really happy—including Ethan. Or at least he was, until you started messing with his mind."

"I wasn't messing with his mind!" David shouts. It's a good thing the dorm is empty right now. "I was just asking him questions and getting at the truth—which is that a lot of things here suck!"

"A lot of things? Like what? That he's on the top bunk? He didn't even care about that until you made a big deal out of it. And, by the way, *someone* has to take the top bunk, David. That's how bunk beds work."

"It shouldn't have to be Ethan!"

I throw my arms up in the air, frustrated. "It has to be somebody! So why *not* Ethan? Especially since he only just got here and the other boys already had beds?"

He turns away from me. "You're wasting my time, and this is my only chance to see my brother. I wouldn't have brought you if I'd known you were going to drag me away from him and second-guess me. If you don't stop being such a pain—"

"Then what?" I step around so I can get in his face. "Then what? You going to break up with me? Tell me you wish I hadn't come with you today? What are you going to do if I don't agree with every single thing you say and do? Be nasty until you win and I lose?"

There's a tense moment while we stand eye to eye, glaring at each other.

He breaks first. He closes his eyes briefly, takes a step back and puts his hands up. "I'm sorry."

I'm not ready to relent. "You should be."

"I know. Just . . . this is all hard for me. I'm worried. Imagine how you'd feel if it were Ivy."

"If I hadn't been doing that all along, I'd have ditched you an hour ago."

That wins me a begrudging smile.

"Come on," he says, flicking his chin toward Ethan's room. "Let's go back."

"Promise you'll stop trying to make everything seem bad?"

"If you'll promise to forgive me for being a jerk."

"Deal."

We go back to the room and push the door open.

There's been an explosion—clothes are scattered all over the floor, and Ethan's at the dresser dragging out more.

"What's going on?" David halts in the doorway. I'm stuck behind him, looking over his shoulder.

"I'm changing drawers," Ethan says. "It's not fair that Ethan W gets the top ones, so I'm moving his clothes to my drawers and mine to his. I had to take everything out first. That's the only way to do it."

"You can't just move his clothes," I say. "You have to ask him first."

"But it's not fair! David said so."

"Chloe's right, though," David says. "We have to discuss it with him and Sammy first."

"You didn't tell me that!" Ethan's voice starts to rise. "I didn't know. Am I going to get in trouble?"

"No," I say. "We're going to help you put the clothes back the way they were. Which are yours, and which are the other Ethan's?"

He stares at the piles. "I'm not sure anymore," he says unhappily.

"We can figure it out," David says. He kneels down. "I recognize these tops."

I flip through some pants. "These have name tags that say Ethan Wilson."

"They probably belong to the other Ethan, then," Ethan says, calming down a little.

"Odds are good," I agree gravely.

We manage to get the clothing back in the drawers—maybe not with a hundred percent accuracy, but close enough.

"If he wants to keep the top drawers, it's okay," Ethan says when we're done. He was pretty stressed during the process, but now that the clothing's all back and the drawers are closed, he's doing better. "I don't really care."

David avoids my glance, but to his credit, he looks a little ashamed of himself. And he doesn't argue.

THIRTY-EIGHT

WE LEAVE THE DORM, and Ethan shows us the gym, where he proudly informs us that in one month he's already doubled the weight he can curl, then the community room, which has an enormous flat-screen TV and a bunch of pinball and video games, then the computer room, and then his little corner patch of their big community garden, where he's growing lettuce and beets.

"But you don't eat vegetables," David says.

"Sammy says food tastes better when you grow it yourself."

"It's true," I say. David rolls his eyes and makes a snorting sound. "It *is*," I insist. "I once had a tomato plant, and I hate tomatoes, but I ate the one little tomato I succeeded in growing, and it was delicious. Then the plant died."

"I didn't want to grow tomatoes," Ethan says.

"I don't blame you. It only leads to heartbreak." There's a loud clanging sound. I look around. "What is that?"

"Lunch. On weekdays it's at noon, but on Saturdays and Sundays, it's at one. I want to go eat. I'm hungry."

"I'm hungry too." I appeal to David. "Maybe we could run out for a meal and then come back?"

"Let's just check out the cafeteria first—I want to see what kind of food they're serving here."

Ethan is trotting ahead, so I take the opportunity to whisper to David, "If you say a single negative thing about the food—"

"I won't. Not unless there are maggots in it or something."

"If there are maggots in the food, you will be too busy scraping me off the ceiling to talk at all."

The food doesn't have maggots in it. It's just your basic cafeteria food, not particularly appetizing, but edible. Ethan seems happy enough with the peanut butter and jelly sandwich that's offered as an alternative to anyone who doesn't want the main course of fish and rice. Ethan tells David, me, the two cafeteria servers, Sammy (who's keeping a watchful eye on everything), and every one of his friends who'll listen that he doesn't like fish and doesn't believe that anyone else really likes it either.

Once he's gotten his sandwich, he points to a group of kids at a table. "I sit there. Between Julia and Nicholas."

"Go ahead and join them," David says. "We'll go get lunch and come back after, okay?"

"Okay," Ethan says, and walks off.

"Maybe I should say something to Sammy now about the bunk beds," David says.

I tug on his arm. "I'm starving. Can't we eat first? You can go on the attack later."

"I'm not going to go on the attack."

"Still . . . food first."

In the car, I Google restaurants, and we locate a Subway just a couple of miles from the school. After we get our food and sit down, I tear savagely into my sub—I really am starving.

When I look up, David isn't eating. Just sitting there, staring at the table.

"You okay?" I say. "What's wrong?"

"I don't know." He sinks his face into his hands. "I feel all messed up inside."

"Why? Ethan seems okay, doesn't he? Maybe there are some minor issues . . . but the school's a lot better than I expected."

"I know," he says with a small groan. "I thought so too."

"Then what? What's wrong?"

He drops his hands. "I honestly don't know! I mean, I've spent the last month picturing the worst, and it's not that bad, and I should be happy about that. So why do I feel like shit?" He reaches for his sandwich and unwraps it slowly, then takes a bite without any real interest or appetite.

"Maybe because it's all anticlimactic," I say. "Ethan doesn't need to be rescued. At least not immediately."

"That should be a good thing."

"It should. But we've both been thinking about him so much—especially you—and wondering what would happen when we came. And there's kind of nothing for us to do. For now, anyway."

"Maybe." We eat in silence for a minute. Then David says, "I thought he'd be happier to see us."

"He was totally happy to see you!"

"Not really. I mean, yeah, he thought it was nice I came, but it wasn't like he was sitting around waiting for me or anything." He wipes his mouth with the back of his hand. "Years and years of us always being together, with me doing everything I could to . . . you know . . . help him. And then he goes away, and he's totally fine." He gives a strangled, slightly choked laugh. "Oh, God. Is that my problem? That I'm so selfish I want him to be miserable without me? Am I that big a wack job?" He drops the rest of his sub on its paper wrapping.

"Well, yeah," I say. "But not for *that* reason. You don't want him to be miserable. It's just . . . you were planning not to go away to college because he might need you, right? And then *he's* the one who goes off to school, and he doesn't even seem to miss you. But I bet he *does* miss you. It's just that he's like Ivy—neither of them is very good at saying what other people need to hear."

"But it's more than just what he says. I honestly think I miss him more than he misses me."

"That's because you took care of him. And he's still basically being taken care of, but you don't have anyone to take care of. So you lost more than he did." I nudge his hand with mine. "I'm willing to be taken care of, by the way, if you need someone to fill that void. I could use a little more nurturing in my life."

"I'll try," he says. "But I'm not all that great at being warm and fuzzy."

"I hadn't noticed."

"I think maybe you're being sarcastic," he says, exactly the way Ethan would say it, and I laugh.

"You need to be proud he's doing so well," I say. "It's all because of you."

"So basically you're saying I should let my baby bird leave the nest?"

"Exactly. Now eat your sub so you can regurgitate it for him when we get back."

The afternoon goes better than the morning did, mostly because David stops looking for things to criticize.

Sammy suggests that Ethan show us the "movie studio," which turns out to be a corner of the arts and crafts building with a green screen and a digital camera on a tripod. Ethan tells us he's going to make a movie and that Julia will star in it.

"Maybe also Nicholas," he says. "But I'm not sure about that."

David corners Sammy about the "bunk bed situation," as he calls it, and Sammy explains that they didn't want to move any of the other boys too soon after Ethan's arrival—"Transitions are hard for them, and we didn't want them to associate Ethan with something negative"—but that eventually they'll have the bottom and top sleepers switch places. "I promise you it will be fair and even in the long run."

David nods and doesn't bring up the dresser drawers. Which I take as a personal triumph.

At the end of the afternoon, as we're getting ready to go, Ethan asks us when we're planning to come back for another visit.

"Whatever you think," David says. "Do you want us to come back soon?"

"Yes," Ethan says. "But you don't have to come for so long. I didn't get to do some stuff with my friends today that I wanted to do. But it's okay. I'm still glad you came."

"We'll come for a shorter visit next time."

"Then come back soon. For just a little while."

"You got it," David says, and the brothers embrace briefly. I give Ethan a hug too and say goodbye.

"Hey," I say to David as we continue on to the car, "you know what I just realized?"

"What?"

"Ivy turns twenty-one in a month. If she comes with us to visit Ethan after that, they'll have to let us take him off campus!"

"Wait," he says, halting. "That's, like, totally brilliant."

"I know, right?"

"You may actually deserve to be my girlfriend."

"Jerk," I say.

"Blonde," he says.

On the drive back, he holds my hand tightly whenever he doesn't need his hand to steer. "Thank you for coming with me," he says when we're close to home.

"You're welcome."

"And for keeping me from making a mess of everything."

"It's a full-time job."

"Then why do it?"

"I don't know. I must like something about you."

"Well, don't stop."

"I won't." I hesitate and then say, "That place . . ."

"What?"

"It was pretty nice. Maybe your folks knew what they were doing."

"They just got lucky."

"Maybe." His father had said they'd chosen carefully. I'd dismissed that as the kind of thing he *would* say whether it was true or not. But maybe he'd meant it. "It's good, is all."

"Yeah." There's a moment of silence. "Guess I should start looking at colleges," he says abruptly.

"Yeah—you can go anywhere now."

"I'd still like to be within driving distance of that place so I can visit Ethan a lot and be there if anything goes seriously wrong."

"I'll look nearby too. Maybe we can both end up near our siblings and—" I stop.

"And?"

"I don't want to presume."

"If you think I don't want us to be near each other next year—"

"Then what?"

"Then I take back calling you brilliant."

"Ugh," I say.

"What?"

"This whole liking each other thing. It's disgusting."

"Yeah," he says. "It's totally outside my comfort zone."

"We could stop. You could crawl back into your hole—"

"And abandon you to a meaningless life of high social status and handsome boyfriends?" He shakes his head. "I'd never be that cruel to you."

"Then I guess we'll just keep going on like this."

"Yeah," he says. "It sucks but it's the right thing to do."

THIRTY-NINE

I POST A PHOTO of the two of us on Instagram, which David says is the "most basic thing" I've ever done. "The fact that I'm dating someone who even *has* an Instagram account —"

"We can't all be antisocial psychopaths," I respond sweetly.

Unfortunately, it's a sentiment shared by many of my friends.

"No one likes him," Sarah tells me bluntly one day. "It's not like we're not trying. But he says stuff like that thing today, and you have to admit, it's just rude."

I know what she's referring to. I'd made David sit with me and my friends at lunch. People were having a lively debate about the meaning and the usage of the word *feminism,* and David brought the entire conversation to an abrupt halt by saying, "A feminist is someone who believes in equal rights for women, so you're either a feminist or you're an idiot."

"He was kind of right," I point out.

"It's not what he says, it's how he says it. Can't you get him to at least pretend not to think that everyone else is a moron?"

"Believe me, if I could, I would."

"Don't get mad at me for asking this, but why do you like

him? I mean, I know you guys have the autistic sibling thing in common, but that can't be the whole story."

"It's not." I want to explain, but it's not easy. "You know that viral video that everyone was into a few years ago? About the lion who gets reunited with the guy who raised him as a cub? And the lion, like, licks him and hugs him and plays with him? And it's amazing?"

She raises her eyebrows. "You saying David's a lion?"

"It's just . . . it's easy to get a dog to love you. But it's a lot harder—and cooler—to get a lion to. Especially if you're the only person he doesn't attack."

"I hope there's a sexual metaphor somewhere in this whole lion thing," Sarah says. "Because, honestly, that's the only reason that would actually make sense to me."

"I don't think either of us has a problem with you leaping to that assumption," I say with an exaggerated wink.

"Seriously," she says. "Calling him a lion . . . I have issues with this."

"It's just a metaphor."

"I know. But I don't want you to be involved with someone who could hurt you."

"He wouldn't. Not ever. He thinks the world is a shitty place, but he also thinks I'm the best thing in it. Well, me and his brother."

"Great," she says. "Now you're making me jealous. I'm jealous of your relationship with *David Fields*. Could I be a bigger loser?"

"I'm not even telling you the best parts."

"Good," she says. "Spare me."

There really is a lot more I could tell her. Like how I admire the way David says whatever he wants to without worrying about offending people—I wish I could be more like that. And how I know that his impatience with stupidity would never turn into anger against me or into actual cruelty against anyone—because, deep down, he just wants to defend the weak and helpless and disenfranchised, and it's his fears for them that make him so frustrated and easily annoyed with how wrong people can be.

And how he treats my sister like a human being. Not like a pet, not like an idiot, not like an alien. He includes her, talks to her, listens to her, and occasionally gets irritated with her.

And how when he and I are alone together, his desire for me makes my knees weak and my pulse race. And how I like being the first girl he's ever gotten this close to, ever even kissed.

How all he wants when we're alone in the dark is to please me—to spark my desire until it equals his. I enjoy making him work for it, sometimes even tease and torture him until he's a little desperate, but the truth is . . . the desire's there already. I adore his slim, strong body, his slender hands, his dark eyes, his neat ears, his warm neck. All of him, in fact.

I admired and enjoyed James's body when we were going out, the way you would a work of art that you've been given permission to touch, but with David, it's not like that. He's not a piece of sculpture. He's flesh and blood and bone and skin and everything that's warm and real and passionate.

FORTY

MR. AND MRS. FIELDS visit Ethan and discover that we went to the school without their permission. They're not as pissed as I thought they might be, maybe because Ethan seems fine and David didn't try to kidnap him or anything.

Mrs. Fields complains that the car trip was too hard on the baby, who apparently screamed the whole way there and back. Mr. Fields says they'll leave him with a babysitter the next time they go, but Mrs. Fields is horrified by that idea—the school is too far away, and "if Caleb needed me while we were gone, I'd never forgive myself." She doesn't exactly refuse to go back, but she rejects any possible solution, and ultimately the job of visiting Ethan falls mostly to David.

I'm convinced that both Mr. and Mrs. Fields have hated me ever since we argued with them about sending Ethan away. They're pretty cold whenever I come by their house and, no matter how charming I try to be, they never fuss over me or invite me to dinner the way James's parents always did.

David doesn't care. "It's not like their opinion matters to me. In fact, if they approved of you, I'd be worried."

"I know, but I like people to like me."

"It's your biggest flaw," he says, and I don't think he's joking.

I don't care. I want to be able to go to his house and feel comfortable and welcome.

There is one member of the family who hasn't made up his mind about me, so I throw myself into entertaining the baby every time I go over. I squeeze his chubby little legs and play peekaboo and repeat the *la-la* sounds he makes and bring him stuffed animals to chew on. Mrs. Fields seems a little uneasy with all this enthusiasm at first, but since she believes her baby is irresistible, she doesn't actually question my sincerity. When Caleb laughs and gurgles at me, she starts meting out a few thin, begrudging smiles of her own.

On one visit, I extend my hands toward him invitingly, and he reaches for me. "May I hold him for a second?" I ask Mrs. Fields.

"Have you ever held a baby before?"

"Yes," I say, because I have, but she still hovers warily as I take him in my arms.

I don't want to freak her out, so I just hold him for a minute or two. I bounce him gently and say silly things and blow soft little noises on his cheeks and hand him back. He reaches out to me like he wants more.

Mrs. Fields says, "He really likes you."

"He's adorable." I flash a big white-toothed smile at her.

And, yes, I'm deliberately trying to make her like me, and I'm calculating enough to know that the best way to do it is through her kid, but I also mean it. Caleb is super-cute and pretty good-natured for a baby. What's not to like?

"I just wish he'd start saying words." Mrs. Fields kisses the top of his head. He twists in her arms to keep looking at me, and I scrunch up my face to make him giggle. "I know it's still early, but I'll feel so much better when he starts talking. You know—with the family history and all."

"He seems totally fine to me. I don't think you need to worry."

"Really?" Her face lights up.

"I mean, yeah," I say. "He's a great baby. Even if he's autistic, he's a great baby."

She doesn't seem to find that as reassuring as I meant it to be, but she manages a weak smile, and when I offer to hold him again, she not only hands him over, but asks me if it's okay if she runs upstairs for a minute while I'm with him.

"Of course!" I say. "And, honestly, anytime you need a babysitter, I'm happy to do it. You don't even have to pay me. It would be fun."

"That's very sweet of you," she says.

David is sitting at the kitchen table during this exchange, but as soon as his stepmother leaves the room, he gets up and comes over. "You're shameless," he says.

"Stop it. Look how cute your brother is. Just look at him."

He touches Caleb's little feet. "He is kind of cute," he admits.

"He's perfect."

"If you can overlook who his parents are. And how often he craps his diaper."

"You'd crap your diaper a lot too if you had to wear one all the time."

"Who says I don't?" While we're talking, he's still playing with Caleb's toes and the baby's making noises that are almost words and reaching for David's face.

"Do you ever just play with him?" I ask.

"Not really. Ethan and I are—were—usually off by ourselves. I think Margot preferred that—didn't want to risk all that autism rubbing off on the baby, you know." He blurps a raspberry on Caleb's chubby arm.

"Well, now that Ethan's not around, you should spend more time with him. This kid's got potential to be a decent human being."

"Then he shouldn't hang out with me. I'll ruin him."

"No, you won't—the one thing you're good at is being a brother."

"That's the only thing?" He gives me a wounded look. "I thought I was a fantastic boyfriend."

"Eh, you're okay," I say with a shrug.

One night Ron says to me, "You've been looking for a job, right? How about you come work for me?"

"Doing what?"

"Receptionist—filling in for your mother when she's picking up Ivy. You could come right after school and stay until we're done at six. It would make things a lot less stressful for both your mom and me."

I need the money, and nothing else has panned out, and Mom loves the idea—although I can't tell whether it's because she wants me to bond with Ron or because it frees up her afternoons (maybe it's both), so I agree to give it a try.

It's an easy job. I'm really just answering the phone and giving people forms to fill out, then entering the information online. It's boring, but I can usually get most of my homework done while I'm there, which means I can hang with David after dinner—he has tons of free time now that Ethan's gone.

Things do turn exciting one afternoon, when a patient comes bursting out of the exam room, claiming Ron damaged his shoulder and threatening to sue.

Ron follows him out. He looks pretty unhappy, but he keeps his voice calm as he says that he stands behind the treatment and expects to be paid for his services.

"My lawyer will be in touch!" the guy snarls. He hurls himself out the office door, slamming it behind him.

He's the last patient of the day. As Ron drives us home, I ask him whether he thinks the guy will actually sue. "Probably not," he says wearily. "He just doesn't want me to go after him for the money he owes me. He's been coming for months without paying his bill, and today I pushed him about it. That's when his shoulder suddenly started hurting."

"Will you sue him, then?"

"It's not worth it. Too expensive. Too exhausting."

"So he'll get away without paying you? That sucks."

"Yep," he says. "But what are you going to do?" And when we get home and he pours himself a big glass of wine, for once I don't judge him. I even fill a small bowl with salted almonds and bring them over to him. I know he likes them with his wine.

FORTY-ONE

AFTER DAVID AND I visit Ethan at school a bunch of times, Ivy asks if she can go with us. David isn't sure at first —he thinks it might make Ethan sad—but a few weeks later, Ethan proudly declares that he and Julia are officially boyfriend and girlfriend, so we agree it's probably safe to let Ivy come. Ethan seems to like the idea when we float it out to him.

I wonder how the school monitors physical relationships —whether they let Julia and Ethan be alone together. I have no idea, but at least this time it's not my problem.

When Ivy greets Ethan, he ostentatiously puts his arm around Julia's shoulders before saying hi back. Ivy gazes at them impassively.

She's not twenty-one for a few more weeks, so we can't take Ethan off campus, but we have fun playing Ping-Pong and video games in the community room. Ivy's a little shy around the other students, but she doesn't seem anxious—or at least no more anxious than usual.

We've gotten pretty close to Sammy on our visits—the more I know him, the more I like him—and I've told him a lot about Ivy. He tries to get her to join some of the group activities, but she clings close to my side and shakes her head.

On the way home, I ask her what she thought of the school.

"I don't like Ping-Pong," she says. "The ball always goes on the floor and I have to get it."

"But did you like the way the students live together? How they get to be on their own?"

"I don't know. It's not like being at home."

"Yeah, it's more like being at college."

She's quiet for a while and then she says, "I like home."

So I don't know what will happen, whether Ivy will ever want to leave the safety of our room and her bed and the family TV. Ethan's thriving away from home, but he was always more of an adventurer than she was, and his stepmother wanted him out of their house, whereas Mom likes having Ivy around and says she can't bear the thought of ever having an empty nest.

I keep trying to get Ivy to do more things out in the world. I sign us both up for a ceramics class in Santa Monica, and she seems to like going with me. Neither of us is about to win any art awards, but we have fun making our ugly, useless vases.

I still want Ivy to find someone to love who'll love her back. There's such a yearning, eager heart inside of her. I know that now. We just need to find a young, gay woman with autism who likes to eat frozen yogurt and watch TV.

Maybe that's not the easiest thing to find, but it's not the Holy Grail either, is it?

It's actually Ivy herself who makes a breakthrough in the search. She joins a Facebook group for young adults with autism and comments on someone's status — something about how *SVU* is better than the original *Law & Order.* A girl named Audrey agrees with her but says *CSI* is better than either. The two of them start rapidly commenting back and forth on the thread, and then friend each other so they can message privately, and pretty soon Ivy is talking a lot about how "Audrey thinks this" and "Audrey says that," and it's pretty clear that Audrey has become her guru.

I ask Ivy if Audrey's gay, and she says she doesn't know and should she ask? I tell her maybe to wait a little while longer. I don't want her to lose the friendship, which is real, even if it's online. Audrey doesn't live too far — Fresno — so I figure one of these days when we're visiting Ethan, we'll drive the extra distance and give Ivy a chance to meet her in real life. I've offered, but Ivy says she's not ready yet.

I get it — if things are weird when they meet in real life, it could mess up what they already have, and that's become very important to her.

So we'll wait a little while longer, but whenever Ivy decides she's ready to go — and wherever she decides she wants to go — I'll take her.

ACKNOWLEDGMENTS

I'M DEEPLY GRATEFUL to Elizabeth Bewley for taking on this manuscript and editing it so thoughtfully. It improved dramatically under her guidance. Thanks also to Nicole Sclama, who has been helpful and supportive every step of the way, and to Ana Deboo, who did a top-notch copyediting job.

Alexis Hurley always has my back and does a pretty good job of protecting me from the front, too. I wouldn't want to do this without her.

Johnny LaZebnik read through the galley pages and pounced on each and every sour note, rescuing me as best he could from future embarrassment. (The other kids didn't help, but I still like them.)

Elana K. Arnold merits an acknowledgment on the acknowledgments page for advising me about acknowledgments.

If you would like more information about autism, I recommend checking out the UCSB

Koegel Autism Center at www.education.ucsb.edu /autism.

And finally, one small note: there is debate in the autism community about which term is more respectful, "an autistic individual" or "an individual with autism." I felt my narrator would most naturally use the first term, and intend no statement or offense by having her do so.